P9-CQO-451

THE
SECRET
SISTERHOOD
OF

THE
SECRET
SISTERHOOD
OF
Heartbreakers

LYNN WEINGARTEN

HARPER TEEN
An Imprint of HarperCollins*Publishers*

HarperTeen is an imprint of HarperCollins Publishers.

Library of Congress Cataloging-in-Publication Data
Weingarten, Lynn.
    The Secret Sisterhood of Heartbreakers / Lynn Weingarten. —
1st ed.
        p.   cm.
    Summary: When her boyfriend ends their relationship, high
school sophomore Lucy thinks she will never recover from the heartbreak until she meets three magical girls who say they can heal her, but
at a cost.
    ISBN 978-0-06-192618-1
    [1. Dating (Social customs)—Fiction.   2. Love—Fiction.
3. Magic—Fiction.   4. High schools—Fiction.   5. Schools—Fiction.]
I. Title.
PZ7.W43638Se 2011   2010050518
[Fic]—dc22   CIP
                                                                      AC

Typography by Erin Fitzsimmons
12 13 14 15 16   CG/RRDH   10 9 8 7 6 5 4 3 2 1
❖
First Edition

To the brokenhearted . . .

THE
SECRET
SISTERHOOD
OF
Heartbreakers

One

*I*n the beginning, there she was, sweet, little Lucy Wrenn, standing all alone out in front of her school on the first day of sophomore year, with a seductive little message written on her stomach in Sharpie marker.

Do you want to know what the message was? Well, just hold on there; that part is coming. First, you need to know why she was standing out there, at 7:44 in the morning, humming a very special tune very quietly, face flushed, stomach fluttering, bouncing from foot to foot: she was waiting for someone.

Alex. Her boyfriend. The first and only one.

He'd been away all summer and now, with him set to arrive *any second* she was so excited she truly thought she might puke.

But Lucy had no idea what was coming, that something monumental was about to happen, something that would change her heart, her life, her entire world forever. Something so huge that when she looked back at this moment she would only remember it as the end. Or the beginning. Or maybe a little of both.

But for now, back to Alex.

Oh, Alex, Alex. His image, his sound, his touch, his scent, his everything had been cycling through her head on a constant loop all summer long while he'd been at a ranch in Colorado. Everywhere she went he was as much in her mind as if he'd been standing there in front of her face shouting, "Me me me me me!" It was excruciating, really, thinking about someone that much, but it's not like the poor dear had a choice.

From the very first moment Lucy saw Alex—when he walked into her American History class in the middle of her freshman year, him a new sophomore who'd just moved to town—she loved him. Really and truly, wholly and completely. And it wasn't just because he had a million tiny freckles on his face as though someone had thrown a handful of sand at him, or because he had that adorable little gap between his two front teeth, or because his hands were so beautiful they made her consider the fact that hands *could* be beautiful even though she'd never really thought about that before. And it wasn't just because he stood there, up in front of the class that day, smiling slightly, with a big-lensed, old-school film camera strapped to his shoulder, his hands in the pockets of his olive-green cargo pants, looking like he was on vacation or something. Or because standing there in front of a brand-new class, he looked so entirely comfortable in his own skin she could practically see the calm radiating off of him.

It was because when their eyes met as he scanned the room, she felt a flash light up her insides, like her heart was recognizing something she'd waited for her entire life.

From that day forward, every class period was fully devoted to studying Alex.

When he got bored he would tap his right foot and drum on his desk to a syncopated rhythm. His bashed-up cell phone was covered in a thick strip of green duct tape onto which he'd rewritten all the numbers in marker. Sometimes he would take out and eat a small bag of mixed nuts. He always ate the cashews first.

Each additional detail she discovered about him confirmed her suspicion that even the most mundane thing about Alex was more interesting than the most interesting thing about anyone else.

Looking at him filled her with a fizzling, frantic kind of joy and an almost sickening longing, like she was very hungry or very thirsty, only not either of those things.

But then, one day, something happened. She walked into class and the only empty seat was the one directly behind him. So she sat there, disappointed, because it meant she wouldn't get to watch his face. Only right as class began, Alex turned around and wrote something on her notebook. Just like that, like it was the most normal thing in the world.

It was, Lucy was sure, a mistake. He must have assumed he was sitting in front of one of his many new friends. But still, just the fact that she now had marks from his pen on her notebook was very exciting.

When she finally looked down she saw what he'd written: a bunch of dashes with a big upside-down *L* next to them, the setup for a hangman game. She looked up at him and he nodded at her, a very small smile on his face. *This was no mistake.*

Lucy's heart exploded. She wrote an *A* at the top of the paper, which was, at that moment, the only letter she could remember. A minute later he turned around again; he didn't even glance at her, just wrote the four *A*s where they belonged in the game. Then he grinned at them and turned back toward the board. Lucy picked *O* next and there were two, and then she picked *C*, but there weren't any of those so he drew a head on the hangman's pole. It looked like an egg. They went back and forth like that for the entire rest of class. She figured out the message just before the bell rang. It was MR. BROOME ALWAYS HAS A SPIT STRING, which was not only funny, but felt meaningful since she'd always noticed that too.

The next day, she sat behind him again, breathless, waiting, and the same thing happened, only this time he glanced at her and half smiled before he started writing. They played, and the message was: I DIDN'T DO THE HOMEWORK. When she'd solved the puzzle Lucy leaned over and whispered, conspiratorially, *"Neither did I."*

Even though she actually had.

The next class they played. And the next class. And the next. After three straight weeks of it, she finally let herself entertain the tiniest creeping tendril of a hope: what if maybe, just maybe, he liked her too? And at that point the game became less about figuring out the message and impressing him with her hangman skills, and more about figuring out approximations of date-invitations that would fit into the spaces he'd provided. SPIT STRING AGAIN could have been DEAR MYLUCY, ADATE? And IT SMELLS LIKE PEE IN HERE could have been OH LOVELY WILL YOU ME DATE. She bought adorable pens and tried to make her handwriting as sexy as possible. She waited and she waited.

Now that she'd let herself consider him a real possibility, it was absolutely excruciating.

Finally, one day after class he turned around and said, "Hey, Laurie, are you busy after school? Think you'd mind if I took a few pictures of you?" He patted that camera, which was always dangling off his shoulder. And despite the fact that she had no idea if what he'd just asked her to do was in fact a date, she was so excited she thought her chest might explode. She didn't even mind the fact that he didn't know her name.

That day after school he'd driven them to the park and taken roll after roll of film of her crouching under a gnarled old tree picking dandelions, and feeding the ducks, and swinging on the swing set. He was almost completely silent while he took the pictures. The only time he spoke at all was when he was reminding her not to look at the camera, which she kept doing because he was behind it. When he was done, when he'd gone through three entire rolls of film, he had come over to the swing on which she sat.

"You're fun to photograph," he'd said.

Her heart squeezed in her chest. "Why?" she whispered.

He reached out then, and moved a lock of hair away from her face. "Because you're beautiful."

The thing was, she'd never felt beautiful before. Cute, maybe, or even pretty sometimes. Beautiful? Never.

But in that moment, she did.

Jump ahead five months and one week and there was Lucy standing out in front of the school, with something written on her stomach. Seven dashes and an upside-down L. A hangman game spelling out a mystery message just for him. And she had a fresh green Sharpie marker in her back pocket for him to play with.

Precious, no?

She'd spent the entire summer coming up with it.

So she put on her lip balm and popped a ginger candy into her mouth to settle her stomach. Then spit that candy out so that her mouth would be free for kissing.

And just when she thought she was going to *throw up* or *die* from sheer excitement, Alex's scratched-up navy-blue Volvo with the ski rack on the top came creeping into the parking lot and pulled into one of the spots.

Alex got out. Lucy gasped. Even from fifty feet away he was the most beautiful thing she had ever seen.

He started walking toward school. Her mouth grinned as big as it could grin. She felt her arm lift up and her hand waving on the end of it.

But he did not wave back. He wasn't looking at her so much as right above her, as though he'd remembered her taller and that's where he was expecting her head to be. Well, she would remind him. She would remind him right where her head was!

Lucy's legs began trotting toward him. They broke into a run. Finally she was right in front of him, panting a little, her heart squeezing and releasing, squeezing and releasing. Lucy flung herself into his arms and pressed her body against his. Firecrackers of pleasure exploded up and down her spine.

"Lucy," he said.

"Follow me," she said, and she took his hand.

Lucy led him down the hill and around the side of the auditorium building, which she figured was a good place to go on the first day of school because no one would be there yet. His camera bounced against his hip as they walked.

"What are we doing?" Alex sounded confused, and not necessarily in a good way.

She turned toward him. "We're going to play hangman!" She'd meant to sound sexy and mysterious but it came out sounding weird and maybe a little insane.

Alex looked at her like, "Huh?" and raised his eyebrows in a way that gave Lucy a queasy feeling in her stomach. She pushed through the auditorium basement door, then through another door and up to the wings of the stage. It was chilly and damp back there, like it was a whole other time of day, a whole other season. She flipped on the switch and a lightbulb glowed yellow over their heads. She reached into her back pocket for the brand-new Sharpie she'd tucked in there and then put the Sharpie in Alex's palm and closed his fist around it. She lifted up the bottom of her T-shirt just enough.

She sucked in her stomach. "Okay," said Lucy. "Pick a letter!"

Alex stared at her. For the longest time he just stared. She looked down to make sure he could see the dashes.

"Aren't you going to pick?" She smiled. But he was not moving.

Lucy took the Sharpie back from him. "I'll help," she said. She drew an *I* on her stomach in the first blank. She tried to hand him back the marker, but he made no motion to take it. So she wrote the *M* too. It was hard since she was doing it upside down. The letter came out lumpy.

She looked at him and nodded. His face was frozen. She wrote the *R*. She hoped it looked okay. Her hand was shaking a little.

"You can guess at any time!"

But he didn't guess, so she just kept going.

She wrote the *E* and the *A* and the *D*. She finished off the final letter—the *Y* with a curlicue flourish. She'd filled in the whole puzzle. "I guess I won," she said. She grinned.

He was still just blinking at her, this confused look on his face. "I don't get it," he said finally. He squinted at her stomach, at the I-M R-E-A-D-Y. "What's your stomach ready for . . . *you're hungry?*"

Lucy started to laugh. "No," she said. "I mean, it's not my

stomach that's ready. *I'm* ready."

He blinked.

"For . . ." She nodded and opened her eyes wide. *"You know . . ."* He must know. ". . . for us to . . ." She leaned over—did she really have to say it? "Lose our virginities together." She lowered her voice for "virginities" even though there wasn't even anyone else around to hear. As soon as the word was out of her mouth, she wished she'd chosen a cooler word for it, although she did not know what that would be.

She leaned back and looked at him then, his beautiful face dimly lit by the weak yellow light, the smooth slant of his cheekbone, the curve of his lip.

This was the part where he was supposed to be overcome with love, where he was supposed to take Lucy in his arms and tell her how wonderful she was and how much he'd missed her. How happy he was to be back with her. How he never wanted to be apart from her again.

But he didn't. So they stood there, just stood there, breathing together. Lucy imagined the air moving between them, filling his lungs, then hers, then his, then hers.

"Lucy . . . ," he said slowly, finally. And he started shaking his head. "I can't."

"I know I had sort of not been ready before." It was, she thought, so sweet of him to be concerned. "But I waited for you the whole summer and that was enough. . . ."

"Hold on. . . ."

"My parents are going away this weekend. It's their anniversary so they're going to some special place with a lot of fancy cheese to, y'know, rekindle things. I guess seventeen is the cheese anniversary or something, ha-ha. I spent most of the summer convincing them to go and to let me stay by myself. . . ."

"Wait . . . ," he said.

". . . just for this! So it would be the perfect time really. . . . You could come over and . . ."

"Stop . . . ," he said. "Lucinda. Stop."

And then finally she did stop, because he never called her Lucinda. No one did. Lucinda was a woman's name and she wasn't a woman. Not yet anyway.

"Listen," he said. He took a breath. He actually looked nervous, which she'd never seen him look before. "We have to break up."

She stared at him, waiting. She thought maybe he was setting up for a joke. "Why would we *have* to break *up*?" Lucy started to smile as she waited for the punch line.

"I wasn't gonna do this until after school so I wouldn't make the first day all weird for you or whatever. . . . But you're standing here now and you just did all that stuff to your stomach, so I guess I should just . . ." He sighed and looked down and shook his head and reached up and started fiddling with this blue glass bead that was on a leather string around his neck, which Lucy had never seen him wear before. And suddenly something occurred to her—the necklace she'd sent him. The one she spent two hours picking out the beads and tiny pieces of carved shell for? The one she had strung on her porch by candlelight and moonlight because it seemed more romantic to do it that way, even though it made her eyes hurt, and she had whispered *I love you* to each bead and shell so that maybe when he wore it he'd know what she had always been too shy to say? How come he wasn't wearing *that*?

"I'm really sorry," he said. He took his hand away from his neck and tipped his head to the side.

He looked so beautiful like that with his head tipped to the side.

"Why?" Lucy's voice went up an octave, like she was imitating a cartoon character.

"I don't know how to explain it," he said finally. "I just don't feel like we should still be doing this." He motioned back and forth in the space between them. The *this* that they should not be doing was *them*.

"But you were gone," Lucy said.

His face softened. He took a breath and she felt a flash of hope because, wait! What if he was just getting ready to shout *GOTCHA!* or *SUPER EARLY APRIL FOOLS!* or to indicate in some way that they were on a game show where boyfriends and girlfriends get big prizes for fake-dumping each other?

He breathed out; the pause ended. He just shook his head and went back to fiddling with that damn leather necklace. They stood there until Lucy became vaguely aware of a bell ringing in the distance. It was the first-period bell signaling the fact that the first day of her sophomore year had officially begun.

"So this is just *it* . . . then?" she asked.

Alex put his hands in his pockets and raised his shoulders up to his ears, a slow shrug. "I guess so."

"Oh. Well." Her voice was still too high, not really her voice at all. "Thanks for letting me know."

"We'll be friends, okay?" he said. And it was that phrase, that sad and most pathetic of overused letdowns delivered in a voice still so sweet, that finally did it.

Lucy's heart began ripping apart inside her chest. She could actually feel it, the heavy red meat of it stretching and stretching until one by one those tendons popped. Lucy looked Alex in the eye one last time; then she did the only thing she could think to do in this totally-not-sense-making world. She said, "Well! See you later, then! I guess it's time for class!" And then she turned and started walking as fast as she could even though the thing was, actually, their first-period class was one they'd signed up for together. Lucy didn't want to cry in front of him.

"Wait!" he said. "I just . . ."

She stopped. She didn't turn but she held her breath, filled suddenly with the sick and terrible hope that he'd made a mistake maybe or changed his mind. It wasn't too late!

"I just don't want you to hate me," he finished.

Lucy shook her head. Because what she was feeling was so, so far from that. Because of course she didn't, because of course she never could.

So she just kept walking, and as she went something occurred to her, something so terrible and so perfect she actually laughed: Lucy had solved the puzzle wrong, her very own game on her very own stomach. The answer wasn't I'M READY.

It was I = IDIOT.

Two

*L*ucy managed to hold it together until she reached the bathroom. She stood in front of those cracked enamel sinks and an anguished cry escaped her lips. Within seconds, she was sobbing so hard she could barely breathe.

As she was crying, what she was thinking was: *this just doesn't make any sense.*

She'd thought about him every second all summer long. During the day she'd seen his face everywhere, on the faces of strangers, in the corner of her vision. Once a hint of him in a particularly human-looking potato. At night she tried to remember the placement of every freckle on his skin, and one night, one night she'd missed him so much, Lucy lay in her bed and held her own hand, and tried to pretend she was holding his.

She'd sent him emails every day, and letters in the mail every few days, and a bunch of presents too—pop-up cards she'd learned to make by watching a video on the internet, a T-shirt she'd had printed for him with a picture of an old-school camera on the front, a semi-failed attempt at banana bread, and once when she was feeling particularly saucy her very cutest, newest bra, which she'd only worn once.

One night when she couldn't sleep for missing him so much, she'd written a song for him on her guitar. The chorus went:

> *I feel you here when you're not*
> *I see your face in the sky when you're not here*
> *I hear your voice in my head when you're not here*
> *You're always here, you're always here.*
> *You are you are you are*

It was the only song she'd ever written. It was silly maybe, but it was from the heart and it was all true. Lucy loved to sing but she'd always been scared to sing in front of *anyone* other than her best friend, Tristan. But over the summer while she was missing Alex so much, she'd decided that maybe after they'd lost their virginities together, she'd finally be able to share the singing part of herself too. And this was the song she was thinking she could sing for him first.

She'd been practicing it all summer, had found herself humming it nearly constantly. It became a part of her as much as he was a part of her.

And he was as much a part of her as her very own damn heart.

Okay, so she hadn't heard from him much over the summer, but she hadn't really worried about that because he was not a very stay-in-touch type of person. And besides, he was on a ranch in Colorado and it was probably hard to get cell service and internet access there, what with all the horses and everything. Besides, all the while that Lucy was imagining him, she knew he was imagining her too. She felt it in her heart.

So then what had happened?

Lucy turned on the faucet, put a scratchy brown paper towel under the water, then lifted up her T-shirt and started scrubbing at the dark green letters.

Lucy was standing there like that, scrubbing and crying, when the door swung open behind her.

Her heart stopped. She froze.

"It doesn't have to be like this," a voice said calmly, simply.

Lucy looked up. There stood a girl in a gray silk minidress, a pile of long chains around her neck with different things dangling off of them: an orange crystal, a green feather, a gold vial, a small black key. Her hair was bleached almost white and hung around her face in long layers. She had dark, arched eyebrows, light gray eyes, a pointy chin, sharp cheekbones, and a space between her two front teeth. She was striking and a little bit scary, like a wolf that had decided to take the shape of a person. Lucy had seen her around. Olivia something; she was a senior.

She was staring at Lucy.

"What doesn't have to be like what?" Lucy said.

The girl then shook her head as though Lucy was a slightly slow child to whom one must explain things gently. "Whoever he is, however you feel now, it could all be different than it is."

"I don't know what you mean."

"Well, you don't yet." The girl smiled. "But you will."

She reached into her purse and pulled out a square of burnt orange silk, delicate like the wing of some exotic bird.

She held it out to Lucy. "Dry your tears with this," she said.

Lucy stared at it.

"Go on."

Lucy brought it up to her face. The material felt cool and smooth against her cheek.

The girl watched her and then gave Lucy this nod, as though they had a special understanding. Then the girl put her bag on her shoulder and turned to leave.

"Don't you want this back?" Lucy asked.

The girl turned back toward Lucy with that same mysterious smile on her face. "Keep it," she said. "I don't cry over boys."

Then she winked and walked out.

Lucy stood there, holding the scarf up to her cheek—it smelled like spices from someplace far away. She didn't feel so upset anymore. She felt . . . strange. Like she knew something important had just happened. Only she had no idea what it was.

She stared at herself in the mirror for one moment more. And then, for reasons even she was not quite sure of, she ran to the door, pushed it open. She wanted to talk to that girl again to ask her what she'd meant by what she said. "Hey!" Lucy called out. "Wait!" But the hallway was empty. Somehow that girl was already gone.

Three

*L*ucy did not like to lie, but it was awfully easy to convince the nurse she was sick and could not go to her Photo I class. A few vague hand motions and a facial expression that implied "stomach problems" and there she was left all alone in the dimly lit Band-Aid-scented sickroom. She stayed there for all of first period, through homeroom, and second period and halfway through the next class too. She lay there, just curled up on a cot, staring at all the painted-brick, graffiti-covered walls:

I JUST BARFED IN THIS BED

E4 4eva

Hope yur enjoying the bio test suckaaaas

Someone had drawn a little parade of muffins, marching up the wall. And under that, two crabs holding claws with a heart drawn around them.

Bells rang. Time passed. When the nurse came in to check on her, Lucy pretended to be asleep. Finally around noon she emerged from the cocoon of the sickroom, blinking in the bright afternoon sun.

Out on the main lawn she saw the WELCOME BACK, VAN BUREN VULTURES! sign strung up on the lunch building, saw the other students milling around in their back-to-school outfits, saw a couple of freshmen standing in front of the main office, a short curly-haired girl tipping her head to the side, beaming up at a skinny boy who was gesturing wildly with his long, gangly arms.

The air was so full of newness, of excitement, of possibilities, of beginnings.

Just not for her.

It was when Lucy saw the guy reach out and touch the girl's hair, awkwardly put a stray tendril behind her ear, and grin, embarrassed, because he just couldn't help himself, that Lucy's legs decided to start walking away. They walked her down around the side of the lunchroom, out back behind the school, past the track and the football field, and they just kept going. Her flip-flops caught on branches. She didn't slow down. She walked and walked, the tears streaming down her cheeks. She took that scarf out of her pocket and brought it up to her face, dried her tears. But when she pulled it away, she caught a glimpse of something on the fabric. A flash of black.

There were words written on that burnt orange silk. The ink looked fresh, and although she knew this wasn't possible she could have sworn those letters weren't there before, as though somehow her own heartbroken tears made them appear.

Midnight tonight.
Old Orchard Road
The Big House Down at the End.
Come alone.
We can help.
SSH

Four

If there's an upside to having a broken heart it's this: a broken heart makes you brave.

Just before midnight, with her parents lying in their bed asleep, Lucy, who'd never snuck out even once in her entire life, got up, walked right out her front door, and pulled it shut behind her. Down the driveway she went, heart aching, head swimming, the tiniest tendril of guilt curling in the bottom of her belly, but she did not look back.

When Lucy had finally gotten home from school that day, after almost two hours of walking, she'd gone up to her room, taken out her Alex Box, and looked at everything that was in there: all the hangman games, a letter he'd written her once during class and signed with what looked like a misshapen heart, a cashew, a framed photo he'd taken of a little bird sitting on a rusty nail and given her as a present, a book about a mountain-climbing expedition that he liked and thought she'd like too, a pair of socks he'd let her borrow when she'd walked on hers in damp grass.

She'd been looking for an explanation in that box, but all that she found was evidence of his having once liked her, not clues to why he no longer did.

When her mom got home from work and asked Lucy how her first day had been, Lucy just said she didn't feel very well, had a stomach-something maybe. "But I'm sure I'll be better by Friday," Lucy had added. Her mother was all excited about the trip she was taking with Lucy's father that weekend. Lucy didn't want her misery to leak out onto their happiness, since theirs was so rare and would be, Lucy knew, so fleeting. Besides, Lucy did not want to talk about what had happened because in order to explain that Alex had broken up with her she'd have to first explain who Alex *was*. And she knew it would hurt her mother's feelings to find out that Lucy had had an Alex in her life and never said a word about it. So Lucy let her mother bring her flat Coke and chicken rice soup, which Lucy would not be able to eat. Then Lucy texted Tristan, asking if he could drive her somewhere late that night. He said yes. She lay there and watched the clock.

And when it was time, she went.

Tristan was already waiting for her in the truck, leaning back, window down, two lollipop sticks sticking out of his mouth like skinny twin tongues.

"Well, hello," he said. "Fancy meeting you here." He grinned as though being up and out at midnight on a school night was totally normal, which for him it kind of was. Tristan had terrible insomnia. So most nights while everyone else was in bed, Tristan was driving around, trying out the pancakes at a diner in a random town, or parked somewhere playing the blues on his harmonica. Tristan had gone to first grade twice (the first time had been the year his mom died), so even though he was just starting sophomore year with Lucy, he could already drive. And he didn't even have to sneak out because his dad had only two rules: don't get hurt, and don't get arrested. Beyond that, Tristan could do what he wanted.

Lucy walked around the front of his truck to the passenger side. She knew how she must have looked to him then—eyes puffy, face blotchy. But Tristan wasn't the kind of guy who'd pry about stuff, so all he said was, "Where to, little buddy?" and moved a couple harmonica boxes from the seat to the cup holder to make room for her.

"Old Orchard Road," she said. "Some big old house down at the end."

He crunched through one of his lollipops and put the stick onto the dashboard, where it lay with a dozen like it.

Lucy leaned back against the seat as the trees whizzed by,

her hand stuck out the window to catch the wind. She knew he wouldn't ask her anything else. But she supposed she needed to tell him.

She took a breath. "Alex broke up with me this morning," she said. It was strange hearing herself say those words out loud. They both did and did not sound true.

She turned toward Tristan, who was slowly shaking his head. "Oh, buddy." This was his serious voice. He didn't use it often. "I'm really sorry," he said. But he left it at that, didn't try to pretend he understood what she felt like. Of course he didn't. Tristan had never been in love. He'd never even had a girlfriend.

Not that he hadn't had options. Although Lucy could never see him like that, she knew that a lot of girls thought Tristan was cute, in a lanky-body, floppy-haired, twinkly-eyed, mismatched-socks sort of way. He was friendly and liked to talk to strangers so he met people wherever he went, and some of those people were girls and some of those girls got crushes on him. Occasionally he would hook up with one if she was cute enough and chased him hard enough, but it never amounted to more than that.

Sometimes a girl he hooked up with would get it in her head that he was going to be her boyfriend and then get all confused when he didn't want to be, even though he'd warned her from the start that he wasn't interested in anything serious. "But people hear what they want to hear," is what he'd always said. It wasn't that he didn't believe in love at all, it was that he didn't believe in love for *himself.* He didn't think he was capable of falling in it, and he was fine with that.

When Lucy first started dating Alex she'd felt sorry for Tristan, sorry that he'd never gotten to know the beautifully delicious pain of loving someone so much. But, she realized now, as they drove down those dark streets, the flip side of that beautifully delicious pain was a pain that was not beautiful or delicious at all. Maybe Tristan was lucky.

"This *hurts.*" Lucy's voice cracked. "I really love him."

"I know you did," Tristan said. He took a deep breath, like he was going to say something more. But then he just exhaled and drove.

Lucy wondered if what Tristan wasn't saying had to do with something that Lucy knew that Tristan didn't know she knew: he'd never really liked Alex. Not that he'd admitted that of course, but when someone's your best friend, you can tell things like that. After the first time she'd introduced them, tried to make them friends, Tristan had said something about how it seemed that Alex bowled Lucy over a little bit. "I don't mean to judge," he'd said. "I just hope that when the two of you are alone he lets you talk a little more is all. . . ."

Lucy had nodded and said that yes he did. But she'd felt protective of Alex and of their new relationship and did not elaborate. Tristan never brought it up again.

Tristan pulled over. They were there. Up ahead was a big,

black metal gate and beyond that were dozens of tall trees lining a dark driveway so long that Lucy couldn't even see what was at the top. "I guess this must be the place," he said.

"I'll just get out here," she said.

"You don't want me to come with you?"

Lucy shook her head, even though a part of her actually did.

"Hold on one second." Tristan took some things out of his pocket—a harmonica, a few lollipop wrappers, a paper clip bent into a spiral, and a little cellophane-wrapped something. He placed the cellophane thing in her hand and closed her fist around it. "There," he said. "For protection."

She looked down. Resting on her palm was a plastic-wrapped toothpick.

"Y'know, in case there are very tiny vampires up there," he grinned. "Or poppy seeds."

Lucy got out of the car, shut the door behind her, walked up to the gate, and went through. Her hands were tingling. She didn't know why.

Left foot. Right foot. Left foot. Right foot. She concentrated on walking, on not feeling anything but the crunch of the gravel under her feet. She couldn't see the house yet and when she turned back she couldn't see the street behind her either. There was only blackness all around her, and the moon up ahead.

She kept going in the dark, humming her Alex song so

quietly that even she couldn't hear it. The driveway curved left and she followed it, and finally, finally, a house rose up in front of her, incredibly tall and very old. The front was covered in dozens of windows, beautiful, but eerie.

Alex would have loved to take pictures of this.

Lucy's eyes adjusted. The front yard was filled with weeping willows that looked like giant beasts with their fur hanging down to the ground. She climbed up a slate walkway that led to the front door. She reached out and lifted the heavy brass knocker. She paused, frozen somewhere between knocking and not. As though somehow she knew even then that once she let go, there'd be no turning back.

And then let go she did. Metal slammed against metal. *Whatever is going to happen, let it happen.*

The door swung open as though someone had been waiting for her inside. Olivia, the girl from the bathroom, stood there staring at Lucy. Her face spread into a slow, brilliant smile.

Then she grabbed Lucy's wrist and pulled her inside.

Five

Olivia dragged Lucy down a long, long hallway, around a corner, up to a set of huge double doors. There was a rush of sound as though an entire ocean lay behind that glossy old wood.

Olivia flung the doors open and pulled Lucy into an enormous room with a high domed ceiling, dimly lit by a dozen Moroccan-glass lanterns. Huge windows lined the back wall, draped on each side with yards of printed silk. There were people in the room, a few dozen maybe, lying across couches, seated on silk pillows, standing in front of the giant fireplace, drinking from silver cups.

"Ignore them." Olivia waved her hand. "We're trying something out here, and they were all already coming before I knew about your . . . situation."

Olivia pulled Lucy through the room, and out a side door. And then they were in an enormous backyard edged in twisted, towering trees.

"We're over there." Olivia pointed toward a gazebo in the grass, in the center of which was a small flickering light. She started to pull Lucy forward again, but Lucy's feet refused to go.

"Who is *we*?" Lucy's voice came out quiet, more scared sounding than she'd wanted it to.

Olivia shook her head, as though this should have been obvious, but by the light that shone through the door, Lucy could see that she was smiling. "The Secret Sisterhood of Heartbreakers. We've been waiting a long time for you."

"Wait," Lucy said. "What?" She stopped, suddenly dizzy. "For *me*?"

But Olivia didn't answer, just pulled Lucy out into the lush grass and toward a large gazebo. Two girls were already inside, a white candle flickering between them.

Olivia sat down on the floor and motioned for Lucy to follow.

"Well, here we are," Olivia said. "Your heart is really, truly broken. Congratulations."

The wind blew. Lucy could see the other two girls' eyes shining in the dark. "Then why are you congratulating me?"

she said quietly. "I feel like I'm dying."

Olivia shrugged. "Of course you do. Most peoples' hearts could never break as deeply as yours has, honey muffin. But you should be grateful for that. There's . . . potential in that."

Lucy raised her hand up to her chest and pressed against her ribs where that chunk of mangled meat was barely beating.

"Do you know why you're here?" asked Olivia.

"Because I read the message on the scarf."

"And do you know how that message *got* on that scarf?"

Lucy shook her head.

Olivia just smiled and held out her hand. "I'd like it back now, please."

Lucy removed the square of crumpled silk from her pocket and handed it to Olivia, who placed it in her lap.

"We're about to give you the greatest opportunity that you'll ever have. We can make it so your broken heart heals back like that." Olivia snapped her fingers. The candle flickered. "And then it will be so strong it will never be broken again."

Lucy wanted to say something, but her brain wasn't giving her the words. "I . . . ," she said. "What?"

"And then you'll be one of us," Olivia went on. "Part of an ancient secret sisterhood. And the entire world will open up to you, full of possibilities . . ." Lucy could hear Olivia starting to smile. "And magic."

"But . . ." The words came slowly, dripping from Lucy's lips one letter at a time. "I mean, that's not . . . possible."

"Why?"

"Because . . ." Lucy stared at her. Was she kidding? Was she crazy? "Things don't work like that."

Olivia let out a laugh. "What do you know about the way things work, kitten? You believe what you've been told. But what if the people who told you about the world only understood part of the story?"

This was absurd, Lucy knew that of course, but she found her mouth opening in spite of herself. "Tell me how it works then."

"It's simple, really. You make someone fall in love with you sometime within the next seven days . . ."

"In seven days? That's ridiculous." She tried to make her voice sound tough, to keep herself from crying. But all she could think was that she'd been alive for more than fifteen years, and in that time she hadn't gotten a single person to fall in love with her. Not one single one.

"Oh, sugar pie," Olivia laughed. "A person can fall in love in an hour, in an instant. Haven't you ever seen a movie or read a book or even *looked* at another human being? Everyone is *desperate* to fall in love. It's quite sweet really. Just give them a tiny push at the edge and they'll go hurtling into the depths of it. It's easy. Of course"—she smiled—"it certainly helps if you have magic on your side."

"Right," Lucy said. "Magic." She couldn't believe she was even having this conversation. But then again, she couldn't believe much of anything that had happened that day.

"Getting someone to love you is only the first part," Olivia said. "Once he loves you"—her voice was calm and smooth—"you break his heart."

"I don't understand."

"In order for your heart to heal, you have to find a heart to break. A Chrysalis Heart."

"What's a Chrysalis Heart?"

"It's the one that changes you. The one you break so yours can heal. Keeps things in balance."

"So I'm just supposed to go out and *break a heart*?"

Olivia nodded. "Of course in order to break a heart first you have to win it. . . ." Olivia turned toward the other two girls. They were farther from the flame, and Lucy couldn't make out their faces. She could see the outlines of their bodies. They were leaning back, stretched out like cats. Olivia smiled a sly smile. "And winning hearts, well, that's something we happen to be experts at. If you want to become a Heartbreaker, we can teach you too."

"But why?" Lucy's voice said. "Why would you do that?"

"We have our reasons," Olivia said simply, finally. Then she reached behind her and lifted up a small satchel and out of it took a delicate gold chain with a small gold vial dangling from it. It looked familiar. "You can collect his brokenhearted tears in here." She swung the necklace back and forth. "They're so powerful, one is really all you need."

"Need for *what*?"

"To power the potion that will fix your heart, make it unbreakable, and make you one of us. You came here because you thought we could help you, right? Well, this is how."

Lucy stood up. This must be some sort of really messed-up joke, and a video of the whole thing would appear online tomorrow. No one could actually believe this, could they?

"So break a boy's heart and bring us his brokenhearted tear and then"—Olivia's eyes flashed—"you'll see."

"But that's so cruel! Even if I believed *anything* you're saying, which I don't, I wouldn't want to do that." What was she even *doing* here? Coming had been a mistake.

"Well, it's your choice. And your loss. But this isn't cruel." Olivia wasn't smiling anymore. "It's natural. Nature is dark and light, birth and death. Everything and its opposite. And in nature there are predators and prey. The hunters and the hunted. The heartbreakers and the heartbroken. The beautiful thing is that Nature lets us choose which we want to be. Most people never make the choice though because they don't even know they have it."

The candle flared up and Lucy could see their faces then: their smooth skin, their plump lips, their shining eyes. They were luminous.

"We are not indiscriminate when choosing hearts to break,"

Olivia said. "We only break the hearts of those who deserve it, and those who could benefit from it."

"Benefit?" Lucy said. "How?"

"Pain softens us and opens us up. To have one's heart broken is to be connected more deeply with the earth; it is to experience *life*. To be more fully human."

"Well, if it's so great, then why would I even want an unbreakable heart?" Lucy's voice cracked. "Why would anyone?"

"Having a broken heart makes you human. But there are better things to be than that." Olivia looked down and for a moment her face registered a flicker of an expression Lucy couldn't place.

"Oh, so you guys are like witches or something?" Lucy half meant it as a joke.

"Not exactly," Olivia said slowly. "Then again . . ." Someone let out a laugh. "Not exactly not."

Olivia reached down and picked up the silk scarf. She pinched it between her fingers and held it over the candle. The orange flames reached up and licked it. She held on to it for one second more and then tossed the flaming fabric into the air. Lucy watched as it rose up above their heads, tiny embers raining down. The scarf vanished in a puff of smoke.

But in that smoke, Lucy saw something that she could not possibly have seen yet somehow did: in that smoke was Alex's face. The sweet line of his cheek, the beautiful hollow of his eyes, the unmistakable curve of his mouth, right there in silver, white, and gray, hovering above their heads. Lucy gasped and raised her hand to her lips.

Then the wind came and swept that delicate smoke away.

Olivia leaned forward and blew the candle out. "Now if you'll excuse us." She stood up. "We have a party to get back to." She motioned toward a low iron gate. "If you walk through that and follow the slate path around the house, you'll find your way back to the road."

"Wait!" Lucy pointed straight up, where only the faintest wisp of smoke remained. "How did you . . . ?"

Olivia laughed a sweet, tinkling laugh. It sounded like a set of bells, the ones that jingle when a door is being opened.

"Good night," Olivia said. "Oh, and honey cake." Her voice was pleasant, soft, soothing. "If you tell anyone anything about what you just saw or what we just told you it would make us very, very unhappy. And trust me, you don't want to see us unhappy. So . . ." She raised her finger to her lips, her mouth spreading into a slow smile behind it. "Ssh."

Olivia and her two friends walked toward the house.

Six

*L*ucy stood there in that big, open space as the three girls disappeared inside, jaw slack, eyes wide, pupils the size of pinpoints even in the almost dark.

The wind blew, but she could not feel it. She was aware only of the dizzying sense of floating and spinning, of suddenly not understanding anything. Or maybe just beginning to realize just how much she hadn't understood all along.

Lucy raised her hand to her lips.

What the hell was that?

There had to be a logical explanation. It was a clever illusion of some kind, a projection from a mini–movie projector perhaps, or a hologram!

There was probably an explanation, there probably was. *But what if . . . ?*

Lucy tried to laugh at herself for even entertaining something so absolutely ridiculous. She shook her head hard. But she could not shake out what she'd seen.

She walked toward the house, toward the large windows, lit up red from inside. She pressed her face up against the glass where one set of curtains was parted. Lucy had the funny sensation, then, of being trapped in a made-up world, as though only what was inside that house was actually real.

Lucy scanned the crowd; the people seemed to be around her age, maybe a little bit older. She didn't recognize most of them but there was a girl on the couch who went to Van Buren. *She was also one of the girls in the gazebo.*

This information came to Lucy in a flash. And, she suddenly realized, she'd seen Olivia, this girl, and another girl together at Van Buren many times.

This girl's name was Gil and she was a junior. She and Lucy had been in the same American History class when Lucy was a freshman. It was the class where Lucy first met Alex.

They'd never really talked, but staring at her now through the window, Lucy felt a rush of warmth and friendliness toward her. First the rush, a second later the memory of why:

The moment after Alex had first asked to take her picture, on that day five months and one week ago, before Lucy realized what exactly had happened, she was met with not joy but a sudden wave of terror. Heart-stopping, pupil-shrinking, stomach-tightening terror. Somehow she'd managed to nod a yes to Alex's invitation. But when he left the room on his way to his next class, Lucy had stood there not smiling but shaking.

A shock is still a shock, even if it's a good one.

Lucy had looked up and locked eyes with this sweet-looking girl. The girl had smiled at Lucy and nodded ever so slightly. *This is good,* the nod had said. *This is real.* She'd done it at the exact right moment in the exact right way to help bring Lucy back to earth.

When what had happened finally hit her, when her disorientation morphed to giddy, blushing joy, Gil was still there. And her smile was so genuine and warm and full of understanding, as though somehow without the two of them having spoken, Gil understood absolutely everything. Lucy had had the sudden urge to reach out and hug that girl. But, of course, Lucy didn't. And she'd forgotten that she'd even wanted to until that very moment standing outside Olivia's window staring in. Gil was sitting on a green velvet couch, her legs tucked under her. As Lucy watched Gil, Gil was watching the room with calm interest.

She was not beautiful, or sexy, or even that pretty. She was clean and wholesome looking, like someone who used a lot of soap. She was a few inches taller than Lucy, with narrow hips and a flat chest. She had very normal features and brown hair in a pixie cut. Something about her eyes seemed warm. Off to the side five guys were staring at her, each with a look on his face that Lucy understood perfectly because it was the way she'd always looked at Alex.

Just then, a flash of black and white passed in front of the window, and Lucy leaned back. This was the other girl Lucy had seen the first two with, the one from the gazebo. She had dark brown hair streaked with gold, almond-shaped brown eyes with thick lashes, a slightly-too-big mouth set somewhere between bursting out laughing and telling you to go fuck yourself. She was five-nine or five-ten, all sleek muscles and flawless skin. She was wearing a black-and-white-checkered dress like a mom from the fifties, except it was way shorter than a fifties mom would have worn, and instead of teetering little heels she was wearing the world's most broken-in cowboy boots. She was gorgeous but somehow unstable looking, like a fast-moving roller coaster about to careen off a too-small track. Lucy watched as the girl threw her head back and took a shot of something. The ends of her hair reached all the way down to the top of her butt.

Lucy stood there staring at the three girls, feeling an itch at the base of her skull, as she tried to pull up memories of the other times she'd seen them together. What had they been doing? Walking toward a beautiful light blue antique convertible. Laughing, their heads tossed back. Had there been any indication of *who* they *were*? She thought maybe she'd had a feeling about them, but that the feeling had been so slight that only now in retrospect was she aware of having had it.

In the room, someone flipped on a light and everyone turned toward the oak doors that were now open. A guy marched in. Lucy could hear his muffled voice through the thick glass. He was tall, broad shouldered, suede jacketed. He had a big, square head, face contorted with pain.

Lucy recognized him too: this was Ethan Sloane. He was a Van Buren junior famous for being crazy, but not in a social outcast way, more like in a hot-bike-messenger-on-a-rehab-reality-show sort of way. He'd run for student council president the year before and his campaign speech consisted of him playing a song on the guitar and then, at the end, shouting, "Don't vote for me, politics is bullshit!" Afterward, everyone had cheered for a full two minutes and forty seconds, which Lucy knew because Tristan had timed it. There were a million rumors about Ethan Sloane. According to one he'd had an affair with the beautiful new just-out-of-college English teacher and was the reason she left in the middle of the year. According to another he'd once gotten caught cheating on his girlfriend with two of her friends at the same time. His excuse had been that he was so high he thought both of them were her.

But the Ethan Sloane who was marching toward Gil at that moment did not look like the kind of guy who'd once been arrested for smoking pot in the parking lot of the police station and got himself released by flirting with the cop, as he supposedly had. This guy looked like he was barely able to stand, barely able to speak. He was sinking in on himself.

Lucy watched as Ethan crouched down, grabbed Gil's hand, and pressed it to his chest. His lips were moving; it looked like he was saying, *"Please, please, please."*

But Gil shook her head again, slowly, blinked her warm eyes. She looked sorry when she yanked her hand free. But not as sorry as Ethan did.

It hurt Lucy to look at him. She could feel his breaking inside her own chest, feel the crumbling of his heart in her heart. He tried to reach for Gil once more, but that big, beautiful girl stepped between them. She stood with her hands on her hips, then pointed toward the door, and opened her enormous mouth. *"GO."*

Ethan stood up, made his way toward the door, bumping into people as he went, like he was drunk, or sick.

Gil looked up then, glanced toward the window light where Lucy stood. And even though it was dark outside and light inside and therefore the window glass should have been a mirror to Gil, Lucy felt their eyes meet, felt a flash of something.

The wind blew then. The trees said *ssh.*

Everyone was watching Olivia, as though looking for a cue of what to do next. Someone lowered the lights. She picked up a small remote from the mantle and music started. Lucy could feel its rhythmic beating through the windows, like the house had turned into a heart. Olivia began to dance, hips swaying, arms raised up over her head. The tall girl joined in, and then Gil did too. Everyone watched them and one by one began to dance until the entire room was a pulsing mass of arms and legs.

Lucy put her hand on her heart and pressed where it hurt the most. She felt something happening, there inside her chest: a sliver of space was opening up, and the thinnest beam of light was peeking through.

Lucy walked through the creaking gate.

She followed the slate path in the silver light, down under the dangling branches of the weeping willows. She made her way across a small clearing, and down more stairs. And she felt a strange calmness come over her, as though what had been moving very fast in her was slowing down now. The moon seemed brighter then; she could feel it shining through her clothes and skin, making its way toward her heart, and sinking in through the cracks.

It was then that she heard the howling. A wounded animal cry, growing louder as she went. And then she saw the source of it: Ethan Sloane, hunched over, on the steps, sobbing into the sleeve of his jacket.

Lucy felt a pang in her chest for him, wished she could say something to him. But, of course, she couldn't.

She hopped off the stairs, into the grass beside them. She ran, her hair catching wind and flying out behind her. And she didn't stop running until she reached the road.

Back down at the truck, there was Tristan, seat back, feet propped against the dash, playing his harmonica. Lucy stood behind the fence, and closed her eyes for a moment and listened to those notes, bending. These were not ragged cries, but a mournful wail, the jagged edges smoothed into something beautiful.

Had Lucy heard this just twenty minutes before, she would have had the strange sensation she always did when listening to music that perfectly matched her mood—as though the thin wall that separated her body from the world around her had dissolved, as though she was just a sound wave vibrating in the air, weightless and part of everything. The merging power of music, it was why she loved it so much. It was why music felt like magic.

Tristan stopped playing and squinted into the dark. "Lu?"

Lucy unhooked the gate and walked out.

"You survived," he said. "I thought maybe the poppy seeds got you." Tristan put his harmonica back in his mouth and played a blues prompt:

Ba duuum ba dum

This was Lucy's cue to improvise some ridiculous blues ditty like the "I'm Out of Gum Blues," the "Where're My

Shoes Blues," the "My Friend Tristan Won't Stop Bluesing Blues." Since Tristan was the only person Lucy wasn't scared to sing in front of, she was happy to do it any chance she got.

Tristan played it again: *ba duuuum ba dum*. He held one hand out toward her.

But she couldn't. Not now. Lucy shook her head as she got back in the truck.

Tristan dropped his harmonica in the cup holder. "Everything go okay up there?"

"It was . . ." Lucy stopped. "Weird."

"How so?" He started to drive.

"Tristy." Her voice sounded strange, like she was hearing herself from very far away. "Do you believe in magic?"

Tristan smiled. "Well, of *course*." He took a lollipop out of the cup holder. He held it between his thumb and forefinger, then waved his other hand in front of it. "Poof!" He wiggled his fingers. The lollipop was gone. Then he waved his hand one more time and the lollipop was back. "TA-DA!"

It was the same trick he'd been doing for years. Usually Lucy loved it, if for no other reason than Tristan's goofy enthusiasm. But in that moment all she could do was try and force a smile.

"Right," she said. "Of course." She leaned back against her seat.

As they drove, images flashed through Lucy's head: the party, the girls in the gazebo, the smoke, Alex's face, Olivia out there in the dark with that look in her eyes and that smirk on her lips. *It certainly helps if you have magic on your side.*

Lucy gasped as she suddenly realized what these words actually meant. It was so obvious she couldn't believe it had taken her until now to comprehend it. Olivia was offering something Lucy had not even known was possible until five minutes before, something out of fairy stories, out of dreams. *Olivia was offering magic.*

Lucy's breath caught in her throat as an idea began forming. What if instead of using the Heartbreaker magic to win a heart and break it, Lucy used the magic to win a heart and keep it? Not just any heart, but the one she'd had and needed back.

Lucy shook her head. That she was sitting there thinking this, considering this, was completely crazy. She knew that. But she also knew this: some of the very best ideas seem completely crazy . . . until they work.

Lucy felt herself nodding slightly as a smile she was barely aware of spread across her lips.

A couple minutes later, Tristan pulled up a few feet from Lucy's driveway.

"Well, I'll be out driving around so . . ." Tristan stopped. "If you want pancakes or need another toothpick or want to rob a bank and need a reliable getaway vehicle . . ."

Lucy so wished she could tell him what she'd seen up there.

What she'd just decided. Instead she reached out and gave him a hug. "Thank you for bringing me there. You are the world's best friend," she said.

"Eh," he shrugged, reaching for his harmonica again. "Tell it to the judge!"

She shut the door behind her and he slowly drove away, steering with one hand, playing the harmonica with the other. Lucy stood there smiling as she listened.

A second later her phone vibrated in her pocket. A text from Tristan, who had sent her a text every night for as long as they'd had phones.

Bu duuuuum bu dum, it said.

Lucy laughed and shook her head.

Then she tiptoed back inside.

Seven

On the second day of her sophomore year, there was Lucy, standing all alone out in front of her school with something written on her stomach in Sharpie marker. Two letters, the ones that wouldn't wash off in the shower that morning even though she'd used a loofah!

M

A

She wondered if it meant something that those were the letters that were left.

My Alex. Magic Abounds.

She put her hand on where those letters were and closed her eyes. . . .

It's early spring. Lucy and Alex are on their way to Alex's house where Lucy has never been before. Lucy is in the middle of telling some story that she wishes she were not telling, something that she saw at lunch and what it made her think about the way people are when they are looking for a seat and how some people look so nervous, and some people don't look nervous but you can tell they are anyway and . . . She is rambling, she knows; she wishes she could stop. She's glad when he interrupts.

"Did I tell you about the ladder I found?" he asks.

"No!" she says. "But please do!"

"Well, I found this ladder last night. It was in the garage. The people who lived in the house before left it there."

"It's so good to have a ladder," she says. Before she can cringe at herself, he smiles at her like she's being adorable. He tells her yes, it is good, he's really glad he found it, and he plans to use it to climb up on his family's new roof so he can take pictures from up there. Climbing stuff and then taking pictures of whatever was down below was his favorite thing to do with his friends at his old school. "Photo safari was what we called it," he explains. "Because we would really climb anything— trees, buildings, water towers, telephone poles. Shit, it was really crazy some of the stuff we did." He grins and shakes his head.

Lucy is scared of climbing most things, ladders especially because she doesn't quite trust those skinny little rungs. She is also scared of what climbing usually leads to, which is heights.

But, but! When they turn onto his street and he suggests that they should go on his roof and try out the brand-new, very old ladder, she smiles and does her best impression of a casual person saying, "Fun!" And tries not to throw up.

When they get there, he does not suggest going inside. He parks in the driveway and goes into the garage and drags out a terrible-looking rusty thing that may have once been green but certainly isn't anymore. He carries it over to the roof and leans it against the side of the house. "Hope it's sturdy enough," he says, and then pounds one of the rungs. Maybe he knows she's scared and he's teasing her a little. She forces a laugh, but it comes out sounding like a cough.

Alex starts to climb, takes the steps in twos. His camera bounces against his leg. He disappears onto the roof.

Lucy takes a deep breath and puts her flip-flopped foot on that first rickety rung. She is glad Alex is already on the roof so he can't see her legs shaking. When she reaches the top, she is dizzy and sweating. She sits down and scoots backwards up the roof. The shingles scratch the back of her legs. Alex is far away, crouched at the edge, taking pictures of the backyard from up above. She watches him and feels the love chemicals pump through her. She loves watching him take pictures, the way his face looks when he squints one eye to look through the lens, the way his beautiful hands look when he clicks the shutter. After a while he stops and lowers his camera and stares out, a funny expression on his face. He looks so artistic and deep.

"What are you thinking?" Lucy asks.

"It sucks not having those guys here with me, my friends back home, I mean."

Lucy's heart squeezes. "But you'll see them soon though, right?" She is trying to be cheerful and encouraging. "Like on breaks and stuff?" He nods, but she has the feeling he hasn't quite heard her.

He wanders off, as comfortable on the roof as he is on the ground. Lucy watches as he takes more photos—the top of the chimney, a tree branch, this one spot where a few shingles have fallen off and a little bird is sitting on a rusty nail. Later he will give her a print of this bird, framed, as a gift. He will tell her that the bird reminds him of her and she will know somehow he means this as a compliment. But she does not know any of this yet; instead all she knows is that he is just over there but seems very far away right now.

"We could go visit them," Lucy calls out. "You know, like a road trip!" Only he is too absorbed in that nail, that bird, and doesn't respond.

Lucy feels an intense, sickening sense of loneliness, of missing him even though he is only ten feet away. A hot, creeping ball of jealousy scampers up her back on its pokey little legs and burrows into her. She is, she realizes then, jealous of his friends back home. Jealous because he misses them and is wishing he was with them even though he's there with her. But her jealousy takes hold and starts leaking outward. And suddenly she is jealous of that *little bird even, because he is looking at it the way he looked at her that first time at the park. And because he is talking to it in the quiet, gentle voice she thought was just for her. "Aren't you pretty? Aren't you a pretty little thing."*

Later, she will grow to find this feeling familiar—this jealousy toward whatever his camera is pointed at that isn't her. But in that moment it shocks her and fills her with shame. To be jealous of a bird, *well, that is just the most pathetic thing in the world.*

Eventually when that bird flies away, Alex comes to her. Lies back on the roof next to her, arm behind his head, one knee up, staring up at the sky. She lies back too and leans her head against his chest and it kind of makes her neck ache but she stays like that. And he says, "Hey," and smiles at her as though he's only then realized she's up there with him. But that he's glad she is. "Come here," he says in that voice. And she snuggles in closer. He puts his hand on her stomach, rests it there absent-mindedly. His fingers are against her bare skin where her shirt had come up a little bit and she could cry with relief now that he's touching her. She imagines that her skin is dissolving and that his hand is becoming part of her, that he is part of her. They stay there like that for Lucy has no idea how long. They stay there until Alex says suddenly, "Did you know that when they decided to move they didn't even consult me?" She knows he must mean his parents. His voice sounds strained. And that is new. "They kind of just told me as an afterthought.

Like for practical reasons since they needed me to pack up my stuff."

Lucy is shocked out of her bliss, but her shock is quickly swept away by an overwhelming wave of tenderness toward this boy whom she loves so much. And anger at anyone who would ever hurt him. There is so much that she wants to say. But the words get caught in her throat.

"You are too wonderful to ever be anyone's afterthought," she says finally.

He does not answer, but pulls her close to him and hugs her in a way that feels different from any hug they've ever shared before. She holds on tight to him and to this moment. But after a while she can feel him float away again. Alex sits up, coughs. His voice is back to normal; he says they have to get off the roof because it's getting dark and they might never be able to get down if they don't do it now. And she thinks, Stay up here forever, that might not be so bad, that might not be so bad at all. *But she is silent as they make their way back down to the ground.*

Lucy opened her eyes, she pressed her chest for all she'd lost. *And all that she planned to get back . . .*

She watched the mass of bodies moving toward her, making their way up from the parking lot toward the school. There was a heart beating inside each one of those bodies. Lucy imagined that she could see each of them beating through their chests, a messy, red muscle, pushing their blood around, making them go.

She focused on the faces one by one and for the first time since she laid eyes on him, she begged the universe to keep Alex away, afraid that if she saw him before she truly had a plan to get him back, the mere sight of his beautiful face would cause the deep, black hole of her heart to open right up and its vast emptiness would devour everything.

Instead she asked the universe to please, please bring her one of the Heartbreakers first.

A second later, it did—the giant, gorgeous, scary one. But a few feet behind that girl there was Alex with his hands in the pockets of his green camo pants.

The universe has nothing if not a sense of humor.

Lucy tried to take a deep breath. But her lungs would take no breath at all. She knew what she had to do.

She walked over to the sidewalk and stood there as the people passed. They were fifteen feet away, ten feet, five feet.

Finally she breathed in and as she exhaled she said, "Hi!"

They both looked up. That girl started to smile; her mouth looked huge. Alex was staring at Lucy. "Lu . . . ," he began.

His voice made her stomach hurt but she forced her

eyebrows up, as though somehow bumping into him at the school where they both went was the most unlikely thing in the world. "Oh!" she said. "It's you!" No one had ever sounded faker.

Her heart was pounding so hard in her chest, it was like it was trying to escape her rib cage and squirm its way to him.

Lucy turned toward the girl, her back to Alex. "Uh, could I talk to you for a second?"

The girl was still smiling, and Lucy felt grateful for that, felt her insides start to uncoil. Maybe this was a good thing, actually, maybe Alex would see her talking to this girl, this cool, older girl, who was smiling right at her, and be impressed. Think, *Hmm, maybe there's more to Lucy than I thought.*

The girl said, "Of course, baby." She stepped off the sidewalk and started walking toward a tree on one of the grassy dividers that split the parking lot into sections. Lucy turned and followed.

She could feel Alex watching her; her skin warmed as though his eyes were the sun.

They stopped; the girl crossed her arms. Lucy's heart was hammering.

"Yesterday," Lucy said, "I made a mistake."

The girl stared at her. She was nodding ever so slightly. "Go on."

Lucy felt her throat start to close, like it was trying to

squeeze back all the lies she was about to tell. Lying, she knew, was bad enough, but lying to a girl who would be scary even if she didn't have magic powers, which she did, seemed completely and utterly insane. But here Lucy was, about to do it. Do broken hearts make you brave or do they just make you stupid?

But *what choice did she have?*

She couldn't tell the truth, of course, and it's not like she could get him back on her own.

It was a miracle that Alex had liked her in the first place. He was the first boy who ever had.

Still standing there out in the bright early morning sun, Lucy felt even more confused about what she'd seen the night before, about exactly *what* had happened. But she knew what she needed to say, which was this:

"I made a mistake yesterday. When I didn't take you guys up on your offer to teach me, you know, about the . . ." Lucy spoke slowly, hoping the girl would fill in what Lucy wasn't saying. But the girl just stood there looking at her, a little smile on her lips. Lucy could not tell what type of smile this was. So she just went on. "I was overwhelmed and I kind of wasn't sure if you guys were kidding or not—ha-ha—but I need to learn. I mean, I'd like to learn"—she lowered her voice to a whisper—"to win hearts, so that I can . . ." *win back the one I want,* "break one." Lucy looked up. "Please."

The other girl was fully smiling now. "I hear what you're saying there. I totally see how all of that could have happened." She nodded. Lucy felt a flood of relief. "The reason it happened . . . ," the girl continued. She held up her hand—her very large and very strong-looking hand—and raised one very big finger and beckoned Lucy close, closer. So close their noses were almost touching, and then she tapped Lucy on the tip of her nose, as though Lucy were a little baby bunny. ". . . is because you're a fucking idiot." The girl smiled again, even wider but so sweetly. "Yesterday you won the lottery." She put her arm around Lucy's shoulders and pulled Lucy in. "And then you took the winning ticket and you threw it in the trash. So my question for you is this: why on earth would we want to team up with someone who has such poor judgment? I mean, who would do a thing like what you did?" She squeezed Lucy's shoulders. Her hands were so strong it felt like she could squeeze straight through to the bone. "A fucking idiot, that's who!"

Hot panic crept up the back of Lucy's neck. She pressed her palm against her stomach where her hangman game had been. She needed the perfect string of words that would make this girl change her mind, make her reconsider. But all she could think to say was: *But I didn't understand then!* And *I made a mistake!*

"*Oooooh, I would neeever want to do that,*" she whined. "*It's wrong. It's croooooo-well!*" She balled her fist and stamped her feet like a tantrum-y toddler. She laughed until she abruptly stopped. "You don't understand much, do you, Lucy?" And then she turned and walked away.

All Lucy could do was stand there shaking her head. Because the girl was right: Lucy didn't understand anything. She didn't understand anything at all.

Eight

Except for this: it was time to go to class, the one she'd signed up for with Alex.

"Our school administration is a bunch of idiots," he'd told her the previous spring during class sign-up week. "They have some stupid rule that you can't use the darkroom unless you're enrolled in a photo class here, and they make you take the classes in order, which means I have to take Photo I if I want to use the darkroom here at all. It's total bullshit because I probably know more than most of the teachers."

"I could take it with you," Lucy had offered quickly. "That would be fun, right?" She pressed her lips together, practically vibrating with excitement at the idea of it.

Alex nodded. "Okay, sure," he'd said. He'd smiled. "Yeah, fun, definitely. I'll teach you everything you need to know."

Alex liked that, teaching her things. And Lucy liked being taught by him.

Alex had tried to show her the basic stuff in the week before he went away for the summer: how to focus, set the shutter speed, that sort of thing. "Take some good pictures for me," he'd said. "You'll need *something* to do while I'm gone, right?"

But during that entire week she couldn't focus on anything other than how much she was going to miss him. All she heard was *I'm leaving, I'm leaving, I'm leaving* every time he opened his mouth.

He'd demonstrated on his own fancy, professional-type camera, which was very different than the embarrassing neon-blue-and-pink one (with SAY CHEEZ! printed on the strap) she'd borrowed from her mom, who had used it as a kid.

Basically this all added up to Lucy having pretty much no idea what she was doing. She just turned the knobs and poked at the buttons. She didn't know anything about lighting or composition or any of the things Alex said were really important. But she figured that was okay; she wasn't trying to be an artist. When she saw something that gave her that feeling, that strange *ping-y* feeling that made her want to take a picture—like a man in a business suit eating an ice-cream cone for example, or a kid running crazily for the bus—she took one. And that was it. But every time she pressed the shutter all summer long she'd reminded herself that when she saw that picture again, she'd be with Alex. That was why it mattered.

Only now, as Lucy hurried down the empty hallway toward the photo room, she realized the film canister she had clutched in her sweaty hand was all she had left.

Lucy pushed through the gray door to the photo lab. That weird darkroom smell curled up her nose. Mr. Wexler was at the front of the room lecturing. He was a grizzly-looking man with a bushy white mustache, always drinking out of a brown clay coffee mug. There was a rumor the coffee was actually whiskey.

No one looked up as she came in.

"A good photograph shows us as much about the photographer as it does about the subject," Mr. Wexler was saying. "You give me a picture of a woman and I can tell you who took the picture, and how they feel about the woman just from the way the light catches her skin. A good photograph isn't decoration, it's a doorway into someone else's . . ."

Mr. Wexler continued on. The entire class was watching him. Lucy stood near the front of the room searching for Alex.

And there he was, standing near the back. She could not look at him and see him as anything other than her boyfriend. When he'd broken up with her he hadn't seen her in *months* but their connection was real and a connection like that doesn't just dissolve for no reason. So maybe his memory wasn't as good as hers, maybe he didn't remember her quite as well as she remembered him. What if she just needed to remind him?

Lucy edged into the crowd, slowly started working her way toward Alex. She had no idea what she planned to do when she got there, but she couldn't help herself. She squeezed between two freshman guys and got caught on one of their backpacks. She stepped on a girl's foot. "Sorry," Lucy whispered. "Excuse me, sorry, sorry." Her face was burning. She just kept going.

There was Alex, staring at the front of the room. He looked sort of lost.

She was almost there when Mr. Wexler started giving his tour of the room, and the class began to move. "Film closet!" he said. "Light box!" He probably said a bunch of other words too, but she did not register any of them. No, all she registered was the pounding of her heart as she made her way closer to her love.

"Alex," she whispered. "I need to talk to you." But Alex was watching Mr. Wexler. He did not turn.

"And now it's time to visit the most magical spot in this whole damn school," Mr. Wexler said. "The darkroom." He led the class around the corner. "Crowd in, people," he said.

The room was hot, the lights were red. Someone made a club-music-imitation *nnnnst nnnnst nnnst* sound and a few people laughed. Lucy worked herself in behind Alex.

"Hi," she whispered. He still didn't turn. Mr. Wexler was saying something about "stop bath" and "fixer." She moved over a couple inches. Their arms were touching. Her fingers grazed his. He still did not turn, but he did not move his hand either. Surely, he had to have felt that. Surely he must have known she was there. She thought she saw him smile. Yes, he knew she was there and he was glad; he was relieved that she hadn't given up on them so easily. He had probably just broken up with her because he missed her so much over the summer and didn't like feeling that vulnerable. That was something that happened to guys sometimes, right?

Suddenly someone bumped into Lucy, tossing her forward into Alex's back. Her cheek pressed against him, right between his shoulder blades. She could feel the soft fabric of his T-shirt against her skin. She closed her eyes. And she sighed.

Mmmmmm.

She could feel the vibration of the sigh working its way up from deep within her chest. A cross between a breath and a hum, that sigh. It said everything. How much she loved him. How much she missed him over the summer. How much she'd been looking forward to this moment, *needed* this moment. She stayed there, sighing against him.

Alex reached his hand back, touched her leg. Then turned around. She smiled.

Alex blinked in that red light. "Lucy?" he said. He looked confused. Then annoyed. Then like he just felt sorry for her. "What are you *doing*?"

Lucy gasped. Oh God. Her jaw dropped. She was filled with a sick and terrible panic, like she'd woken up from a nap to find that the house was on fire.

What *was* she doing?

All she could do was stare back, and raise her hand to her mouth and shake her head. "I have no idea," she whispered.

Nine

*L*ucy had had some embarrassing moments in her life:

When she was in third grade she'd fallen down in the mud and this really mean boy said it looked like she'd crapped her pants.

When she was in sixth grade, someone had bumped her lunch tray and she'd gotten ketchup all over her white sweater and that same awful boy had said it looked like she got her period out her boobs.

In seventh-grade Earth Science, while reading out loud in class, she had mispronounced the word *organism* in a very bad way.

But nothing *even came close* to what had just happened. To what she had just done.

Lucy rushed back through the crowded darkroom, into the photo lab, out into the hallway.

After this moment she knew nothing would ever be okay again.

She would need a miracle to fix any of this. To make the world a place she could live in. Or make her a person who could live in *it*. A miracle . . . or magic.

The problem was, *she had had her chance*. She had had her chance and she'd blown it. Surely she would not be given another.

Lucy flip-flopped her way into her homeroom, positioned herself over an empty chair, and crumpled down into it. She felt, if not relief, then a slight resignation. At least she was with her people now.

Homerooms at Van Buren were arranged alphabetically, and Lucy always felt a kinship with her fellow *W*s. They were the end of the alphabet people, the weirdos. They were the type of people who, if they heard a girl quietly humming to herself with a slightly frantic and desperate tone, wouldn't question it. They'd know that that's just what a person needs to do sometimes.

So, even though normally she would never hum where anyone could hear her, that's what Lucy did as she leaned back against her seat, her Alex song vibrating through her closed lips. She let her head tilt slightly to the right, and then she saw something so strange that her mouth dropped open and her humming just *stopped*: sitting there with her fellow *W*s was someone who did not fit. Not a wacky, wistful *W*. But a sexy, suavely serpentine, maybe-even-a-little-bit-scary *S* right there amongst them:

Ethan Sloane.

Was she in the wrong room?

No.

Were *S* and *W* still different letters?

Yes.

So then what the heck was he doing there sitting between Shana Wilson, who always smelled like a sneeze, and Lucy herself, a girl who had just *sighed* all over the back of the guy who dumped her?

They were *W*s. *He* was not a *W* . . . yet, in that moment she felt weirdly close to him. In that moment he was not the Ethan who she'd heard all the stories about; he was Ethan whose heart was broken, just like hers was. Who maybe had been driven so crazy by his heartbreak that he had simply forgotten his own name.

"Jason Wolf?"

Ms. Eamon, homeroom supervisor, was up at the front of the room taking attendance.

"Here."

"Jessica Wooster?"

"Present."

"Lucy Wrenn?"

"Here," Lucy said. She turned toward Ethan. *Poor guy,* she thought. In that face, in that formerly happy, always cocky face, she now saw a reflection of her own.

"Ethan Wrigley?"

"Yup." Ethan Sloane raised one finger up in the air, like he was at a restaurant signaling for the check.

"Excuse me." Lucy leaned over. Normally she'd be too shy to talk to him, but now she felt like they were just the same. Even if he didn't know it. "Didn't you used to have a different name?"

"My parents' divorce became official over the summer," he said. His voice was flat, like he'd told the story so many times he was repeating a speech from memory. He neither knew nor cared whom he was telling it to this time. "And we live with my mom now. She said she didn't want to have to see or hear or say his last name ever again, so she made us change ours. She's insane. So now I'm here."

"Heartbreak can make people crazy." Lucy lowered her voice meaningfully. She wondered if he knew she had seen him the night before.

He shrugged, tipped his head to the side, and smirked. He

looked exactly like the old Ethan, the old Ethan she never actually knew. It was a look of casual not caring, so smooth that for a second she wondered if she had imagined everything she'd seen.

But broken hearts cannot lie, *at least not to each other* . . .

He turned his head slightly, and then . . . there it was. Was it the quick twitch of the jaw? A tightness around his eyes? Something gave him away and her heart thunked in response.

"I guess so," he said.

Lucy stared at him, forced herself not to avert her gaze because she could feel something happening between them. She could feel him beginning to understand that she understood. Even if he was not entirely aware of it.

"Well, welcome to the club," she said slowly.

He blinked again. "What club?" He looked a little suspicious then and maybe even a little scared.

"Oh, you know . . ." She stopped.

He started to nod slowly.

She tried to smile. "The *W*s."

"Right." But he looked different then, his mask was gone.

Ethan brought his arm up to his face and coughed quietly into the crook of his elbow. And right then, Lucy saw something on the sleeve of his brown suede jacket—a matted area, darker than the rest. Around the edges of the dark stain was a faint white crust, like evaporated seawater.

Or whatever is left after tears dry.

An image flashed into Lucy's head. Ethan, the night before, sobbing heartbreak tears all over his jacket.

She got an idea, a stupid idea, a crazy idea, but it was all she had so she had to try.

"Hey." Her face was burning. "Can I see that for a second? Your jacket, I mean?" The words came out in a pinched jumble. She heard them as she said them.

Ethan gave her a funny look. "Yeah, sure," he said. He held out his arm.

"No, I mean, can you take it off so I can see it?" What the hell was she doing?

He raised his eyebrows.

"Please. It's just that it's . . ." She paused. *What could she say?* "Important."

And then how to explain what happened next?

Was Ethan just used to girls wanting his jacket? Was he so heartbroken that he wasn't even thinking?

All Lucy knew was that Ethan Sloane was doing it. He took off his jacket and held it out. Lucy took it. It was heavier than she'd expected it to be.

In one swift motion she stood up, tucked the heavy suede jacket under her arm, and headed for the door.

Ethan was staring at her. "THANK YOU!" she shouted. "I'LL GIVE IT BACK LATER, I PROMISE!" Then she turned and ran faster than she'd ever run in her life even though she'd been doing an awful lot of running lately. She ran straight down the hall, and when she turned the corner she saw Ethan standing in front of the door to homeroom watching her. He wasn't even trying to stop her. Over the stomp of her feet and the beat of her heart, she couldn't hear anything else.

Ten

*I*t wasn't until lunchtime that Lucy finally found Olivia in the senior section of the cafeteria, which Lucy had never been in before. Olivia was sitting at the far corner, leaning back with her feet up under the table resting on the seat across from her. She held a book in one hand and an onion ring in the other.

Lucy walked forward, her stomach in knots. All last year if someone had told Lucy to even set foot in the senior section, she would have been too scared to do it at all. But now, here she was deep in it, standing right there in front of Olivia, and no one seemed to care at all.

Lucy opened her mouth. Without even looking up, Olivia spoke.

"I heard you had a little chat with Liza this morning." Olivia moved a lock of her white-blonde hair away from her face and glanced at Lucy. Liza, Lucy realized, must be the name of the beautiful one. The one who had been so mean earlier. It seemed strange that she would have a regular person name.

Olivia looked down at the jacket that Lucy was clutching to her chest with both hands. Lucy thrust it out toward her.

"Lumpy suede isn't really my thing . . . ," Olivia said. But she was smiling ever so slightly.

"He cried on it," Lucy said. She was too loud. Olivia's eyes flashed. Lucy lowered her voice to a whisper. "I was walking back down to the road last night and . . . I saw him crying on his sleeve. And then I was with him in homeroom and I thought maybe you would want it because . . . of what you said about tears . . . ." Lucy stopped. Olivia stared at her. Maybe this was insane. Maybe it all *had* been a joke. And now here Lucy was standing with some guy's stolen jacket, not understanding that the joke was over. She felt hot prickles creep up the back of her neck and she watched Olivia's face. Waited for her to burst out laughing.

Instead, Olivia raised her eyebrows, and in a voice so quiet Lucy could barely hear her, she said, "You know these are useless to you. We can't fix you with these. It has to be tears you earned yourself."

"Okay," she said. "I mean, I didn't think I could use them for me . . . I was just trying to make up for last night. . . ." Lucy looked down. "I thought you might want them."

Olivia said coolly. "Once we harvest the magic from a broken heart, there is no more. Any additional tears are useless. Which is good, I suppose, because otherwise every time we break a heart we'd have to stand around for a week with a cup. Gil already got the magic from Ethan's heart when she broke it, which was weeks ago."

Lucy nodded. "I'm sorry to bother you." She stepped back, her face burning. What should she do? What *could* she do? She turned to go.

"Wait," Olivia said. Her voice was a whisper. "Your attempt to help was not particularly helpful. But the effort is endearing. Meet us after school. We like you again," Olivia said. Lucy could feel Olivia's smile coursing through her. "For now."

The rest of the day crept by in slow motion. Lucy went to her bio lab, to her English elective. During her free period she went back to the photo room, and Mr. Wexler showed her how to develop a roll of film. Then European History, Advanced Algebra. In each one she made up vague excuses to explain her absence the day before, and because she was the kind of girl she was, everyone believed her completely and without question.

When the final bell rang, Lucy walked out front. Olivia, Liza, and Gil were across the parking lot, standing around that perfect, baby blue convertible. She started toward them.

Beeeep.

Lucy looked up.

Tristan pulled right up to the curb, window down. He leaned far back in his seat, eyes shaded under a dark brown army hat, looking like he hadn't gone to class at all, but had in fact been sitting there relaxing all day. One arm was hanging halfway out the window. In his hand was a long pink ribbon at the end of which was a big, shiny Mylar balloon.

"Well, hello there, little lady," he said. He tugged the string, and the balloon bounced.

"What's that?" Lucy pointed to the balloon. Written in giant, light blue letters, the same color as the sky, CONGRATU-LATIONS, GRADUATE. She raised her eyebrows. "Graduate?"

"Well, they didn't have 'Good Riddance, Fucko' in stock," said Tristan. "So this seemed like the next-obvious choice. Now hop up in here, little lady. Uncle Tristy is going to take you and this here balloon on an extravaganza of exciting adventures. Yes, that's right, I said *extravaganza!*" He swooped his arm. The balloon bounced some more.

"That sounds so fun, Tristy. But . . ." Lucy looked up where Olivia, Liza, and Gil were still standing by that car. Gil had her hand raised up to her eyes and she was squinting toward them. When she spotted Lucy, she waved. "I . . . can't come."

"Okay," Tristan said easily, the way he said everything. "Whatcha doing?"

Lucy wanted so badly to tell him the truth. Oh, how much, how very, very much she wanted to. The words were flinging themselves against her cheeks, trying to slip their way out between her clamped lips. Lucy swallowed hard, forced them down. "I'm supposed to do something with them."

She pointed to where the three girls stood.

Tristan craned his neck to see.

"You are?" He sounded confused. Which made sense. Lucy could not remember the last time she'd had an after-school plan with someone other than Tristan or Alex. It wasn't that she was a complete social outcast; it's just that she was sort of invisible. Every so often she'd make a plan with another girl from one of her classes. Usually the plan revolved around doing homework. Once a couple girls from her homeroom had asked her to go shopping but she got a stomachache and couldn't go. Tristan was basically her only friend.

"Yeah, the short-haired one and I had a class together last year. They asked me to hang out with them after school." Lucy bit her lip. It wasn't exactly a lie. But it wasn't exactly not a lie either.

For a moment they both stared at the three girls standing by that beautiful, old car. It looked like the sun was shining brighter on them than it was on anything else.

Tristan turned back. "That tall one is *mmmf*." He waggled his eyebrows and stuck his tongue out of the corner of his mouth, a joke imitation of the kind of guy who would do that and mean it. "Wanna do something tomorrow?"

"Yes, please," she said.

He held out the balloon. "I believe this belongs to you, graduate."

Lucy turned toward the girls, then looked to the balloon, then back to them. She imagined herself walking up to them with that balloon and started to blush.

Tristan nodded, understood without her saying anything. He smiled. "Have fun, kiddo."

"Thanks." She forced a smile back.

Tristan opened his fist. The balloon rose up out of it. "It's better this way anyway," he said. "Balloons really hate being tied down."

Lucy wasn't sure what to say when she got to the car, so she pretended to cough until they noticed her.

Gil reached out and squeezed Lucy's hand. A jolt of friendship went all the way up Lucy's arm into her chest where her empty heart soaked it up.

"I hope your fake cough isn't contagious," said Liza.

Olivia gave a sly half smile. She got in the driver's seat. Liza took shotgun. Gil pulled Lucy next to her in the back.

"Swap time," Olivia said. The three of them took out their phones and passed them clockwise. Then they started scrolling through each other's messages.

"Jason M misses you and wants to know your shoe size," Liza said to Olivia. "Pete wants to make sure we're coming Saturday. Clarkson says, 'hahahahahahaha' with about ten exclamation points. Kyle says a friend of his is having a party tomorrow and that also he is reading a book he thinks you might like and wants to know when he can meet up and give it to you." Liza turned toward Olivia and rolled her eyes. "And some guy from a three-one-oh number can't stop thinking about you. Who's that?"

"Three-one-oh's L.A.?" Olivia shrugged. "No idea."

Olivia was looking down at Gil's phone. "Gilly, Rowan wants to know if he bought you a ticket to visit him in Australia if you'd use it. Jason says he's sitting next to someone really smelly and that you're lucky smell-o-texts haven't been invented yet. Mikey wants to know what you're up to this weekend and if you like paella. Ethan sent you a heart emoticon, but he did it wrong, used an eight for the top instead of a three."

"Oh, that's sweet," Gil said.

"It's not. It's ridiculous," said Liza.

Gil shook her head. "Sammy and Ian F want you to come to a party on Saturday. Evan says he bought you something that he thinks you'll like and then he wrote a wink face so

I guess that means it's dirty. And Scott called you sixteen times. And . . ." The sound of lightning striking filled the car. "Now seventeen because he's calling you again." Gil handed Liza her phone. Liza tossed it in Lucy's lap.

"Tell him I'm not going to make it this afternoon. Imply that I might be with another boy."

Lucy looked down. SCOTT—NOT BROKEN YET was blinking on the screen.

"It's a phone," Liza said. "Pick it up."

Lucy lifted the phone to her ear. Hit TALK. Her palms were already sweating.

"Hel—" she started to say.

"Oh, thank *God*." The voice coming through the phone was deep, not a boy's voice but a man's voice. "I've been calling you and calling you. Did you get any of my messages?"

"He-hello?"

"You're still coming this afternoon, aren't you?"

"This isn't . . ."

"Sorry, sorry. That came out wrong. I don't mean to sound demanding . . ." The voice paused. "It's just that I planned something special for this afternoon and I wanted to make sure you . . ."

"Um, this isn't Liza."

Pause.

"Oh." The voice coughed. "Who is this?"

"This is Lucy, Liza's . . ." She paused. "I'm Lucy. Liza wanted me to . . ." Lucy looked down at her lap; she could feel them watching her. "Liza wanted me to tell you that she can't make it this afternoon."

"Tell him about the other guy," Liza whispered.

"Oh." There was a long pause. "God. Okay. Right. I should have figured that maybe. Uh, what's she doing?"

"I don't know. She just said that she can't make it. She's . . ." Lucy felt her heart squeezing for whoever this was. "She's sorry."

"Oh," he said. "Um. Oh. Well. Okay. I left her a voice mail and emailed her and stuff too, but I'm not sure if she got it. I think my phone's been weird and you know how unreliable email is and everything. Can you tell her that I left her voice mails and that I'll call her back again later?"

"Okay."

"Promise me you'll tell her that?"

"I promise."

"Did she get the bunny cake?"

"I don't know."

"The orchid?"

"I don't know."

"Did she like the singing telegram? I wasn't sure if she was one of those people who was scared of clowns or not. . . ,"

"I don't know." Lucy could feel Liza glaring at her. "I'm sorry."

"Sure," the voice said. He sounded crushed. And then, "Hey, did something happen with her mom again? Is *that* what's going on?"

"I don't know what's going on," Lucy said. "I . . ."

"Tell him about the other guy!" Liza hissed.

Lucy looked down.

"Give it to me." Liza reached out and grabbed the phone. Then she pressed what looked like a blue ice cube against Lucy's neck. Lucy felt a sudden intense coldness in her throat.

". . . think she's out with some friend of hers, Justin something. I don't know. Tall, muscle-y, do you know him?" Liza said into the phone.

Lucy stared and her mouth dropped open. *Liza was talking in Lucy's voice.* Lucy tried to speak, but no words would come out. She brought her hand to her freezing throat. Liza continued. "She said she'll be back late. I'll tell her you called though. Byeeeee!"

Liza hung up.

"There," she said.

Olivia turned toward Lucy. "I'm really so sorry, sugar lump, that should not have happened. *We do not use our magic on our potential sisters.*" Olivia looked at Liza. "Liza *will not do anything like that again.*"

"*What?*" Liza said. "She was messing it up!" But she sounded like a little kid arguing with her parents when she knew there was no point in trying to fight.

For a second the car was silent.

"So what did he say to you?" Liza asked.

Lucy opened her mouth. She felt her heart trying to pound its way out. Sweat sprung out all over her body. Her throat was still so cold. She couldn't speak.

"Liza!" Olivia said sharply.

Liza reached out and tapped Lucy's throat again. Lucy felt a melting and then her words came. "He wanted to know if something happened with your mom," Lucy said. Her hands were shaking.

What had Liza done to her?

"He *what*?"

Lucy flinched.

"How the hell does he even know . . ." Liza shook her head. She bit her lip and looked out the window. "Anything else?"

Lucy was breathing in tiny little gasps. "He-he also a-asked me to tell you he called and texted and would call you tomorrow. He asked if you got the flowers he sent and the . . ."

Liza shook her head. She laughed. "God, how pathetic." She looked at Lucy again. "Who told you to tell him I was *sorry*? Do *not* tell a guy that I said I am *sorry* unless I *tell you* to tell him I said I was sorry. What's *wrong* with you?"

"I'm sorry, I . . ."

Olivia glanced at Liza. "Is Scott ready?" Her words were laced with meaning.

"Almost." Liza nodded, then went back to her phone. "Tall Chris put us on the comp list to see some band on Friday night. But it's like some emo band. And emo-boy-heartbreak tears are hardly worth anything. Whatever."

Lucy put her hand against her throat. *What had just happened?* "What did you do there?" she said. "What did you do to me?" But Liza didn't answer.

Olivia flipped on the radio. A song Lucy knew came on and Olivia turned it up loud. Lucy felt her whole body sizzling. Lucy sang along quietly to calm herself. She closed her eyes, the wind blew her hair. *These girls are magic.* If she'd had even the slightest hint of a doubt left, she didn't anymore. They had power. They could destroy her. Or they could give her everything she wanted.

Ten minutes later they pulled up in front of a bunch of row houses a couple of towns away from their clean, little suburb. The lawns were all bare and the paint on most of the houses was peeling. A woman was pushing a pink baby stroller toward them. As she passed, Lucy realized the woman was no older than Lucy. They got out of the car and walked up to a blue house. There was a guy with a shaved head and a goatee sitting on the stoop. He looked like he was in his forties. He had a can of something in a paper bag.

Lucy could feel the guy on the stairs watching them with sleepy eyes. He gave Olivia a nod, like he knew her. Olivia walked inside. And when Gil passed he smiled and said, "Babybabybaby," but it was sweet somehow, not skeevy.

And Gil said, "Herbiiiiiee," and he caught one of her small hands in his big ones and brought it to his lips and kissed it. Gil squeezed his shoulder and then walked inside too.

When Liza was standing next to him he didn't say anything, just stuck out his brown-paper-bagged can. She grabbed it, raised it up to her lips, and took a long, slow swallow.

Liza handed him back the can. The guy held it upside down and a few drops sprinkled out onto the steps.

"I owe you a beer," Liza called out behind her.

And the guy, he just opened his mouth and laughed. His teeth were perfect, movie-star teeth, the kind that people have when they have unlimited money to devote to the inside of their mouths.

Lucy stared at the man on the stoop with his dirty hands and his beer can and the sun streaming down on him and his head tipped back and his lovely teeth all lined up in a row and Lucy thought about how Alex would probably have liked to take a picture of him.

Lucy's phone buzzed in her pocket. Her heart leapt.

She wondered if it was Alex reading her mind!

But it was Tristan.

He'd sent her a photo of a balloon with GOOD RIDDANCE, FUCKO written on it in Sharpie. He was smiling next to it, giving a big, cheesy thumbs-up.

When Lucy looked up, the other girls were already inside.

"And oh," Olivia called out, not turning back, "by the way, this is a test."

"A test of *what*?" Lucy said. "What am I supposed to do?" But no one answered.

Lucy hovered in the doorway.

Three guys were in the room in front of her looking like they belonged in an ad for surf gear or skateboards. There was one sitting on the couch leaning forward, tan arms wrapped in leather bands, one lying down on the couch with his shoes off, and one cross-legged on the floor, sun-bleached hair flopping in his face. They were beautiful, all of them, and had that ease about them that implied not that they didn't know what they looked like, but that they knew and didn't care.

Lucy just stood there blushing.

There was, Lucy had long ago realized, an art to entering into rooms where groups of people were already having fun. One joke, one question, one clever observation was all one needed to cross the invisible line between person-by-the-door and person-in-the-room. This would have been hard for Lucy even on a good day, but then, with the wounds of a broken heart festering inside her chest, it felt completely impossible.

"Oh no, no you don't!" Gil said sweetly. Gil sat cross-legged on a giant blue cushion on the floor, holding a video game controller. Projected on the wall in front of her, a guy in a silver space suit was fighting a many-headed monster. He was projected so big that he was the size of an actual person. One by one she was making the spaceman knock off the monster's heads. The screen flashed. The monster screamed and fell off the cliff. The game was over.

"Sheeeeeeeeeeeeeeyat," Leather Bracelets said. "We've been trying to do that for like a month."

Barefoot Lying on the Couch sat halfway up, "JACK! JAAAACK!! You owe Gil a hundred bucks."

"Damn it!" a voice called from the other room. Lucy realized then that Olivia and Liza were nowhere in sight.

Gil laughed and shook her head.

Liza walked back in from the kitchen. Behind her was a tall guy wearing jeans and a short, pink bathrobe with frills around the neck. He was holding two frosted martini glasses, both full.

Leather Bracelets looked at the martinis and raised his eyebrows.

"Liza asked for one," Bathrobe said. "She came in here and said, 'Where's my martini?' Just like a mean husband from the fifties."

"Dude," said Sun-bleached. "That wasn't asking, that was demanding."

"She's a demander," said Bracelets. "A demandstress."

But they were smiling. What was Lucy supposed to be doing? Whatever it was, she was quite sure that hovering in the doorway was not it.

"Where I'm from," said Lying on the Couch. He had a slight southern accent. He crossed his legs at the ankles and stretched out his toes. They were very long, like fingers almost. "Where I'm from we just call that a bitch."

Liza smiled. "Where you're from, honey, they've just started walking upright. I don't think they've gotten around to inventing words yet." Then she raised the glass in his direction, like she was toasting him and they all laughed. She brought the glass to her lips and tipped it back.

"How is it?" Bracelets asked. The glass was empty. "Was it . . . ?"

Liza wiped a few droplets of liquid off her lower lip with her middle finger. It looked both suggestive and mean. "Vile." She licked the tip of her middle finger and gave him back the glass.

"Speaking of . . . things," said Bathrobe. He turned toward the big video screen where the end-of-game sequence was still going—now the spaceman was standing on a pedestal with fireworks exploding behind him while one at a time hot lady characters walked up and tossed their bras at him. Bathrobe shook his head slowly, then turned toward Gil and bowed low. He pulled a fistful of bills out of his bathrobe pocket and held them up over his head.

Gil just laughed. "I don't want your money, Jackie."

Bathrobe/Jack shook his fist in the air. "No, no, you have to take it. Otherwise I will feel like a bet welsher. Which is even worse than being broke."

"Take it, Gil," Liza said. "Or these assholes will make fun of him forever and the pharmaceuticals he'll need to get over it will cost *way* more than a hundred bucks."

Bathrobe/Jack grinned and stuck his tongue out at Liza through his teeth.

"The girl's right though," said Lying on the Couch. "We assholes will do that."

Gil took the crumpled-up bills. "Okay. Okay, okay." But she was shaking her head.

Lucy leaned her head against the door frame. She did not even need to know what she was being tested on to know that she was failing.

Olivia walked slowly back toward the kitchen. "Come on, Gilly," she said. Gil got up and followed; so did Bracelets and Sun-bleached and Liza. And then it was just the three of them, Lucy in the doorway, Bathrobe/Jack holding the martini, and Lying on the Couch.

There was paint chipping on the door frame; she picked at it with her pinky. A little flake came off and she pressed it into the pad of her thumb with her nail. It split in half. No one was saying anything. She looked up.

Bathrobe/Jack was watching her. He rubbed the top of his head. "We haven't offered anything to our guest." He tipped his martini toward her. Liquid sloshed out onto the floor. "Maybe she wants this delicious handcrafted imbibeable."

"Um," Lucy started to say very quietly. She was staring down at the floor. "No thank you." But when she looked up, she realized they hadn't heard her.

"Well, our guest hasn't even come in the room yet," Lying on the Couch said. "She's just been standing at the door watching us. A little creepy if you ask me."

"She can hear you, B," Bathrobe/Jack whispered loudly.

"How do you know that? She appears to be mute. Maybe she's deaf too." But he was smiling at her. Her heart pounded. "Actually I don't think she's mute," Lying on the Couch/B said. "Muteness is really rare."

"So you're saying she just doesn't want to talk to us?" Jack asked. "Why wouldn't she want to talk to us?"

"I don't know," said B. "Maybe you should ask her."

Jack reached into his bathrobe pocket and took out a plastic magic wand like the kind that comes in magic sets for kids. Lucy stared at it. Her stomach tightened.

Jack waved the wand. "Speak!"

Lucy pressed her lips together, sure that at any second her

mouth would open and words would start pouring out.

He waved the wand again. Nothing happened.

"Um?" Lucy said.

"Ha! It worked!" Jack shouted. He thrust the martini up in the air and more of it sloshed out. "I *am* magic. I knew it!"

But in that moment Lucy knew it was all just a joke.

"Well?" B said.

Lucy's heart pumped blood to her already hot face. "I don't know," she said. It was all she could think to say. "I'm sorry. I'm. . ." She didn't know what to say after that, so she just stood there.

Jack tucked the wand behind his ear. Then he raised his eyebrows and nodded. "Fair enough. You don't know. I don't either." And then they just stood in silence.

A moment later Olivia, Liza, and Gil came back into the room.

Liza grabbed B's butt. Gil and Olivia hugged the boys goodbye. Lucy just stood there awkwardly until Olivia walked out the door and they all followed.

The guy who'd been sitting on the front steps was gone. His empty beer can was sitting on its side on the pavement and there was a little puddle next to it, as though he had melted and that's what was left.

"Well then," Olivia said.

"Well then," said Gil. She turned toward Lucy and smiled.

"This was such a waste of time," Liza said. "Except for

Gilly's hundred bucks." She marched ahead and got in the car. She turned back, stared at Gil. "Which you probably slipped back in his pocket when you were hugging him good-bye just like you did after our last five bets."

"I felt bad!" Gil said.

"You would have made the best pickpocket on earth. If only you didn't keep getting it backwards." Liza was shaking her head. "Well, now it was a *complete* waste of time. And just so you know, Lucy"—Liza glared at her—"you got an F."

"No, no you didn't," Gil said. "It doesn't work like that; you weren't being graded." She turned back toward Liza. "Lucy was nervous," Gil said. "That's natural."

"It's not natural." Olivia shook her head as she got in the car. "Understandable? Maybe. But not natural. We were not all meant to be so afraid of each other. She was afraid because she's been conditioned to be afraid."

"She was *afraid* because sweet wittew baby bunnies are always afwaid," Liza said. She got in shotgun and stuck her long legs out the open window.

"Liza! You're being mean." Gil got in the back. Lucy got in too.

"What?" Liza flipped down the mirror and stared at her excruciatingly gorgeous face. "It's true."

"She isn't one thing or another thing." Olivia's voice was calm and low, but there was something in it that made Lucy's heart beat faster. "People are endlessly changeable." Olivia turned toward Liza. "You of all people should know that."

Olivia started to drive.

"But what were you testing?" Lucy said. The wind was rushing around inside the car now and she wasn't even sure if anyone heard her. She tightened her stomach, spoke louder. "I didn't even know what I was being tested on!"

Gil turned. "We needed to see where you were starting from is all."

"And now we know," Liza said.

"But I had no idea what I was being tested on," Lucy repeated. She felt suddenly sick.

"So what," Liza said. "Grow the fuck up. You've had like what, fifteen years to prepare for this?"

"It's not about fair or not fair. Life is what you make it; *everything* is what you make it." Olivia laughed. "Put that on a poster with a cat! That wasn't just a test, it was also lesson one."

"Yes, lesson one," said Liza. "Have a personality."

"Did you happen to notice how incredibly hot those guys were?" Olivia asked.

"Yes," Lucy said.

"They're used to girls being scared of them or too polite or just fawning. Did you notice how much they all seem to love Liza?"

"It's not just because I'm hot," Liza said. "Actually, it has nothing to do with it."

"It's because of the sass factor. She makes them work for it and she's a little mean."

"So the lesson is to be mean?"

"Not *mean* mean exactly," Gil said. "There's a difference between being mean mean and being fun mean. Liza's fun mean." Gil paused. "Most of the time." Liza reached her hand back without turning around and made a grabbing motion. Gil giggled. "Mean mean hurts feelings and that's not the goal here, fun mean adds a little sizzle to everything and makes all interactions into a game. You toss something, they hit it back. They toss something, you hit it back."

Lucy blinked.

"This concept should not be new to you," said Liza. "It's called flir-ting." Liza turned toward Olivia. "This is a waste. She's not going to be able to do any of this. I mean look at her, she's practically shaking right now. And she doesn't even know what flirting is! If you really want a fourth we can find someone else. . . ."

Lucy wanted to ask her—a fourth for *what*? But she was scared to.

"*Liza,*" Olivia said. There was a low warning tone in her voice.

"I think you might be surprised, Li," Gil said gently. "Besides, we said we'd help her." Gil glanced at Lucy. "I want to help her." Their eyes met. Gil smiled a warm, secret smile. Lucy felt something happening inside her chest: a softening, an opening. Suddenly Lucy saw in Gil's eyes a reflection of herself, not as a dump-able mute, but as someone worth fighting for, someone worth trying to save. And for a moment Lucy thought perhaps she understood what it was that made guys, unattainable guys like Ethan, love her enough to let themselves break.

"Well, there's not enough time," Liza said. She crossed her arms. "Not enough to fix this one . . ."

Gil's smile had wrapped a delicate bubble-cushion around Lucy's heart. But Liza's words popped it and put a heavy steel clock in her belly. And that clock started to tick.

Tick tick tick.

Because the thing was, Lucy *agreed* with Liza. Six days was nothing. No time at all. In six days she'd be back on her own. Alone forever unless she had their help.

And their magic.

"What if you give me some of the . . . ," Lucy started to say.

Tick tick tick. The clock ticked in time with the pounding of her heart.

"We don't just 'give' you anything," said Olivia. "Anything you get from us, you have to earn. You have to prove that you're worthy of it."

"How do I do that?" Lucy said, too quickly.

"By doing everything we say, obviously." Liza snorted. "Quick, meow like a kitty."

Gil shook her head. "It's not like that." She reached out and squeezed Lucy's shoulder. When Lucy turned, Gil winked.

Olivia pushed down on the gas and the car sped up smoothly. Faster and faster they went until the trees transformed into a green-and-brown-vibrating stripe and it felt like they were flying. Lucy closed her eyes. She felt the air rushing past her. "Six days is an eternity," Olivia said. "Anything can happen. . . ."

Eleven

At night Olivia's enormous and eerily beautiful house made a strange kind of sense. It was a house for having secret moments, nights that feel like a dream, and dreams that feel real. It was a house for doing things in that time between sundown and sunup when the world is covered in a velvety black blanket, under which you can do whatever you want.

But in the slowly fading, late afternoon sunlight, it didn't make any sense at all. It was too tall, too not-quite-now-ish. It felt like the air in the house had been in there a long time, not in a sad and musty way, but in a meaningful way, like every bit of it had circled through who-knows-how-many other peoples' lungs, like by breathing it you were mysteriously connected to them all.

A pile of packages had been left on the front steps—a light-blue leather box ringed in gold, three huge bouquets of flowers, a giant paper bag with gold twine handles, a basket wrapped in peach cellophane. The girls stepped over them as they walked inside.

"What *is* all that stuff?" Lucy asked.

"Gifts from our guests last night," Olivia said. "We tried something that may have worked a little too well."

"What'd you try? Some sort of spell?"

"No," Liza said. "We made them some really fucking good rice pudding."

Lucy blushed.

"Your parents must be really cool letting you have such a big party and on a school night and everything," Lucy said. As soon as Lucy heard herself she blushed even more. She sounded like a six-year-old.

"Yeah," Olivia said. "Right." She laughed and walked up the stairs, Liza following close behind.

"Her parents are dead," Gil whispered. "Olivia lives alone."

"She *does*?" Lucy said. "But . . . how?" She looked at the back of Olivia's white-blonde head.

"After her parents died she moved in here with her grandmother, but her grandmother died a little over a year ago so now she lives here by herself. She has her grandma's credit cards and bank info and can forge her signature so . . . she does."

"That's really s—," Lucy started to say.

Gil looked up the stairs; Olivia and Liza had already disappeared down the hallway. Gil put one finger in front of her lips and gave Lucy a little push up the stairs.

They headed down a long hallway lined with many doors, all of which were closed. Lucy was brought into an enormous bathroom with a claw-foot tub and a cream-colored velvet daybed. A large, crystal chandelier like you'd see in a fancy hotel lobby hung down into the center of the room spraying tiny points of light. Before Lucy even had a chance to think, *A chandelier! In the bathroom!* she felt herself pressed down into a straight-backed chair.

Olivia raised her hand. She had long, strong-looking fingers. She snapped them.

Six serpentine arms moved around Lucy in unison, as though the three girls had merged into one ancient many-armed goddess.

A hand slid Lucy's ponytail holder off and her light brown hair fell around her shoulders. In another hand, silver scissors appeared. *Sssssshk ssshk shhk*, the blades slid against each other, like a metallic-winged dragonfly fluttering, fluttering around her head. Wisps of hair began to fall, landing on her arms, her shoulders, her bare legs. She stared at a few strands that lay there on her thigh, pieces of herself that were not attached anymore. Another hand brushed those discarded pieces of Lucy off her leg, onto the floor.

Lucy's sad broken heart pounded painfully, pushing blood out. What were they *doing* to her?

"Wait, are you . . . ," she started to say. She didn't even know what she was asking.

And someone said, "Ssh."

She closed her eyes to quiet her heart.

She would trust them. She had to.

The air smelled of sweet chemicals mingled with flowers and spice. Someone applied something to her head, thick and cold.

A cream of some kind was rubbed onto her cheeks, her forehead, her nose. Her eyelids. Her heart squeezed again. Blood rushed in. Memory pumped out.

She's in her backyard with Alex as the sun is going down. It is getting chilly but they're not going inside. She is on her back and is intensely aware of everything that's under her—the dirt, lumpy and hard, grass on top, softer, and above that, the thick down comforter that naughty, naughty Lucy has dragged outside and spread out on the damp grass. Later she will have to hide it as she sneaks it back into her bedroom. Her mother, who does not often get mad, might be mad if she sees it. But Lucy is not thinking about this now, nor about how Alex is leaving for the summer in just eleven days. No, for the first time in a very long time she is not thinking about anything. She is just there,

*out there on the lawn with her boyfriend and a dozen blinking
fireflies, which she can't see because her eyes are closed now. She
feels something softly tickling her cheek. She opens her eyes, finds
Alex staring at her, tracing her features with a blade of grass.
He smiles and brushes her hair back from her face. "If I were a
painter and I were painting you," he says, his voice low, "this is
where I would start." Gently with his blade of grass he shows her.*

Time was passing. Time had passed.

A voice said she was done.

Lucy opened her eyes. She was led over to a huge cream-
colored sink with a giant gold faucet and from the neck up
everything was rinsed. Someone patted her face with a towel.

Hot air blasted into her hair.

"All right, gorgeous," said Gil. "Olivia and I have to go
do something downstairs. Liza is going to help you with the
rest."

"Wait," said Lucy. She reached up and touched her hair.
It felt smooth. She pulled a lock of it toward her face. What
had been a light, mousey sort of brown was now dark, almost
black with hints of eggplant and cherry.

Gil smiled. "Don't worry, Liza will be nice to you." She
looked up at Liza. "Won't you?"

"I'm always nice," Liza said. But she wasn't smiling.

Gil squeezed Lucy's shoulder, and followed Olivia out.

Liza pulled out a big black toolbox and opened it. Inside
was an assortment of jars and tubes and pots and brushes.

She picked out a thin brush and a jar of what looked like black ink. Lucy's heart began to pound.

"Oh, calm down," Liza said. "The pleasure I'd get from giving you a henna unibrow would not be worth what Olivia would do to me if I did it." She shook her head, then pointed the brush at Lucy. "But don't think it didn't occur to me. Close your eyes." She was leaning so close Lucy could feel Liza's breath on her face. "The good thing about you is that you don't really look like one thing or another. Open them." Liza leaned back. "Close them. Me? I look like a fifties pinup girl. I have big tits and a big ass. I have a sweetie-pie-looking face. That's just what I look like. Okay, open them. You, on the other hand, you're totally blank. You could be anyone. Stop moving your mouth." She put something on Lucy's lips. "Blot." She took out a big brush and started pulling Lucy's hair back.

Lucy's phone vibrated.

Liza reached out and grabbed it off the counter. "Ooooh, a text from a booooy."

Lucy's heart began to pound. Alex? Liza held the phone up over Lucy's head as Lucy reached for it.

"Who's Tristan?" said Liza.

"My friend." Lucy's heart sank.

"Your *friend*?"

Lucy reached again.

Liza raised one eyebrow, put one freakishly strong hand on

Lucy's shoulder, and pushed her back down into the seat. "I am assuming this Tristan is a dude, correct?"

"Right."

"Does he like girls?"

Lucy nodded.

"Well. Then he's not your friend."

"I don't know what you mean."

"Guys who like girls aren't ever just *friends* with them. The only time a guy and a girl can ever be just friends is if the guy is gay. Otherwise there's something else going on."

Lucy shook her head. "It's not like that." She felt her face begin to flush. "We've been friends forever. We're like brother and sister."

Liza started laughing.

"Well, isn't that some adorable bullshit." She looked down at the phone and read. "'Hope you're having fun over there, slugger.'" The phone vibrated in her hand. "Oh look, another one. 'PS Found something really cool, must show you later.'" Liza looked at her. "Hmmm?"

Liza then held up Lucy's phone. "Smile, slugger." She snapped a picture and started texting. "Of course. Don't I look like I'm having fun?"

"Wait!" Lucy said. "Don't send that!"

"Too late." Liza pressed a few more buttons.

Liza handed her back the phone so Lucy could see the photo she sent.

There on that screen was a picture of a girl.

Lucy's little mouth dropped open into an O as she stared at her.

If you looked at the old Lucy, and slowly started turning around in a circle, by the time you were facing her again you might have forgotten what she'd looked like. Or so she thought anyway.

But the girl in the photo was . . . not the kind of girl you'd forget.

Her eyes were big and green, lined with the thinnest stripe of jet-black liner; her lashes looked thick and dark. Her sexy mouth was stained a deep matte red. Her dark, shiny hair was pulled back into a sleek ponytail, which somehow seemed to have changed the shape of her face. This girl had *cheekbones.*

What would Alex say if he saw her like this? She tried to imagine how she'd feel sitting there talking to him, all her words coming through this lush lipsticked mouth. But she just couldn't.

Tristan's reply popped up on the screen. *Whoa, bud, you look like a Russian spy posing as a hostess at a fancy cocktail bar.*

"All right, enough," said Liza. She snatched back Lucy's phone and stuck it in her back pocket. "That's one person you can be. Now let's try something else." Liza released Lucy's hair from its ponytail. She wiped off Lucy's lipstick and removed the mascara from her bottom lashes. Then she rubbed the tiniest bit of petal-pink blush on the tops of Lucy's cheeks and a dab of berry-colored gloss on the center of her bottom lip.

"Let's see what your completely platonic brother-friend thinks about this one," Liza said.

"Don't." Lucy reached out for the phone, but Liza held her in her chair with one hand and held the phone up with the other. "Seriously . . . ," Lucy said. But it was too late. Liza took another photo and sent it. Lucy turned toward the mirror.

She looked completely different this time. Sweet and innocent on the surface, but with a simmering layer underneath. The blush made her face look flushed, like she had recently been doing something face-flush-worthy. Her lips were plump and shiny, like ripe fruit.

"Guess your *buddy* wasn't into it." Liza made a frowny face and put the phone down. "That's okay. Someone else will be. You can be anyone now," she said. "Whoever you need to be."

"But who do I need to be?" Lucy said. Although what she really wanted to say, but didn't, was "Who do I need to be to get Alex back?"

Liza half smiled, then shrugged.

"Wash your face," she said. "Then we start again."

Half an hour and four faces later, Liza left Lucy with dewy skin, flushed cheeks, smudgy eye makeup, and her hair combed into a strangely sexy, tousled pile.

Olivia and Gil were back in the bathroom. Liza was putting cat's-eye liner on Olivia.

"You look amazing," Gil said, then leaned over and whispered into Lucy's ear, so no one else could hear her, "just one last thing." And she gave Lucy's neck a little squirt of perfume. Lucy breathed in deep. It smelled like ginger and something she could not name.

Lucy moved her hand up to touch her face, to make sure, just to make sure. The hand in the mirror moved too.

"Well," Liza said from across the room, "I *am* sort of a miracle worker. So long as she never has to talk to anyone, she'll do just fine. Maybe it's time to start telling everyone she really *is* a mute."

"Liza," a voice said, "maybe it's time for you to shut the hell up."

Lucy gasped because suddenly she realized something: it was her own voice that had said it. Out of her very own mouth.

For a moment, the room was silent. No one moved. Perhaps they had all stopped breathing.

This was very bad. A horrible mistake.

Lucy opened her mouth, the apology bubbling over the edges of her lip, ready to dribble down her chin. "I . . ."

And at the same time Liza opened hers and a single syllable slid out. "You . . ."

But they were both drowned out by something else, a tinkling, jingling sound that filled the entire room. A delighted laugh. Olivia's. "See, Li-Li?" She draped one arm around Liza's shoulders. "People change faster than you think. . . ."

Twelve

n old country song was playing on the stereo.

"Sad times with my baby baby gone, I'll sing this song till she comes back home."

It was an hour later and Gil had led them into a big room filled with row after row of pool tables. Hanging over each one was a yellow glass lantern. The place smelled like chalk and something musty.

"What is this place?" Lucy asked.

Liza pointed to a sign over the bar, RANDY'S BILLIARDS, and rolled her eyes.

Lucy looked around. The walls were covered in huge black-and-white photos of people playing pool in the forties and fifties. Lucy stared at one of a woman with long, dark hair and dark-painted lips holding a cue, poised for a shot. There was a row of guys behind her all staring.

"It's a little run-down," Gil said. "But it's always ninety-nine percent guys, which is why we brought you here. And Randy, who runs it, is nice so . . ."

As if on cue a big grizzly bear of a man stepped out from behind the bar. He was wearing a plaid shirt and a cowboy hat and had a cigar chomped between his teeth. "What's this you're saying, Miss Gillian?"

"I was just saying that yours is the best pool hall I've ever been to," Gil said. "But that the owner's a big ol' jerk."

He grinned and shook his head. "No more betting, little lady," he said. "You hear?" He pointed his cigar at her, and then up to a sign on the wall. NO GAMBLING, it said in peeling red letters.

"No more smoking, big guy." She pointed to the big NO SMOKING sign right next to it.

He winked and shook his cigar at her. The smoke curled up.

He handed Gil a stacked set of balls. "Take sixteen. On the house for my favorite sharks."

Gil smiled and kissed him on the cheek, then walked toward the back; Olivia, Liza, and Lucy followed.

As they walked, every guy looked up; some smiled, some nodded, some tried to pretend they were less aware of the girls than they obviously were.

"You know those guys?" asked Lucy.

"Well, not all of them . . ." Olivia smiled. "Yet."

"We like to come here to try stuff out," Gil said. "It's a good place to practice all sorts of things. And there's hardly ever any girls here. . . ."

"Not that we're afraid of a little competition," said Liza.

Liza and Olivia wandered off.

Gil led Lucy over to one of the tables where two guys in their midtwenties were in a heated game. One was walking slowly around the table, staring at it, like a hunter stalking his prey. He was wearing a thin black T-shirt stretched across the muscles of his back.

"A hundred bucks says my friend here can make that shot for you," Gil called out. "Left corner pocket." On the table were one white ball, two striped balls, and a black ball off to the side.

"Yeah, right," said the guy's opponent. He let out a laugh. "Even I wouldn't be able to make that shot. And"—he smirked and smoothed his greasy-looking goatee—"I've never missed a shot in my life."

"Well, then let your friend make the bet and win the money."

Goatee snorted. "Hell, this little thing gets that shot, I'll give you a hundred bucks too."

"Sounds good to me," Gil said.

"I'm in," said the guy in the black shirt.

Lucy stared at Gil. What was she *doing*? "I'm a terrible pool player," Lucy whispered. She'd played pool all of once in her entire life, with Tristan two summers ago. The balls kept bouncing off the table.

"I think you might be better than you think," Gil said.

"No, but seriously," Lucy said. "I don't think you understand how bad I am."

Gil took the cue from the guy in the T-shirt. Then she reached into her pocket and pulled out a little blue square of chalk. She poked the cue into the chalk and twirled it around. Then she put her hand over Lucy's hand when she handed her the cue. Lucy stared at her fingers; they were tingling.

"Go on then," Gil said.

She could hear the two guys snickering. "Must be some trust-fund babies we have here," Goatee said. "Eager to get rid of Da-da's money."

"Hit the white one into the black one, bounce it off that wall, that wall, and then get it in the pocket in the back on the left," Gil whispered.

Lucy held the cue. Her hands were shaking. She looked down at the table, pulled the cue back, then brought it forward toward the white ball. The balls swished across the table propelled by a force far stronger than that with which she'd hit it. *CLACK!* The white one connected with the eight ball.

It sounded like a gunshot. The eight ball bounced off one wall, another wall, and then sailed smoothly into the back left pocket. Lucy had made the shot.

For a second they all stood there. Lucy and the two guys had their mouths hanging open.

Finally Goatee let out a low whistle.

"Pay up, boys," Gil said. She held out her tiny hands. Lucy stood there blushing. But when she looked up, she stopped. The guys were staring at her. They weren't annoyed or suspicious. They were . . . awed.

No one had ever looked at her like that before. Not in her entire life. If only Alex had been there to see what had just happened.

They piled their cash into Gil's outstretched hands. Then she crossed her arms and handed each the others' money.

"Take your girlfriends somewhere good this weekend, okay? They deserve it for putting up with your asses." But her tone was sweet and she was smiling.

They stared at the bills, wholly and completely confused.

"Come on, Luce," Gil said. She linked her little arm through Lucy's and pulled her away.

"How did you *do that*?" Lucy asked. She turned back toward the table where the guys were still watching her. Goatee gave her a little smile and a nod.

"I didn't," Gil said. "You did." She paused. "But . . ." And she brought her finger up to her lips.

Gil led Lucy over to where Olivia and Liza were talking to a group of four guys. They were standing around the pool table, all skinny with tattoos and dark jeans. They looked like they belonged in a boy band.

Olivia and Liza stepped away from the table.

"You're going to meet some of our friends now," Olivia said quietly to Lucy. "Just do your best to make each one of them like you."

"With your newly sparkling wit it should be no problem," Liza said. She was at least one-eighth smiling.

"Gillykins, go introduce her to . . ." Olivia pointed toward a guy in the corner at a table by himself.

He had dark hair, a sweet-looking face, black button-down shirt and gray suit pants, glasses with thick, black frames and dark gray eyes behind them. He was leaning over the table. He took a shot and missed. He stood back up. He was tall, but held himself like he did not know that. He was wearing a red plastic watch.

Gil walked Lucy over. The guy smiled shyly.

"This is Lucy," Gil said to him. She looked up at Lucy. "And this is Colin."

"Hi there." His voice was soft but deep. Alex had a low voice. Sometimes when she was leaning with her back to his chest and he was talking, she could feel his words vibrating inside of her, like music with a heavy bass. Lucy felt her throat tightening and swallowed hard.

This guy who was not Alex smiled uncomfortably.

"I'm Lucy." Lucy tried to force herself to smile too, but it didn't quite work. "Um, I mean, obviously." She coughed out a strangled laugh.

"I'm Colin," said not-Alex.

"Right," said Lucy. The lump was working its way up her throat again. What was she doing here? Here at some strange pool hall in the middle of the day trying to flirt with this guy who wasn't Alex?

Olivia walked over. "Gil," she said. "I'm going to take Lucy for a second." Olivia brought Lucy over to Liza who was sitting to the side. Gil stayed with Colin. Lucy saw Gil reach out and gently touch his face. She held her hand there for a moment. She whispered something and he closed his eyes.

Then Gil left him and walked over to Liza and Olivia at table sixteen.

Lucy felt the hole in her chest start to open up again. It felt huge, like the sinkhole she'd seen a picture of once. If she didn't stop it, the whole world could fall into it.

"Lesson two," said Liza. She held out two fingers and pursed her perfect lips. "Remember when we said you don't have to be so nicey-nicey? Well, that doesn't mean you should make it seem like you're disgusted by everyone. Really, that's only adorable on some people." She smirked. "And you are not one of them." Liza stood up, leaned over, and took her shot. A ball narrowly missed its pocket.

"But I," Lucy started. Her voice broke. "I wasn't disgusted by him. I was just . . ."

"We know," said Olivia. "You miss the guy who broke your heart."

Lucy shrugged and looked down.

"What, you thought we didn't know that? So you miss him." She shrugged. "So what? Everyone else doesn't have to know that."

"I can't change how I feel," Lucy whispered.

"Yeah, but you can change how you *seem* like you feel. A successful Heartbreaker is an amazing actress," said Olivia. "Only most of her performances are for an audience of one. Every role is different of course, because everyone likes different things. But you know what pretty much every guy responds to?"

Lucy shook her head.

"Tits!" said Liza, throwing her arms up. A few guys nearby looked over. One shouted, "Woo!"

Olivia grinned and shook her head. "Being liked. Which is not the same thing as being worshipped or fawned over or obsessed about or lusted after, by the way. The thing is, you can't be fake about it."

"How can I be acting and not be fake?"

"By convincing yourself you actually feel it," said Olivia. "Your face does a lot of things you're not conscious of doing, and other people aren't conscious of noticing, but on some level they do notice, and these things affect all our interactions. For example, when you're looking at someone you like, your pupils expand. That's just biology. Hard for *you* to control on your own, but if you look at someone and are able to pull out some feelings of warmth for them, your pupils will follow. And the other person will feel that, without being conscious of it, and they'll like *you* more. So find something to like about him, whoever he is. Or if you have to, pull up feelings for someone else—even for your ex. Don't fight them, go with them, and then just send them in your target's direction."

"I'm not sure I understand," said Lucy.

But Olivia just nodded at Gil who went and got Colin. "Colin, this is Lucy."

Lucy took a breath.

"Hey," said Lucy. "Um, nice to meet you, again."

He stared at her in confusion. "Have we ever met before? I'm pretty good with faces. . . ."

Lucy laughed, expecting him to laugh along with her. But he didn't, just chewed on his lip, looking nervous.

Gil was standing behind Colin. "I think maybe you're confusing Colin with someone else, Lucy," she said. When their eyes met, Gil winked.

Lucy's entire body was tingling.

She looked at Gil again. She stared into her eyes. *What did you do?*

Gil mouthed, *Go.*

So Lucy did.

She closed her eyes and inhaled. She pictured Alex's face. Let the love wash over her. She thought about his jaw, his chin, his lips. She stopped when she got to his ears.

Oh, how she loved those sweet, delicate things. Tristan once told Lucy it looked like he'd glued dried apricots to the sides of his head. But Lucy loved them precisely because they did not quite fit with the rest of him. Once she'd told Alex how much she loved them, and he'd mumbled something in reply about how small ears ran in his family. It was the only time she'd ever seen him look embarrassed.

Thinking about Alex's ears, she felt that wave of love swell until she thought she might drown in it. Then she forced her eyes open and she stared at Colin's face, ears first.

There was a tiny freckle in the middle of his left one, where an earring would be if he had one. If she loved him, she would love that freckle. And what else? She took in his whole face, and instead of seeing him the way she saw everyone—as flawed in the ways in which they were not Alex—she tried to imagine what he would look like to her if he *was* her Alex. What if his face was her very favorite face out of the billions and billions of faces on this planet? She'd love the way his smile only came in quick flashes, like he was embarrassed about his teeth. She would love the way one of them was slightly crooked. She'd love the fine white scar where his lip met his chin.

Lucy felt something around her eyes release, like the feeling you get if you've been looking at too-bright lights and finally look away.

"Lucy's a friend of ours," Gil said. "Isn't she gorgeous?"

Lucy started to blush, but Colin blushed much faster and redder.

"Colin, we're all going out tomorrow night," Gil said. "You should come."

"Okay," Colin said. He looked down at his shoes, gray canvas sneakers; a piece of rubber was flopping off the side of one toe. He looked back up and at Lucy. "Hey, that was a really amazing shot you took before," he said quietly. "Over there, I mean." He pointed toward the table where Goatee and his friend were racking up another game. "I've always wanted to be able to play like that."

"Me too," said Lucy. She smiled.

He smiled.

"I guess I should get back to my game," he said. "I mean, I'll need to practice if I'm ever going to play you."

Gil linked her arm through his and walked him back to his table. When she returned, Olivia and Liza were with her and Gil was beaming.

"Good job," she said. "Seriously. And I sensed a . . . a thing between the two of you. Maybe he could be your . . ."

"Gil," Olivia said sharply.

Gil looked down.

"But wait." Lucy could barely breathe. "When you touched his face before, and then he didn't know who I was. Was that . . . ? I mean, that was . . . wasn't it?"

Gil shot Lucy a look. Lucy immediately regretted saying anything at all.

Olivia spoke slowly, her tone was cold and hard. "Gil should not have done that." And then she looked at Lucy. "And *you* should not be asking about it."

Lucy swallowed.

Olivia nodded. "Try them next?" She pointed toward two guys at the back of the room.

Gil grabbed Lucy's hand and started walking her over.

"I'm sorry," Lucy whispered. "I didn't realize . . ."

Gil just shook her head. "Ssh," she said.

They were at the table now. The guys stopped their game when Gil walked up. The first one gave her a cheek kiss. The second one picked her right up so her legs dangled a foot from the ground. He put her down and Gil punched him in the arm.

"Lucy, this is Eric and Stephen," she said. "They like to show off how tall they are." Gil stuck her tongue out at Eric, the one who'd picked her up. Then she leaned over and mock whispered, "The reason they have the same face is not because they're two versions of the same hotness robot, but because they're twins. Stephen and Eric, this is

Lucy. She's our new friend."

"Nice to . . . ," Lucy said. But when she looked at their faces, she lost her words.

"Hey," Eric said. "What's up? You're a new friend of the girls', yeah? That's cool. Always nice to meet a new friend of theirs. So, are you into pool?"

Lucy stared at them. They looked like a model or a famous person, only more so. And twice: bright green eyes, sculpted cheekbones, lush mouths. Their face didn't stab her in the heart the way Alex's did. But still.

Gil cleared her throat.

Lucy kept staring. She knew she was supposed to say something, but she could not get her mouth to go.

"Well, anyway," Gil said finally. "We'll let you boys get back to your game." She stood on her tiptoes and kissed each of them on the cheek. Then Gil led Lucy back to Liza and Olivia's table. Olivia motioned for them to follow her. The four of them walked into the bathroom.

It was a huge room, all brown and orange tile like it had been decorated in the seventies and never touched since.

"Gil, lock the door," Olivia said. She turned toward Lucy. "You were intimidated by what they looked like, am I correct in assuming that?"

"Scared, distracted, I don't know," Lucy said. "Are they models or something?"

"Well, obviously," Liza said.

"Which means exactly nothing." Olivia hopped up onto the counter and crossed her legs. "You know the phrase 'beauty is in the eye of the beholder'? Well, that's not true. Beauty is in the mind of the beholden."

"What does that mean?"

"She who has the strongest reality wins," said Liza.

Gil nodded. "People think about a person what that person thinks about themselves. If you think you're hot, so will everyone else."

"It sounds silly, I know," Olivia said. "Meaningless because it's been so repeated. But such is the nature of many truths."

"Are you saying looks don't matter?" Lucy frowned. "Then why the new hair and makeup and everything?"

Olivia shook her head. "It's not that they don't matter *at all*. It's just they matter a whole lot less than people think. The most important thing is believing you're beautiful. The benefit of improving one's looks lies largely therein."

"But what about people who think they're hot but then no one else does?"

"Well, there are exceptions obviously, but usually when what you believe is someone's perception of their own hotness seems out of whack with what the majority of people think, that person doesn't *actually* believe they're as hot as they're trying to pretend they are."

Lucy raised her eyebrows.

"If they *really* thought they were that hot, you wouldn't

think they were wrong to think it. Because you'd believe it too. The proof that they don't think it is the fact that you're not buying it. Be confident and believe in your own beauty. That's the big secret. Turns out the deodorant commercials were right." She smirked.

"But how do you get yourself to believe something you don't actually believe?" Lucy asked. "You can't just decide you're the most gorgeous person in the world and then think it's true."

"It's not about telling yourself you're the *most* gorgeous person or the smartest person or the funniest person, because guess what, snap pea, you aren't."

Lucy looked down.

"I don't mean that meanly; I mean that realistically. You're just not. And I'm not either. And neither is Gilly or Liza."

"Well, that's debatable," said Liza.

Olivia smirked. "There *is no contest*. You need to change your way of thinking. Stop putting everything in a hierarchy. There is no prettiest or ugliest or smartest or best. The world likes to pretend that there is to sell us stuff. But there isn't. So stop buying the bullshit. Tell yourself a different message. Because you already *are* telling yourself things. Every day all day long you're telling yourself things about who and what you are. But you've gotten so used to hearing the things you tell yourself about yourself that you're not even aware that you're doing it anymore."

"It's like how you can't smell your own shampoo," Gil said.

"Or your own shit," said Liza.

"Stop looking in the mirror and thinking to yourself, 'Oh, my nose is too round. Oh, my skin isn't perfect.' Focus on the things you like and ignore the rest. Look at yourself like you're someone you love."

Lucy stood there trying to process all of this, or any of it, but Olivia wasn't done. She took a breath and lowered her voice.

"Whenever you feel insecure or unsure or self-conscious or scared, just focus on tapping into the energy at the center of the earth. You have a heart, the earth has a heart too, down below, bubbling with power and beauty. Suck it up into yourself, like a tree taking food from the soil. It's there for you at any time. Just concentrate and close your eyes."

"But I don't . . . ," Lucy started to say. "I'm sorry, I don't understand."

"Well, of course not." Olivia waved her hand. "Don't try and understand it here." She pointed to her head. "Somewhere deep in there"—she pointed to Lucy's heart—"you already know all of this. This is ingrained in you and has been since before you *were* you. So just do it. Right now. Close your eyes."

Lucy did.

"See that blackness that you think of as flat? Well, it's not, it's a tunnel and it goes down. And if you go down far enough into the darkness you will reach the other side, and beyond that is pure energy and light, an endless supply for you to tap into. With your heart cracked open it should be easier to get to it."

Lucy breathed in. She looked at the back of her eyelids.

"Stop trying," Olivia whispered. "Just let go."

Lucy felt her eyelids twitch.

Lucy smelled something then, that spicy scent, gingery mixed with something else. The scent got stronger.

Someone touched each of her eyelids, just lightly. And they stopped fluttering.

Lucy felt herself inch forward. In the world she knew, it was not possible to be inching forward into mysterious blackness and at the same time be standing in the bathroom at a pool hall. Then again, in the world she knew, words did not appear on silk scarves, and faces did not appear in smoke, your voice could not be stolen, and when a boy met you and shook your hand he would remember you a minute later, even if you were as forgettable as Lucy.

Which meant only one thing: the world she knew was not the world she was in.

So if they said that she could somehow soar to the center of the earth, what was stopping her?

Lucy let go.

She moved faster and faster. Deeper into the blackness she went. Up ahead, there wasn't a light exactly but there wasn't not a light either. It looked like the moment before a strange kind of dawn that she'd never seen before. But somehow it felt familiar. She stared deeply into it until she couldn't see it anymore. When she breathed in she felt it curl its fingers up her nostrils, into her lungs, filling her up.

Her eyes opened and her smile spread.

Olivia looked at her, calmly, coolly, from her perch on the counter. Something about her expression had changed. Lucy couldn't pinpoint what it was exactly, but she could feel it when Olivia's eyes met hers. And then Olivia nodded ever so slightly. A centimeter up, a centimeter down, it was almost imperceptible. But to Lucy, in that moment, it was everything.

Olivia hopped off the counter. They led her back out into the main room and over to a guy who'd just sunk the eight ball.

"Asher," Gil said. "There's someone here I need you to meet. . . ."

Thirteen

*I*t's not that no one had ever looked at Lucy before, it's just that usually when they did it was by accident, or just briefly, or she never even noticed. But on the third day of her sophomore year, something was different—as she made her way up the slate walkway she could feel eyes on her. Lots of them. A tickle of a glance here, a tingle of a glance there, looks coming from every direction.

To her right two floppy-haired junior guys were staring at her. When they noticed her noticing, they nudged each other and smirked. To her left a senior was standing with his girlfriend, but he kept glancing at Lucy over his girlfriend's shoulder. Up ahead the cross-country team was on an early morning run. Three of the runners turned back to look at her after they ran past.

But *why?*

Lucy looked down at her dress to check for embarrassing stains. But, no, the fabric was spotless. Okay, so the light-blue thigh-skimming jersey thing that Olivia had shoved into her hand the night before, which she'd yanked over her head that morning, was composed of significantly less fabric than she was used to wearing. But it was not any tinier than what lots of girls usually wore.

Lucy took out a little compact from her bag.

But everything looked fine. There was a line of charcoal pencil on each of her eyelids, a swipe of mascara on her lashes. Her lips were a red-y plumb-y color courtesy of a small pot of gloss she'd smeared on with her pinky. But it didn't even look like makeup; it just looked like her lips had been recently kissed.

Only they hadn't been kissed in a long time. Lucy remembered exactly when that was.

The day before Alex leaves for the summer, he and Lucy go to the hiking store to buy things he thinks he might need—a fancy aluminum water bottle with a mouth big enough to fit ice, a clip for his keys, waterproof sealant to spray on his hiking boots. She follows him around the store saying things like, "Oh look, a camping stove!" "Chicken and rice in a bag, who could believe it!" She is pretending to be excited because he so obviously is. But this feels like death to Lucy, like the end of the world, his leaving. And pretending otherwise is exhausting.

Eventually she can't do it anymore. She becomes quiet and the corners of her mouth drag down. He catches her by the arm in front of the two-person tents. "Hey," he says. "Don't look so sad, okay?" She nods and forces a smile but neither of them believes it.

He's excited for this trip, that's the thing. She tries to imagine trading places with him, what she would feel like if she were the one leaving. But the truth is, it's impossible to imagine that she would ever plan a trip that would take her away from him.

She follows him through the sleeping-bag aisle, through the belay-clip aisle, thinks about him leaving her. He touches items one by one, and it seems like part of him is already gone. It makes her feel that empty, starving, hollowed-out feeling she gets sometimes. She tries to control her face the best she can, but it is no use.

When they are done at the store the sun is falling and he tells her he has to go home. He's getting up at 5:30 a.m.; 6:30 is when the taxi will take him to the airport. A taxi, not his parents, a fact that does not surprise Lucy given what she knows about his parents. But it still makes Lucy feel so incredibly tender toward him she almost can't stand it.

They are quiet in the car. She does a silent countdown: five minutes left before he gets to her house, three minutes, two minutes. She cannot help but cry a little as he turns onto her street. He parks in the driveway, gets out of the car, and walks around to her side. He opens her door and takes her hand and helps her out of the car. He does not usually do this, but she cannot even enjoy the extra-special attention he is now paying her, because she knows how soon it has to end.

They stand there, holding hands, in front of his car in front of her house. He turns toward her then, takes her face and cups it gently, looks her in the eye. "It's going to be okay, Luce," he says. "It is." He leans in. And then . . .

Lip to lip, hot breath and tongues. They have done this a hundred times before, but every time his lips touch hers, it feels like a surprise. No memory of a kiss, Lucy has decided, can ever do justice to what one actually feels like.

And there is nothing on earth Lucy loves more than kissing Alex. Her body tilts and presses against his, her arm snakes up around his neck, she runs fingers through his hair. He sighs into her mouth.

She smiles into his.

Because here's the thing—Lucy, who is not cocky about anything on earth, who second- and third-guesses herself about everything, is sure of only this one thing: Lucy just so happens to be an amazing kisser.

She is not really sure how this happened since Alex is the first and only person she's ever kissed. Then again, there are some things we do that don't need to be taught—how to smile, how to cry, and for Lucy, kissing feels like this. Like something she was born to do.

She channels every bit of love for him from her heart, out through her fingers on the back of his neck, his lips to hers, in her saliva and tongue. She needs him to remember it, this, what it feels like, what she feels like. She puts everything she has into this kiss that they are sharing outside her house with the sun going down and a warm, late June wind swirling around them like ribbons.

And then the kiss is over and they lean back. He keeps her face in his hands and looks at her, as though he has just been returned to earth from somewhere far away. "I'm really going to miss you," he says. His voice sounds thick, and in that moment she knows that he means it. Her insides fill up, no more empty spaces. Just like that.

Lucy shook her head and snapped her compact shut.

That was then. But she is here now, at Van Buren. Here. At school. And their last kiss was a long time ago.

But if she does everything right, the next one might not be . . .

Two senior guys walk past. They both stop talking and neither can take their eyes off her. And in that moment Lucy suddenly knew one thing for sure: it wasn't the makeup that they were looking at, nor the dress. No, they were looking at her.

And they were not the only ones.

In the parking lot, Lucy gave Ethan Sloane back the jacket, which he accepted without even looking at, because he was too busy staring at her. He was full of questions like, "Are you new here? Do you want me to show you around? Do you want a bite of my apple?" If she hadn't known better, hadn't known his heart was broken, she would have sworn he actually seemed to be flirting.

As soon as she walked into school, this guy Xavier, who Tristan was friendly with, gave her a big hug. "Lucinda! Heeeeeey, babe, please tell me every little thing about your summer," he had said. As though they were the sort of friends who discussed such things, even though he'd never spoken directly to her in her life.

While she was standing at her locker, a guy she'd shared an art class with two years ago, who everyone called Big D, walked up and told her a long story about his summer in Florida, and offered to show her a cell-phone slide show consisting of pictures of him at the beach with his shirt off.

And when she dropped her bio notebook as she shut her locker, this guy Mark, the volleyball team captain with the big, round, volleyball head, dove down onto the floor to catch it. Then he looked at the front where she'd written *bio* and said, "Hot handwriting!" without even a hint of irony.

It was fun, the attention was, she had to admit that. But they weren't who she cared about. Who she cared about, she had yet to see.

Lucy stopped off in the bathroom, on her way to Photo I, stomach jangling like it was filled with a handful of pennies. She reapplied that berry gloss and looked herself in the eye.

"Not bad, sugar face," she said to the mirror. She winked at her reflection before she walked out.

Ten minutes later, the new Lucy walked into the photo room where the old Alex was snipping a long ribbon of negatives. His camo shorts hung loose on his hips, his faded olive T-shirt stretched across his shoulders. She remembered how soft that shirt had felt under her cheek that time when they'd been lying on a blanket in her backyard. But there was no trace of her face there, no trace of how much she loved him anywhere on his person in fact, which suddenly struck her as so terribly, incredibly sad, she had to turn away.

Lucy looked around the room, where everyone was bustling doing this and that; what were they supposed to be doing that day? What were all these people doing who were not standing there imagining their face pressed against Alex's hard chest?

They were making contact sheets is what, those sheets of mini photos that showed a tiny version of every picture on the roll. Mr. Wexler had taught Lucy how to make them when she came in during her free period the day before.

Lucy took out her sheet of negatives. She didn't care what was on there, just went into the darkroom, put a strip of negatives into the enlarger, flipped on the light so it shone down through her negatives, and projected tiny versions of all her photos down onto the paper.

She stared at the little pictures—she focused on one she'd taken in early evening in mid-July when Tristan had driven them twenty miles into the middle of nowhere where, strangely and wonderfully, two saxophonists and a drummer were set up in the middle of an empty field, playing music just as the sun was going down. It had been hot that day, so hot that nothing seemed real. She'd watched them in a daze, feeling the sweat dripping down her back.

"I was just driving around one day and saw them," Tristan told her. And then he'd grinned, all big and cheerful. "That's the thing I love about driving, you go for long enough you always find something, even if you weren't looking for anything in the first place. They're really friendly guys. I talked to them last time. They don't have anywhere else to practice so they come out here to play."

Lucy had taken out her camera and stood there shyly. Tristan had nudged her forward. "Seriously, Lu," he'd said. "Go as close as you want. You don't need to be scared. They really won't mind."

So she'd run up and snapped a picture. And that picture told such a story of something she'd planned to try to explain to Alex—about the beautiful cool of the music slicing through the thick, hot summer air, how she'd sung along quietly, words she made up right on the spot, and it felt like magic (although maybe she'd leave out the singing part, since he didn't really know she did it).

And there were dozens of other stories for him on that roll. She'd hunted them out, swirled them around in her head, polishing them like bits of sea glass to give him when he got back.

Lucy flipped off the enlarger, then slid the photo paper into the different vats of chemicals, one by one, until the photos she'd taken began to appear. When she was done, she came back out into the main room. Alex was at the light box staring at his own contact sheet—she peeked over his shoulder. She caught a glimpse of a field, horses, a lake, someone in a barn. Photos from the summer he'd had without her.

She was still so embarrassed about the day before, but her embarrassment was overridden by the unbearable ache in her chest that only eased when she was close to him. Her face was burning as she put her stuff down next to his. She knew she needed to say something.

"About yesterday," she started. "I'm sorry about that. That was an accident." Except she said it so fast it came out like one long word: AboutyesterdayI'msorryaboutthatthatwasanaccident.

Alex turned slightly. "Oh, hey," he said. "What did you say?"

"About yesterday . . . ," Lucy whispered.

"Sure, fine, no worries." But it sounded like he was just trying to appease her to get her to stop.

Lucy stood there. She closed her eyes for a moment and concentrated on pulling power up from down below, holding it in her belly, and radiating it out. Her hands began to tingle.

She inched in closer so her elbow was just barely grazing his.

He looked at her, then started backing away. She took a deep breath.

"I really love that photo!" she said too loud.

He smiled a little and then nodded.

"Which?" His voice softened.

"Um." She stuck out her finger and pointed at random. "That one."

They stood side by side staring at it.

It was a photo of a few people dragging a canoe into a lake. The shot had been taken from high up above, at the top of a hill perhaps.

When Alex took that photo, had he known he would be ending things with her? Had he known he would be coming back to break her heart?

Lucy felt heat on the back of her neck, sharp claws digging in, and was immediately sick with jealousy of everyone in those photos even though she could not see a single thing about them other than that they were people with arms and legs and that one was wearing flip-flops and two were wearing hiking boots.

"They look so tiny," she said. "Like little toy people." Her voice squeaked, as though she was just a little toy person herself.

She felt herself begin to deflate. She was projecting no power or glow. There was nothing but raw need oozing out of her.

"Yeah." He nodded. "And I like the way I captured the light here"—he pointed—"through the trees onto the lake. And the composition is excellent because the focal point of the photo is . . ."

While Alex went on, Lucy forced herself to breathe. Sometimes when Alex was talking about something he cared about, it was almost like he forgot about the fact that he was talking to another person. But that was okay; Lucy had never really minded that. Her heart slowed, and as he talked, she tuned out and closed her eyes. She concentrated on breathing. On taking strength and power from the center of the earth, on radiating something else back out. She breathed in; she was beautiful. She breathed out; she was strong. She breathed in; she was a goddess. She breathed out; she was luminous.

She felt her pulse slow and her lungs open up to hold more air. Her shoulders pulled themselves back and she licked her lips. Alex was still talking. He was pointing out photos one by one. But Lucy wasn't paying attention. Her skin was tingling. Something was happening.

Suddenly Alex stopped. And finally, finally he looked at her.

"Your hair is different," he said. She breathed deeply and felt a lock of it fall in her face. She swept it back behind her ear.

"True," she said.

"And you're wearing a dress."

Lucy looked down. "Yeah, I don't really know how that happened. I could swear I put on shorts this morning."

Alex smiled with half his mouth. "You look nice, Luce."

Lucy waved her hand and shrugged like it was nothing as a lightning bolt of joy hit her straight in the gut.

Suddenly she smelled something sweet and sharp. She turned. Mr. Wexler was behind them, holding his coffee cup in one hand, stroking his yellow mustache with his other. He was looking over their shoulders.

"Not bad," he said.

Alex turned too, a pleased little smile blooming on his lips. But Mr. Wexler was not looking at Alex's nature photos, his artsy still lifes, his shots of the moon and people in the lake. No, he was looking at Lucy's half-crooked contact sheet full of the things she'd wanted to show Alex.

"Me?" said Lucy.

"That one." Mr. Wexler pointed to a photo in the center of the page. It was barely anything, just Tristan smiling at her over a sundae. She wasn't even sure *why* she'd taken that picture, except that something in her told her to.

"There's something there," Mr. Wexler said. He tapped it with a gnarled, tobacco-stained finger.

"Thank you?" Lucy was embarrassed to be thanking him in front of Alex, as though the thank-you implied she must agree.

"Don't thank me," Mr. Wexler said. "Thank *this*." And he reached out and pointed at Lucy's eye. "And maybe a little bit of *that*." He pointed at her heart.

Lucy stood there trying to think of how to respond, but before she could, Mr. Wexler had walked away.

Lucy turned back to Alex. He was looking down, suddenly quiet.

"He's obviously drunk," Lucy whispered.

Alex shrugged. "Maybe." But he didn't sound happy anymore. Lucy looked down at his photos again. She scanned his contact sheet for another one to compliment.

There was one right in the center of the page, three pairs of legs, all bare feet, scratched-up knees, bits of dirt and cut grass and leaves stuck to their skin. One of the six ankles was wrapped in a complicated-looking anklet made of flat carved beads; another ankle had a bug bite right near the bone. There was a pile of backpacks and reusable water bottles off to the side. And the photo was taken from such an angle that you could see that they were standing on the edge of a cliff and that there was water down below.

It wasn't particularly complex or thought provoking, she

had to admit. It looked like a page from a camping gear catalog.

"I love that one too." Lucy pointed. Then looked up hesitantly.

"Yeah, it's a good shot." Alex was nodding. "It was amazing. We went cliff diving right into the Colorado River after. You should definitely go sometime. I think you'd like it."

"Yeah," Lucy said. "Sounds like it."

Alex went back into the darkroom after that. The corners of Lucy's mouth twisted up into a private little smile. And okay, so, no, the truth was she would most certainly *not* have enjoyed cliff diving. The idea made her dizzy. But that wasn't the point. The point was that he *thought* he knew—that meant there was still a place in him reserved for her, reserved for knowing her. That was the important part.

When the bell rang, Lucy put her negatives into her folder and put it all in the storage closet very, very slowly, waiting for Alex. Finally he emerged from the darkroom.

She tried to find things to occupy herself as the other students filed out of the room: she dropped her negatives on the floor and slowly picked them up; she put on lip balm like she was moving underwater. Scratched her elbow for a long time. As he was leaving she walked out right in front of him.

He caught up with her. "Hey," he said. "Listen. I was thinking and I just wanted to tell you something. . . ."

Lucy held her breath.

". . . and maybe it's too late now but . . ."

"It's not too late," she said quickly. She felt her face flush. Someone was tossing rocks inside her rib cage.

". . . I just wanted to say I'm really sorry for breaking up with you so fast like that and then freaking out at you yesterday too. I mean, I know it all probably seemed really sudden to you, that everything ended like that. I just wanted you to know that . . ." He paused. "Well, it seemed sudden to me too, is all." He was talking in the special soft voice he used to use when they were together, like she was something delicate and he did not want to break her with the force of his words.

Their eyes met then. He smiled almost sadly. It was, she realized, the first time he'd actually looked her *in the eye* since before he went away for the summer.

What is it about eye contact that feels so . . . important? There is no almost there. A half centimeter to the right of eye contact feels like nothing. A millimeter to the left, nothing too. No points unless you hit the bull's-eye.

But he was hitting the bull's-eye then.

They stood there, eyes locked together. She did not have to pull up feelings because they arrived all on their own, a waterfall flood of them coming out from her heart and her gut. Her pupils expanded to take him in. The boy who'd taken her picture and told her things and taught her things. The boy who she held that afternoon on the roof so many months ago. The boy she'd been desperate to know ever since that very first time their eyes met, whom—she realized in that moment—she'd never really gotten to know at all, not fully, not the way she needed to. Because if she had, then maybe she would have the tiniest hint of understanding of how they could be standing there, eyes locked, and to her it could still feel just as magical as it always had. Only somehow it didn't to him.

But maybe it wasn't too late.

"You know if you want to talk about it more," she said. She wanted to ask him what he meant by "sudden." How could it seem sudden to him when he was the one who did it? Was this his way of saying he missed her? That he'd made a mistake? "Maybe we could get together after school or something. . . ."

Alex was not looking at her anymore though. "Hey." His voice sounded different again. He was talking to someone behind her.

Lucy turned. Gil was standing there, a giant iced coffee in each hand. Lucy felt her face redden.

"Hi!" Lucy knew she sounded guilty. And hearing herself sound like that made her face even redder.

Gil stared at Alex, then Lucy, then Alex again. She looked like she was trying to figure something out.

"You were in my American History class last year, I think," he said. "Mr. Broome and his spit strings." He smiled the smile that usually charmed everyone.

Gil just shrugged. "I guess," she said.

"You're Gillian, right?"

"Yup." Gil's voice was flat. She turned toward Lucy. "Thought you might be tired." Her voice was back to normal. "Because of last night." Her eyes flickered. She held out one of the giant iced coffees. Lucy reached out for it; the condensation dripped onto the floor.

"You guys know each other?" Alex was staring at Gil, his head tipped to the side. "Right, because you were in that class too," he said to Lucy.

"Right," said Lucy.

Gil stared at him until he gave a little shrug and a "Well, okay then" and turned to go. "See you ladies later." His eyes met Lucy's one last time before he walked away.

She wanted to scream, WAIT!

"Bye Alex," Lucy said weakly.

"Bye-bye," Gil called out. She sounded sarcastic.

They both watched as he walked away, bag bouncing against his hip. He stopped halfway down the hall to take a picture of an old water fountain.

"What an ass," Gil whispered. She was smiling a sort of smile that Lucy didn't understand.

"Yeah." Lucy sucked some coffee through the straw. She normally didn't drink coffee; she was anxious enough as it was. But this was a gift. It was cold and sweet. "Thank you for this."

"I thought you could probably use it," Gil said. But her voice was just nice then, back to normal. "Liza is skipping today and Olivia never seems to need to sleep for some reason, but *whew.*" She shook her head. "Exhaustion!"

Lucy nodded, but she wasn't thinking about coffee or how tired she was anymore. All she was thinking about was Alex and how it had felt when their eyes met, and the expression he'd had on his face, at once completely familiar, and not familiar at all.

"So, hottie, having a good day?" Gil gave a sly little grin.

Lucy just smiled and shook her head. "It's . . ."

"Wackyland, right? All the attention?"

"But did you . . . ?" Lucy paused. She lowered her voice. "I mean, did you guys do something . . . ?" She stopped and held her breath. She was scared to ask the question. She didn't know what she wanted the answer to be.

Gil laughed like she understood everything. Then shrugged. "Well, that's hard to say, I'm so tired." She held her hand in front of her mouth and mock yawned. "I'm not sure I even remember! And if we did, it was just a teensy-tiny little thing anyway. And it was maybe more of a me than a we. And you should definitely *not* mention it to anyone. And by anyone, I think we both know who I mean."

"I do." Lucy smiled. "Well, thank you then. Thank you a lot."

Gil smiled back.

Lucy's heart was hammering.

So it was magic. And it was working.

"If you ever felt like doing anything like that again," Lucy said. "I mean, you could do whatever you—"

Lucy felt the cup yanked from her hand. She turned. Tristan.

"First you get completely different hair, then you start drinking *coffee*?" Tristan raised the straw to his lips and took a long sip. "It's like I don't even know you anymore, buddy." But he was grinning. He took another sip. "Mmm, sugar, my favorite. But hey, coffee makes you cuckooballs, doesn't it? Who said you could have coffee?"

"I guess that's my fault," Gil said. "I'm the caffeine pusher here."

"Perfect sugar-to-coffee ratio, pusher," said Tristan. "You know your poison."

Gil smiled.

"Anyway," Tristan said. "See you later, dudes. I'm off to have a *special meeting* with the old Van Buren vee pee. Apparently this year everyone is expected to go to class all the time? Huh? Wha?" He made a mock-innocent face. "That doesn't even make any sense!" He threw his arms up in the air and walked away.

"That was Tristan," Lucy said.

"Well, *he* seems fun," Gil said.

"We're just friends though."

"Oh-kay," Gil said slowly. "What else would you be?" She looked confused.

"Nothing, I just . . . Liza told me that guys and girls aren't really friends ever. So I was just making sure you didn't think . . ."

Gil waved her hand. "Yeah, the girl has her theories. Try not to take her too seriously." Gil smiled. "She's actually a total sweetheart deep down."

"Really?"

Gil laughed. "Well, maybe not a *total* sweetheart. But she's not the bitch she seems like either. It's just her life at home is really . . ." Gil took a long slurp of her coffee and tipped her head to the side, like she was trying to decide whether it was okay to say what she was about to say. ". . . Messed up. She doesn't know who her dad even is."

"That's so sad."

Gil shook her head. "Oh, that's not even what's bad over there. The problem isn't a lack of Dad, it's too much Mom."

"Who's her mom?"

"Imagine Liza, but thirty years older, still completely gorgeous, only instead of a Heartbreaker, she's like the exact opposite. She gets her heart broken all the time. Like five or six times since I've known Liza, and a dozen times before that. Not just bruised, but actually broken."

"But isn't it good to have your heart broken? Isn't that what Olivia said?"

Gil looked away. "Not for everyone, not for people like Liza's mom. Glass Hearts are what we call them. Their hearts shatter so easily, over and over. It's an awful thing to see. I have a cousin like that actually." Gil paused. For a second her eyes flashed deep sadness. She shook her head and continued. "Every time Liza's mom's heart breaks she completely falls apart. She stops going to work, won't eat, stays in bed for days. She starts drinking or taking too many painkillers. Or both. She gets fired from whatever job she has at the time so then it's up to Liza to figure out how to pay their rent and keep their lights from getting shut off. Liza tries to act tough now, says it's her mom's problem, that her mom is how she is and that she can't wait until she's eighteen and can leave. But that's not actually how she feels about it deep down. Especially because she feels partly responsible."

"How could she be responsible?"

Gil stopped then, and stood there blinking as though she wasn't sure whether to continue. She linked her arm through Lucy's. "I wouldn't normally tell someone this. I wouldn't normally tell anyone. But . . ."

Lucy felt her stomach tighten. "You don't have to if you don't want to," she mumbled. Her face was getting hot.

"Soon, Liza will be your sister too and you'll need to know this stuff. Liza had a ton of freedom growing up. Her mom basically left her to fend for herself, so one day Liza met this guy. I'm not too clear on the details." Gil took another long sip. "She was at a party, I think. She was thirteen at the time, almost fourteen but she looked about twenty. The guy was twenty-four and she told him she was nineteen and was going to community college and was just staying with her mom to save money. She was a good liar and so they started hanging out. After not too long she was completely in love with him, but one day he found out how old she was. He freaked out and then completely cut her off, like *completely*. That was *it*. He never spoke to her or saw her ever again. She was a total mess."

"And that's when she became a Heartbreaker?"

Gil nodded. "Olivia and Liza were friends, and Olivia's grandmother had just turned her into a Heartbreaker on her thirteenth birthday."

"Olivia's grandmother is a Heartbreaker too?"

"Well, was," Gil said, "but yeah. She taught Olivia everything she knows. Which is how we know everything *we* know. Anyway, Olivia told Liza what to do. And that's where the part with Liza's mom comes in. Liza's mom had a boyfriend at the time, which wasn't out of the ordinary since her mom always has a boyfriend, but apparently this guy was different. According to Liza, he was the most boring guy on earth, but also the only nice guy she'd ever dated before or since. And he was very in love with Liza's mom, wanted to marry her and everything. Anyway, her mom's boyfriend had a son, and Liza's mom and the boyfriend were always trying to get the four of them to be like a little family. Only problem was the boyfriend's son was obsessed with Liza. And Liza hated him. So she broke his heart. His dad broke up with Liza's mom not that long after that, pretty much for his son's sake. And that was it. Liza's always felt guilty about it, thought it was maybe her mom's only chance for her heart to be safe and stop breaking. So now Liza is always making different potions and elixirs to find a new guy for her mom without her mom knowing she's doing it."

"Wow," Lucy said. "I didn't realize Liza . . ."

Gil smiled. "Yeah, she doesn't broadcast that part of herself."

Lucy tipped her head. "I didn't realize you guys used magic for things like that. I mean, I thought it was only for . . ."

". . . for breaking hearts?" Gil laughed. "What did you think, that we just broke hearts to get magic to use to break more hearts?" She shook her head. "Well, what would be the fun in that? We use magic for all sorts of things. But I've already said too much, so . . ." Gil raised her finger to her lips. "Ssh, okay?"

Lucy nodded.

"I guess what I mean is just that Liza is awfully good at hiding who she really is. But because she's so good at hiding herself, she's constantly suspicious of other people and assumes everyone else is hiding things too. Sometimes she's not good at telling the difference between an actual enemy and a new friend. But soon, you'll be one of us, Lucy, and she'll be your sister too, and then she'll love you."

"But how can you be so sure?" Lucy said. Her stomach was heavy with ice-cold guilt. "I mean, how can you be so sure I'll actually become a Heartbreaker? You don't even really know me." She could barely get the words out.

Gil just shook her head. "Lucy," Gil said. "I know you better than you think."

Fourteen

"Music room," said Olivia as she turned a fancy gold knob and swung open the door. Lucy caught a glimpse of a giant, carved harp, a grand piano, a stand-up bass, dozens of other instruments she could name, and many she couldn't.

Lucy wanted to stop, but they pulled her forward.

Olivia opened the next door. "Library." Lucy saw rich wood shelves, stacked floor to ceiling with leather-bound books.

"My room." Olivia turned the orange crystal knob and inside was an enormous bed, covered in green-and-gold silk.

It was a few hours later, Friday after school, and Olivia, Liza, and Gil were giving Lucy a tour of the house. The hallway went on forever. Olivia swung the doors faster and faster, and Lucy barely had time to peek inside.

"What was probably a maid's room a long time ago but is now a guest room . . . empty room filled with nothing . . . cluttered room filled with everything . . . I don't know what this room is for—my grandmother used to keep just flowers in it."

There was one door Olivia walked by without mentioning. It had a small, wrought-iron doorknob and under it was an ancient-looking keyhole. Lucy stopped and stared at it. Olivia and Gil had gone up ahead.

"What's in there?" Lucy asked.

"That's a very *special* room," Liza said. "Only for very *special* people." Her tone was sarcastic, but something in her eyes looked completely serious.

"Oh, really?" Lucy's breath caught in her throat. Somehow knowing all she knew about Liza made her seem much less scary. "Can I see?"

Liza snorted. "The only way you'll see the inside of that room is if you manage to become one of us," she said. "Or if you grow enough balls to steal the key." Liza gave a short laugh. "Of course, the only way that'll happen is if you have the stuff that's in that room." She laughed again. "Come on."

Gil and Olivia were up ahead, standing at the end of the hallway in front of a set of double doors with sculpted brass handles.

Olivia pushed the doors open. The room revealed was easily as big as Lucy's family's living room. All four walls were lined with dresses, skirts, shirts, pants, jackets, shoes, and hats, in every color and fabric that had ever been invented. There were slinky slip dresses and brocade silk suits out of another era. An entire section of men's suits and shirts and pants, but in women's sizes. A half rack of clothes in gold glitter, six pairs of blue pants printed with multicolored reindeer, and shelf after shelf of jeans, boots, and boxes of jewelry. Against the walls were trunks made of leather, wood, and brushed copper, each labeled with a metal plaque.

Lucy felt her phone buzzing in her pocket and was about to reach for it when Gil called, "Dress-up time!" and Liza said "Strip."

They yanked Lucy into outfit after outfit. Zipped zippers and buttoned buttons. Yeses got tossed in one pile. Nos in another.

An hour later, both piles reached waist high and Lucy stood in the center of the room, staring into a stand-up mirror with a glossy wood frame. A sequined headband was wrapped around her head, three black feathers sticking straight up in the air. Gil stood behind her, poking at one of the feathers, making it bounce back and forth.

"But it looks so . . . ," Lucy started to say. "Silly." But then again, what did she know? Apparently not much.

Lucy's phone buzzed again from the back pocket of her

jeans, which were in a ball on the floor. She started to reach for it but Gil was standing in her way.

"I know," Gil said. "It's not quite it. . . ." Gil took the headband off Lucy's head.

Lucy looked over to one corner; five wedding dresses and one ivory-colored satin suit were hanging in the closet. "Wow, someone really likes to get married. . . ."

"Ruby did, six times in fact."

"Who's Ruby?" Lucy said.

"Olivia's grandmother," Gil said. And then gave her a pointed look. A we-did-not-have-that-talk-we-had-earlier look. "This was her house."

"Bought for her by one man while she was married to someone else," Liza said.

"Now *that's* a Heartbreaker," said Gil.

"And one powerful bitch," said Liza.

Olivia's eyes flashed. "She used to be anyway," she said.

Olivia dragged a beautiful, dark wood trunk to the center of the room. There was a brass plaque affixed to the front. *BIRDS* was carved on it in fancy, gothic letters.

Gil opened it. Lucy peeked over her shoulder. From amongst the many bird items within (sparkly pins, necklaces, a nest made of gold wire), Gil selected another headband, this one a simple black band on which was perched a very real-looking bright yellow bird with its wings ever so slightly outstretched. She put the band around Lucy's head. Lucy stared at herself in the mirror. Her bangs flopped over one eye. She pushed them out of the way. The bird looked as though it had just landed on her head, or was just about to fly away. Gil stood next to the mirror and nodded.

"Yeah, that's it, I think," she said. "It gives you a Snow White kind of vibe. And with the hair and everything . . ."

Lucy reached up and lightly touched the bird. "Is it a costume party?"

Olivia and Liza just laughed.

"Insofar as every party is a costume party, yes," said Olivia. "But otherwise, no."

"Oh . . . ," Lucy said. "But it looks . . ."

"I know," Gil said. "Sort of crazy . . ."

". . . but that's the point," Olivia said.

Gil reached out and replaced the yellow bird headband with one with a red bird. Then she took the red one off and put the yellow one back on and nodded. "Yellow."

Olivia stared at it. "Something's missing." She reached down into the box, rifling deep. She stood back up, delicately holding a yellow feather identical to the three that were already sticking out of the bird's tail. "*Four* is the most powerful number in nature. There are four seasons, four phases of the moon, and most important"—she reached out and tucked the fourth feather into the tail of Lucy's bird—"four chambers to a heart." Olivia stepped back. "There."

"A guy is going to fall in love with me because I'm wearing a four-feathered bird on my head?" said Lucy.

"Of course not," Olivia said. "That extra tail feather is just a little nod to Mother Nature. As for the bird, no, a guy won't fall in love with you *because* you're wearing it. But a guy might come talk to you because of it if you manage to stop looking so uncomfortable. . . ." She gave Lucy a sly smile. "The fact that you're doing something different will make people think you *know something* that they don't. And maybe they'll want to find out what it is. Also it gives them something to talk about. You don't have to use a bird, of course." She opened the trunk and began pulling things out as she named them. "You could use a big, sequined apple or a pair of plastic monster hands. It's all just bait." She tossed a handful of rubber eyeball rings onto the floor. They bounced across the dark wood.

Liza walked up behind Lucy with a blue-and-white-checkered dress. "Put this on," she said.

Then she pushed Lucy to the side so she could look at herself in the mirror. "It's like this: Most guys are scared shitless. Even more shitless than you are." She looked Lucy in the eye and smiled ever so slightly.

Lucy fumbled with the tiny buttons, then tied the cotton belt around the waist. She stared at herself in the mirror. She looked like she was about to go work at a fairy-tale-themed diner. Olivia was shaking her head. "Yeah, too polarizing.

Perfect for the guy with a fairy-tale fetish. But fetish freaks hardly ever invest, not with their hearts anyway. . . ."

Lucy started to take the dress off.

Olivia continued. "It'd be awfully convenient if we could just go up to all of them ourselves, but there are still those guys who like to think it's all their idea. The problem is, lots of guys are too scared to approach a girl because they have no idea what they're supposed to say when they get there."

"So what are you supposed to do then?" said Lucy.

"You help them out a little." Liza shrugged. "Wear something they can make a joke about or comment on. Giving a guy an easy opening line is often the difference between him standing, staring, wishing he could talk to you and actually being able to do it. Then—and this is kind of the best part— the fact that he's been able to approach you is going to make the littlest, scrawniest loser feel like a big, brave, manly man. Even though you made it easy for him to do it, that's not what he's going to remember. He's just going to remember feeling like he was hot shit there for a minute, and he's going to want to be around you so he can continue reveling in his hot-shittiness."

"Okay," Lucy said. "But then what happens after that?" She took a breath. "Is that when the magic comes in?"

Liza and Olivia looked at each other and smiled. But Gil caught Lucy's eye. She walked toward her with a navy slip dress. When Lucy took it, Gil winked.

Lucy thought it was a just-you-wait wink, but she could not be sure.

Lucy stood there, the dress hanging limply in her hand.

"That's called a *dreeesss,*" Liza said slowly. "You put it on over your head, Lucy, and then you wear it places."

Lucy shook her head and rolled her eyes. She pulled the dress on. It was made of a thin T-shirt material, clingy and swishy in just the right places. Would Alex like her in a dress like that?

"It's . . . ," Lucy said. She closed her eyes and tried to imagine. She kind of thought he would.

Olivia handed her a pair of navy satin ballet flats that somehow fit just right. Lucy stared at herself in the mirror, wearing that tiny little navy dress, her hair tousled, eyes smudgy and lips looking wet, a bird perched on her head like it was just landing, or about to fly away.

The three were looking over her shoulder, nodding. "Perfect."

Fifteen

At the end of last year, Alex had invited Lucy to a party being thrown by some random girl he had a class with. He said she'd just come up to him and told him she really wanted him to be there. The girl wasn't flirting; she had a girlfriend. She just thought he'd be a good person to have at her party.

That kind of thing happened to Alex all the time—he always got invited places because he just seemed like the kind of guy who got invited places.

It was not like that for Lucy. There was nothing terribly wrong with her, like a bad smell, or fleas, or a propensity for getting drunk and throwing up on things, that would have made her an undesirable guest. People were happy to invite her places when they were trying to pad a Facebook invite or even out a boy-girl ratio. But she was never the top of anybody's list. Not that Lucy minded really. Parties made her stomach hurt. There was always just so much *pressure* to be funny and interesting and loud and fun. She avoided them when she could. But at the end of last year when Alex had invited her to come to one, of course she had to say yes.

Within thirty seconds of walking in the door, Alex started chatting to some guys he knew. Lucy had hovered by his side for a while, but then the guys had started talking about girls and their hotnesses (not Alex, although he'd laughed when someone had made a joke about a very breasty freshman) so she'd gone and gotten a cup of some gross punch stuff and spent the rest of the party taking tiny sips and trying to find ways to look busy. She walked from room to room, pretending like she was looking for someone; she stood in the bathroom line even when she didn't have to go; she texted Tristan a whole lot and called her voice mail a couple times even though she knew she didn't have any.

But that night, walking into that party with Olivia, Liza, and Gil, felt like a whole other thing. Lucy could feel the heat of a hundred eyes on them, but instead of getting that sick feeling in her gut, she felt something else, higher up, a kind of sizzling. It pulled her shoulders back and lifted her chin. And while she did not think that they'd used their magic to make the perfect sexy strutting song start playing just as they came into the main room, the fact was, the song *had* changed, and it *was* perfect. And for just a moment Lucy couldn't help but wonder what it would be like if this really were her life.

It only lasted a couple of minutes though, that feeling. Then she thought she heard someone make a bird noise (although they could have just been sneezing). And she thought she heard someone say the word *nest* (although it could have been *best* or *vest*). She turned to the side and saw two incredibly tall, blonde girls whispering and maybe possibly looking at her.

Her face started burning. She reached up and slid the headband off her head. She held it down at her side. The bird's beady little eyes stared up at her.

Lucy's phone started buzzing inside the little red purse that Olivia had given her to carry. When she was sure none of the girls was looking at her, she opened her purse and looked inside. Four texts from . . . her heat sank: Tristan. The first three sent hours before.

> **Hey, where are you, bud? I'm at the bottom of your driveway . . .**
> **Have already made it through 4 l-pops.**
> **All I have left now is grape. YIK. Are you coming down?**
> **Bud, are you okay?**

She had three missed calls from him too.

Lucy had completely forgotten they'd had plans. *Sorry sorry sorry!!* She typed quickly. *Something happened I am okay will text you later. Sorry. Sorry!*

"Come on, Lucy," Gil whispered. She linked her arm through Lucy's arm and pulled her forward as Lucy tossed her phone back in the bag.

Olivia led the way through the house. People kept calling out her name, Liza's name, Gil's name. They slowed down for hugs and cheek kisses, but they never stopped.

They went through the back door, out onto a brick patio. A group of a dozen or so people was sprawled out around a giant outdoor table, in white plastic patio chairs, sipping from beer bottles. The table was covered in plastic cups. One of the cups seemed to be mildly on fire, but no one noticed or cared. Beyond that was a giant aqua-colored pool lit up from underneath and next to it was a hot tub, the steam hovering over the water, a tangle of bodies in each of them.

"Okay," Olivia said. "So here's what you need to . . ." Olivia suddenly stopped and pointed at the bird headband clutched in Lucy's fist. "What's going on there?"

"It was itchy," Lucy said.

"Look around you, Creamsicle." Olivia pulled her back against the wall of the house. "See that girl?" She pointed at a tan girl barely covered in strips of yellow ribbon. "And that girl?" A girl in a gold bikini was by the pool, obviously posing. "And that one?" A tall girl with huge, dark eyes and a giant Afro was sipping something pink. "You're a beautiful little lemon muffin. So are they. So are most girls whether they know it or not. But beauty alone doesn't get you anything. The point of bait isn't just to make it easy for guys to talk to you and make you look like you 'know things.' It's like a maaaagical visibility cloak. It makes you visible when otherwise you might not be. . . ."

"It's magic?" Lucy said.

Olivia just smiled, took the headband, and put it back on Lucy's head. "There," she said. "Now someone might see you."

"And there's nothing to be scared of when you're with us," Gil said quietly.

"Well, if it isn't my three favorite people!"

Lucy looked up.

"Paisley!" Gil said.

Off to the side a guy was staring at them. He had a wide mouth and wide-spaced, ice-blue eyes, and the way the bones in his face were made it easy to imagine that his skull was in there, but in a beautiful way, not a science-dissection way. A pair of giant, white headphones hung around his neck; the cord was being held by a tiny, gorgeous girl dressed all in white who was perched on his lap.

"Paisley, come meet our brand-new friend," Olivia said.

Paisley stood, lifting the girl up with him, then placed her back in the chair. She held on to the headphone cord. He took the headphones from around his neck and put them over her ears. Then he patted her on the head. She sat there blinking her enormous eyes, her mouth curled down into a pudgy little pout. He turned and made his way toward them, slowly and gracefully like he was doing an underwater ballet.

"Hello, lovelies," he said. He pulled Olivia, Liza, and Gil in for a hug.

"And hello, brand-new friend," Paisley said. "And who might you be?"

"This is Lucy," Gil said. "She . . ."

"No, I'm not *'the bitch'* who *stole* anyone's anything," Liza said loudly. Lucy turned. Liza had spun around and was pointing at a girl with a long, blonde braid draped over one shoulder standing a couple feet away with two friends huddled behind her. "Boyfriends are not brand-fucking-new MacBooks. If anyone's boyfriend left anyone, he did so because he wanted to. And you"—Liza pointed to the friends—"would be wise to put a muzzle on your friend here, lest she embarrass herself with that mouth of hers." Liza reached out and grabbed the girl under the chin and gave the girl's face a little shake. "Anyway." Liza turned just as she was slipping a container of what looked like lip balm back into her purse. She blinked innocently. "You were saying?"

Paisley caught Lucy's eye and raised a perfect black eyebrow. "They're a nonstop party, these girls, no?" He smirked at Lucy. Lucy gave him a tiny smile back.

"When are you going to Tokyo again?" Gil asked. She turned to Lucy and said, "Paisley is being flown in by the guy at Insurance Office."

"Why's an insurance office flying you to Tokyo?"

Paisley laughed.

"Um, hellew, it's a very important club?" the girl in white called out from her chair, where she'd been eavesdropping.

Liza put her arm around Lucy. "Lucy probably hasn't even heard of you."

Lucy stared at her feet. "I haven't heard of a lot of things."

When she looked back up, Paisley was smiling at her. "The less random stuff you hear about, the more room in your ears for music, that's what I always say. The show was supposed to be next week, but they moved it up a week. I'm leaving tonight. Heading to the airport in oh . . ." He tapped the empty spot on his wrist where a watch would have been. Then took a shiny black phone out of his pocket and poked at it. Then shook it. "Hmmm," he said. "Guess it wasn't fire resistant after all. Vivs, sweetie, how much time do I have?" he called out behind him.

"You were supposed to leave fifteen minutes ago," the girl yelled back.

"In fifteen minutes ago, apparently," he said. "Hey, does your bird speak Japanese, Bird Girl? You and birdie want to come to Tokyo?"

"Um," Lucy said. She knew she was expected to flirt back then. To sass it up the way Liza would have. "We can't. Birdie has a fear of flying," Lucy said. She cringed at hearing herself.

But Paisley just smiled. "You—" He pointed at Lucy, swirled his finger around like he was stirring something in the air. "You are refreshingly adorable. I like you." Then he turned back toward the girl in white. "Vivs, would you tell the car service we'll be outside in, like, two minutes?" The girl in white nodded and smiled then, like being asked to do something for Paisley was the biggest honor of her life.

"Finally," she said. "We get to leave this lame place."

"Oh that poor girl," Gil whispered to Lucy, shaking her head.

Paisley turned toward Lucy as he passed. He looked straight at her, then up at the bird on her head. "Hey, little birdie, tell your friend I said it was very nice to meet her. Can you do that for me, birdie?" He reached out and pet it. Then turned to go.

"Chirp chirp," Lucy said. She wasn't sure it was loud enough to hear.

And as he walked, Paisley broke out laughing like this was the funniest joke he'd ever heard.

"Too bad," Liza said. "If it weren't for the obvious, he could have been a good Chrys for you."

"Chrys?"

"Chrysalis Heart," Olivia said. "The one you break that changes you."

"But I'm . . . I mean, I'm sure I'm not his type. I'm not nearly . . ."

"Cool enough?" Liza finished. "But that's entirely the point. I think you misunderstand who likes who and why. I mean, what Paisley wouldn't like about you is your lack of a penis, not your lack of coolness."

"Oh," said Lucy. She blushed.

"Aw, you thought he was flirting with you, didn't you?" Liza said. And then she laughed.

"There are two mistakes so many girls make when they get past the initial flirting stage and are trying to get a guy long term," said Olivia. "She'll think a guy will love her if she's similar to him, so she'll pretend to like the same movies or the same music or the same whatevers. Or she'll think a guy will like her if she fawns over him and giggles and coos at everything he says. Thing is, you can maybe get a guy to like you that way, kind of, a little bit. But if we're talking long-term love, it doesn't really work like that."

Lucy felt her stomach tighten. "How does it work then?"

Olivia smiled. "Pick someone, Li-Li."

Liza tapped her lip. "The dude over there, who thinks it's open-mic night." Liza pointed through the glass doors toward a tall, painfully skinny guy, in a bright green T-shirt with a picture of his own face printed on it. Both his real face and his T-shirt face showcased a mouthful of crooked teeth and a pair of enormous ears. He was standing in the center of a little group of people talking animatedly.

"Gil," Olivia said. "Show her how it's done."

Gil nodded, then looked at Lucy and winked.

"Watch and learn, ginger chew," Olivia said.

They walked through the sliding-glass doors and stood off to the side about fifteen feet away from where he was in the middle of telling a story. The half-dozen people surrounding him were hanging on his every word. "So, this is me," he was saying. He started dancing, arms up, eyes squeezed shut. "And this is her . . ." He stuck his butt out and shook it around. "Moral of the story?" He did some complicated hand gestures that made no sense to Lucy. "Guess that's just what the ladies like." Then he winked. Everyone burst out laughing. A guy reached out and gave him a fist bump. A pretty girl with wavy, brown hair, who'd been standing up near the front laughing loud and hard, was staring up at him blinking her big, round, googly eyes.

"You are *soo freaking funny,*" she said. "Seriously, I just peed a little!"

The guy raised his eyebrows.

"I mean, not in a gross way," she said quickly. "I'm just kidding. I was making a joke too! But yours are funnier."

The guy shrugged. "Thanks, babe." He gave her the up and down, but looked bored.

Olivia leaned over toward Lucy and whispered, "A guy might kind of like a girl at first because she seems to like him for whatever everyone likes him for, for the obvious stuff, but if you want him to feel like you are his air, his water, and his light in the long term, that's not really gonna cut it."

Gil slipped between the guy and the girl. Gil's face had transformed, every bit of sweetness and warmth was gone. "Good job with the jokes there," Gil said. Her voice sounded different too, deeper. "Very clever." But the way she was talking, it sounded like she didn't think he was clever at all.

The guy stared at her with this strange look on his face, part surprised, part hurt, part interested, and entirely confused.

Olivia was standing right next to Lucy; she could feel her breath when Olivia whispered, "For anything more than that first spark, you shouldn't be asking yourself what is he like or what does he like, but what is he missing. What is he insecure about? Show him you have what he lacks or lack what he wishes he didn't have. Or that you can appreciate the parts of him that no one else seems to or the parts he hates but feels stuck with."

Olivia motioned with her chin and they looked back up at Gil. "You're cute enough not to need the jokes though." She said it not like she was giving him a compliment, but like she was just stating a fact.

"I know," he said. "I'm a spicy-hot man steak." He flexed

each of his skinny arms and kissed his walnut-sized biceps.

Gil stared at him, blinked, and did not smile, just shrugged. Then turned and walked back to her friends.

"Okay, so on one hand what Gil just did was a little off-putting. The thing is, he's a guy who's used to being in control socially, who's used to being a step ahead of everyone. And what she just did shook him out of that. He's trying to seem unaffected," said Olivia. "But look at the tips of his ears." His ears were bright red. He said something to his friend, then scratched the back of his neck. "Five-four-three-two . . ."

Olivia whispered "one" and the guy looked up at Gil's back. And the tips of his ears got redder.

"He's a guy who's used to being told his best quality is that he's funny," Olivia said. "He's probably convinced himself that being funny is more important than being hot, that hot guys are idiots anyway. He has decided not to want what he thinks he can't have, which is hotness. It's something a lot of people do as a defense thing, decide they don't want something just because they think it's un-gettable. But Gil has just given him the idea that maybe it's okay to want it. Look at how he's standing now. His back is straighter and his shoulders are back farther. His perception of himself is already changing. If we stand here for long enough, he'll find a reason to come over. He'll find it impossible not to."

"If Gilly wanted to she could have him sobbing onto his

skinny little arm in a month," Liza said. She put her arm around Gil.

Olivia shook her head. "Two weeks. When someone's whole perception of himself shifts because of how you see him, you suddenly become very, very important. When people love you, it's because you've made them fall in love with themselves and the rest of the world. And that's not accomplished through telling them how wonderful they are, but through making both them and the world seem more how they wish it was. Show the bored-by-everything guy how exciting life can be if he's with you. Show the dumb guy who's insecure about his dumbness that he understands the world on a primal level that no one else quite gets. This is a long-term thing; you can do that for your entire relationship."

"But what if . . ." Lucy took a breath. "What if the person is someone you already know? So . . ." She coughed and looked down. "So meeting you can't be what changes things for them?"

Olivia shrugged. "It's never too late to start things over. People have awfully short memories when it comes to feelings. They're practically goldfish."

"And while you're making him suddenly feel like the guy he always wanted to be," Liza said, "little fishy won't even feel your hook sinking deeper and deeper into him, all the way to the center of his heart. Which is where your hook will stay. Until you decide to yank it out."

Lucy winced.

Gil leaned in close. "Just because you know where a soft spot is doesn't mean you have to aim for it. You don't ever have to do anything you think is wrong."

"It's not *about* right and wrong." Olivia shook her head. "It's about nature and how it works."

"Besides"—Liza shrugged—"it's fun."

"We kind of have . . . different philosophies about some of this," Gil said with a small smile.

"But this is all so . . ." Lucy stopped. The idea that something that felt so magical could have a formula, a recipe, struck her as both fascinating and terrible.

"It feels weird to think about it like that," Gil said. "I know. But there are a lot of things that feel like magic just because we don't understand them yet. But understanding them doesn't make them less magical . . ." Gil's phone buzzed and she looked down at it. When she looked up, Olivia said, "Now?"

Gil nodded.

"All right then. Good luck, Popsicle," Olivia said. "We'll see you in a bit."

Liza and Olivia started walking toward the back patio. On the way, Liza snatched a guy's drink right out of his hand. He smiled and followed them.

"Come on, Lu," Gil said. "You're . . ."

"Gil?"

Gil turned. Lucy turned too. There was a guy standing there, staring at her.

"Oh, wow!" he said. "I can't believe it's really you." He grinned at her from behind thick glasses. He was wiry and small, unremarkable looking, except for the fact that his face was blooming into a face-splitting smile. Lucy could practically see the light coming off of him, shimmering gold.

"Hey," Gil said. There was something strange in her tone, something Lucy couldn't place. "Good to see you. But we were just on our way somewhere."

"Okay," the guy said. He paused. "But I miss you, you know." He smiled again, but the light was gone from it now.

"We'll hang out soon, okay?" Gil said. But it was obvious that she didn't really mean it. Gil's face was expressionless.

Lucy stared at the guy's back as he walked away. After a few seconds, he turned and waved. He looked so sad.

"Who was that?" Lucy said.

"Will," Gil said. "We were best friends once."

"Did you . . . ," Lucy started to ask. She bit her lip. She wanted to ask if Gil had broken his heart.

"The opposite." Gil smiled. There was no bittersweet sadness there, nothing in that smile but teeth. "I made the mistake of falling in love with him. I loved him for years, and he loved me too, but only as a friend. And there was nothing he could do about that. So he . . ." She pointed to her heart. "He didn't mean to."

"And that's when you became . . . ?"

"That's when I became a Heartbreaker. My Chrys was this friend of his who I didn't know very well but who always had a crush on me. I still feel bad about that; it really hurt him. We don't have the same rule about Chryses that we do the rest of the time. Anyone's fair game for that."

"And you and Will aren't friends anymore?"

Gil shook her head. "We couldn't be," she said simply. "Will never even knew what happened, that he broke my heart and all that. I think he just thought we grew apart." She cleared her throat. "Anyway!" She took Lucy's hand. "Come on. Someone's here to see you."

"To see me?"

"Yup," said Gil. "Let's go get him. I think he's nervous about coming inside."

Gil led Lucy toward the front of the house.

They passed a girl and a guy talking on the stairs.

"It was really awesome though," the guy was saying. "Like they didn't end up taking our tickets so we got to use them again the next time."

"You know, that's like this time my sister and I . . . ," the girl started to say.

But the guy kept talking. "And so the next time, we went in but we had to change the date on them. I have a friend with really neat handwriting so he . . ."

"They've just met," Gil whispered, "and he's really nervous.

He likes her and he's trying so hard to impress her. She thought he was cute at first but now she's thinking he's a narcissistic ass because he won't let her get a single word in. In three minutes, she'll get up and pretend to have to go to the bathroom and she won't come back. Which is too bad because they would have been perfect for each other. But that will be it. Or would have been . . ."

Gil pulled what looked like a case of mints out of her pocket. As she walked by, she dropped a tiny, black pellet into the guy's drink. He didn't notice.

". . . we ended up getting to go backstage, which I was so excited about."

The guy brought his cup to his lips and took a sip. He put the cup back down and opened his mouth. But no words came out. He opened his eyes wide.

"That's cool. My sister and I got to go backstage at a Monster Hands show last week," the girl said. "It was . . ."

Gil linked her arm through Lucy's and pulled her away. "For five minutes he'll be silent, and she'll finally get a chance to talk. And if they manage not to mess it up, they will fall madly in love." She grinned at Lucy. "Oh, look!" Gil pointed. "There he is."

Standing under a tree near the end of the driveway was Colin from the day before, playing with the strap of his red plastic watch.

Gil leaned over and whispered in Lucy's ear. "Just do

what we taught you, okay?" And then she gave her a little push.

"You're not coming?"

Gil shook her head. "He's here to see you. I'll just be over there on the phone. If it starts going badly, just motion to me and I'll come help, okay?"

Lucy felt her stomach tighten. She didn't want to do this. But Gil was watching and Gil had the magic. Which meant that if she wanted Alex back, somehow this guy was the route to him. So Lucy would try her best. She had to.

Lucy studied Colin, took in all she could.

He was slouching the way he had been the day before, like someone who didn't know how tall he was. And he had his shoulders slightly raised, like he was bracing himself for something. He was fiddling with his watch uncomfortably. So what did that all mean? It meant he didn't feel the six foot two inches of his height. He didn't feel powerful. He felt small. He was scared and uncomfortable.

Lucy cocked her head to the side. She forced herself to smile and in her head she said, *I* own *this place*. When their eyes met, he blushed.

"I like your bird," he said.

"Thanks," said Lucy. "I've trained her to just sit there. As you can see, she's really good at it."

Colin laughed. He looked down at that floppy piece of rubber on his shoe. "So, um, how do you know Gil?"

"From school. We were in a class together last year," said Lucy.

Colin nodded. "I think she might be trying to set us up," he whispered.

"No way," Lucy said. She smiled. Colin was smiling too. Lucy felt something warming inside her.

"So . . . ," he said.

"So . . . ," she said.

"So do you know a lot of other people here? I don't know anyone really," he said. "Parties make me uncomfortable, there's so much pressure to be, y'know, *on* the whole time. It's like being on display."

Lucy had to bite her lip to keep herself from smiling wider. She shrugged. "But that's what's fun about parties, isn't it?" *Did she sound as fake as she felt?* He looked so uncomfortable. Just the way she had at every party she'd ever been to. She leaned in. "Actually, I shouldn't tell you this, but this here?" She motioned toward the house just at the moment that cheers broke out inside and a hot pink bra flew through the open window and landed on a bush. "This is a surprise party for *you.*" She looked up at him. He looked confused. She let her mouth spread into a slow smile. "The fact that it is not your birthday and that you don't know anyone is meant to make it extra surprising." She threw her arms up in the air. "Surprise!"

Colin laughed. A real laugh. He didn't even cover his teeth this time.

"Just think about that if you're uncomfortable: They're all here for your party and if you feel like they're ignoring you, that's only because they're gearing up for the big moment later."

Colin was staring at her with his head tipped to the side.

Suddenly there was a commotion behind them, and Lucy turned. Olivia, Liza, and Gil were walking out of the house. Behind them was a guy in a bright red T-shirt with a bright red face. "You!" he shouted. He might have been cute if he wasn't so red and yelling, "You, you, you, you, you." And so obviously, sloppily drunk. "I have been *looking* for you. I thought you might be here!"

Olivia, Liza, and Gil stood on the lawn below. Olivia stared at him. She shrugged.

"Oh, so you're going to pretend you don't know me?" The guy snorted and sputtered. Spit was spraying everywhere. "Is that how it is? *We were together for the entire winter, Olivia! I first met you here.*" He started stumbling down the stairs. Colin put his hand on Lucy's arm and pulled her gently back, just as the guy went tumbling in front of her.

"I don't know." Olivia shook her head slowly. "That was a long time ago."

"You horrible, horrible, horrible bitch." He was shaking his head. Behind him, everyone was staring. "And you two"—he pointed at Liza, then at Gil—"I know just who you are." He turned to address the crowd. "Stay away from these bitches," he yelled. *"These stupid, horrible, evil bitches will get you. They'll take everything out of you and then when there's nothing left, they'll leave you to die!"*

"I think it's time for you to rest now, sweetie," Gil said quietly to him. "Go back inside." She reached out and put her hand on his arm.

Liza was laughing a little bit.

He started to step away.

"That's a good boy," Gil said. "Just keep going."

Suddenly he lunged toward Olivia, hands out grasping blindly. Like he was trying to grab a piece of her to keep.

But before he could reach her, Gil's thin arm slipped around his neck, and with one little squeeze he dropped to the ground. As he went down, his hand shot out and grabbed Olivia's tangle of necklaces. A chain broke with a tiny pop and fell into the grass with no sound at all.

Olivia looked down at his crumpled face, his mouth opened in an O of surprise. She inhaled and shook her head coolly. She hadn't noticed the necklace.

"Thanks, Gilly." Olivia leaned over and kissed her on the cheek.

Lucy stood there, heart pounding, so confused by everything that had just happened, by every single moment of it.

Gil smiled. "I have a lot of brothers," she said. She shrugged.

Lucy looked down at the guy on the floor, curled on his side, moaning.

"He'll be okay," Gil said.

The broken necklace lay in the grass, a delicate gold chain on which was a small black key. Lucy reached for it. But a fist closed around it first. "Not for you," Liza said. And she slapped the back of Lucy's hand.

"I was just trying to . . ."

"Not for you," Liza said. She handed the necklace back to Olivia who quickly slipped it into the front pocket of her giant leather bag.

Lucy stared at the guy, who was still moaning on the ground. Her heart was hammering.

Liza stood over him, nudged his shoulder with the toe of her boot, and slowly turned her beer upside down, right over his crotch. The beer spread out over his shorts. "Tasted like piss anyway," she said.

But Olivia shook her head, reached out, and gently moved Liza's hand away. "Come on, ladies, let's go back inside." Olivia looked down then one last time at the body on the grass. "Good-bye, Ricky," she whispered. His eyelids fluttered at the sound of her voice.

Sixteen

ours later, Lucy lay in bed, cheek pressed to her purple flower pillow, brain stretching, skull pounding, as though her head had eaten an enormous meal that it did not know how to digest.

So much had happened at the party, but that's not what she was thinking about.

She was not thinking about the way Colin had looked at her, while girls all over the party were staring at him, which he seemed not to notice. Or how a guy had started hitting on her while she was in the bathroom line (which incidentally Colin had seen and was probably the reason for his hasty exit, which Lucy actually felt a tiny bit bad about). Or about how three separate guys had asked for her phone number. Or how funny it had been to be a ray of sunshine for the dude in the I'LL STOP FROWNING WHEN THE WORLD STOPS SUCK-ING T-shirt. And then moments later to be a very deep and introspective wallflower for the perky party host.

She wasn't even thinking about the wonderful moment when Olivia dropped her back at home and said that the next night they had something "really special in store for her," in a way that felt like a promise. A promise that *meant* something.

No.

What Lucy was thinking about, lying in her bed, as the sun came up on that early Saturday morning, a day that was supposed to be her first day as a nonvirgin, her first time waking up in a bed curled against Alex, was this:

Everything she'd done during her entire relationship with Alex had been wrong. Starting with that first googly-eyed look she gave him, right up until yesterday at school.

The problem wasn't that she'd loved him too much; it was that she hadn't loved herself enough. She'd never really understood why he liked her. She tried to be a nice person, and Tristan said she was smart and funny, but Alex was *Alex.*

So to make up for the great distance between what she was and what he was, well, she just ended up doing whatever he wanted all the time, complimenting him constantly, and telling him over and over how he was the most wonderful person the world had ever known.

She'd been his biggest fan.

But he didn't need a fan.

Looking back now, she realized he'd often shrugged off her compliments the way one might do with those of an overly doting aunt.

He wanted the world to be more interesting and exciting. What he was looking for was not a soft place to land, but a cliff to jump from and someone to fly through the air after.

Suddenly Lucy knew that with such intensity that she sat straight up in bed, heart pounding.

She could be the lurch, the tingle, the breathless feeling of hurtling into vast empty space. She could be that free fall. Starting now.

Lucy reached for her phone; she had an idea.

She wrote a text.

> **Alan, great meeting you too. Sneaking in tonight was fun, but if you think that's crazy just you wait. . . .**

She sent it to Alex before she had a chance to change her mind.

Then took two deep breaths. She counted to five. Then wrote another.

> **SORRY!! Oops, meant to send to someone else.**

Hope I didn't wake you up ☺

Was that too obvious? Would he know she'd meant to send it to him all along?

A second later her phone buzzed, which meant Alex was sitting right there with it. Which he almost never was. Lucy gasped. What was he even doing *up*?

It's cool.

What did that *mean*?

Her phone buzzed again.

Glad you had a fun night tho. Oh, and don't worry, I was up anyway. Couldn't sleep. . . .

Lucy's breath caught in her throat.

The old Lucy would have texted back immediately, asked him why, suggested warm milk, wished she had enough guts to offer to sing him a lullaby.

But the new Lucy wouldn't.

So the new Lucy didn't.

Instead she just tucked her phone away and forced herself to concentrate on the feeling of speeding through space, of the wind rushing by her. Of pulling that into herself. Of sending it back out.

Seventeen

"Do you need help steering that thing toward your mouth hole, my friend?" Tristan pointed to her motionless fork, and grinned.

It was morning and there was Lucy, sitting with Tristan in their favorite booth at Pancake Land, totally unable to eat her pancakes. She knew she'd done a good job the night before. But she'd woken up that morning to the ticking of the clock on her nightstand, with a ticking in her belly too, suddenly all too aware of the passing time, which she'd let herself ignore up until now.

Tick tick tick.

It was the start of the fourth day. How had she squandered

so many of her seven days already?

Tick tick tick.

Time was passing much too fast.

Tristan reached out, grabbed the soggy pancake piece off her fork, and popped it in his mouth.

Lucy pressed her hand to her belly. There had been four days since her heart had been cracked open. And somehow she'd managed to survive them. But only because she had had hope and time. She was quickly running out of both of them. . . .

"So what happened to *you* last night, eh?" Tristan said. "Dog ate your homework?" He grinned.

Lucy shook her head. "I'm really sorry, I . . . ," *was trying to get these magical girls to give me some potions,* ". . . completely forgot."

"It's okay, you've got a lot going on up there." He lifted his coffee and motioned toward her head. Then drained the last sip. A half second later a cute red-haired waitress appeared to refill his cup. She gave him a big, blinky-eyed gaze and brushed against his arm as she walked off.

Lucy gave him a look. Tristan shrugged. "What?" He opened his eyes wide and grinned. "The service is just really good here!"

At least half the waitresses at Pancake Land had crushes on Tristan, a fact he vehemently denied (but only denied as a joke, since it was so completely obvious).

"So what'd you end up doing anyway?" Tristan grabbed a handful of sugars and ripped the tops off, dumped half in his coffee and the other half directly into his mouth.

"I was hanging out with . . . those girls actually . . . ," Lucy said. "We went to some party." It was funny how normal it sounded when she put it just like that.

Tristan raised his eyebrows. "Hey, good for you, dude. If popular movies and TV shows have taught me anything, that's how a person's supposed to get over a breakup. Get out there and do a bunch of Jell-O shots off strangers. Nice."

"Ha-ha," said Lucy. "No, it wasn't like that. It was weird."

"Cuddle party?"

"The party was just a regular party, it's just . . . what happened at it was a little funny. . . ." Could she tell him this part? She blushed.

"Spill it, blushy." Tristan smiled. "Sounds like someone met a booooooooy."

Lucy blushed more. "Three guys asked for my number."

"Awesome!" said Tristan. He raised his coffee and waited for her to clink with her peppermint tea. "Good for you, kiddo. Total hotties?"

Lucy just smiled and shook her head. How much was she allowed to tell him? "I'm not actually trying to date anyone. It was more like . . . practicing."

"Huh?"

"Practicing stuff with boys, I guess."

"Practicing for the purpose of what? If you're not trying to date anyone . . ."

Lucy shrugged. She definitely needed to stop here. "Those girls were helping me," she said, as though it was an answer. Even though it obviously wasn't.

"So what's the deal with them anyway? That little one seems nice enough, but I always sort of got the feeling that something *odd* was going on with the wolfy-faced one and the hot one."

"Well, they're . . ." Lucy paused. "They're, yeah, they're definitely weird."

"Look, Lucy," Tristan said. His expression went suddenly serious. "If they're recruiting you into a lesbian sex cult you can tell me." He paused. "So long as they let me join too." Tristan drained his coffee cup again.

Lucy had a sudden troubling thought. "Promise me you'll never date any of them," she said.

"Um, okay?" Tristan said. He raised his eyebrows. "I definitely won't 'date' them, especially not the big, hot one." He made air quotes around "date." Then winked. "But seriously, when do I get to hang out with your new buds?"

"Soon," said Lucy. Even though she didn't mean it.

"Want to invite them to the fair tonight? I will make a special exception for our Lucy-Tristan Tradition if you want. Big-hottie looks like she has good aim. Maybe she can win me one of those giant teddy bears I've had my eye on." Every year since they first became friends, Lucy and Tristan went to their town's fall fair together on the first Saturday of the school year.

"Oh, Tristy . . . ," Lucy said.

Tristan's face dropped. "You can't go?"

Lucy shook her head. "I'm so sorry. . . ."

"S'okay," he said. "This girl Janice wanted to do something tonight anyway so . . ." He looked down at his phone and pressed a few keys. Put his phone down.

They stared at each other for a second. It was awkward. Things between them were *never* awkward.

"Well," said Tristan. "What are *you* doing tonight, Miss I'm-suddenly-too-busy-and-important-for-important-traditional-friendship-traditions?"

Lucy frowned.

"I'm joking my friend, joe-king. Do what you gotta do."

"I'm just going to hang out at home tonight," Lucy said. "My parents are away this weekend, celebrating their anniversary."

"Georgie and Suzanne doing the happy couple thing again?"

Lucy nodded. "For the next ten minutes at least. So I think I'm just going to relax tonight, eat a lot of ice cream on the couch or something. Sulk alone."

"You want a sulking partner? I'll text Jan-Jan back, tell her I'm busy. There was something I wanted to show you anyway. This cool thing I think you'll really like . . ."

Lucy's stomach tightened. "If you were there I wouldn't be alone then, now would I?" She tried to make her voice sound light.

Tristan blinked and scratched his head in mock confusion. "I don't follow . . . ," he said. He moved his hands back and forth between them and moved his mouth around and squinted and shook his head. Then grinned.

Lucy picked up her camera and snapped a picture, Tristan, head tilted to the side, eyes squinting, pointing at the lens.

"All right, enough with the picture taking, Ms. Clicky. Finish your pancakes. . . ." He reached out with his fork, stabbed a pancake, and brought the entire syrup-dripping thing into his open mouth. "Orfsomfonefish going to finif them forfyoo." A line of syrup dribbled down his chin. Lucy lifted her camera again. The flash went off the moment before the syrup hit the plate.

Eighteen

ristan dropped Lucy off at home, where she spent the next few hours pacing from room to room, putting on makeup, and trying to sing loud enough to drown out that clock. It was how the background sounded to everything she did: *Tick tick tick.* But there was just no drowning it.

Finally, Olivia picked her up. And then a few hours after that, Lucy was standing with Olivia and Liza and Gil in front of an old theater.

"What's this place called?" Lucy asked.

"It isn't called anything," Olivia said. "This is where Pete lives."

"Wait, seriously? But what about . . . ?" Lucy pointed to the line of people snaking around the building.

"He has a lot of friends," Olivia said, and she shrugged.

Lucy looked at the people, each one of them so perfectly *something* in their leather, vinyl, fishnets, tattoos, thick bangs, cat's-eye glasses, tuxedo pants, bloodred lips. Lucy stared down at her yellow eyelet dress and little brown purse and the camera around her neck with the SAY CHEEZ camera strap and shook her head.

She glanced back up at the giant building. There was what appeared to be a box office out front with a very skinny man inside wearing a top hat.

"Who's that guy?" Lucy asked.

"Scarecrow." Lucy felt Gil's arm link through hers. "Not a real guy. Don't believe everything you see here tonight," Gil said. "This is a strange place and funny things can happen." She turned toward Lucy and gave her a meaningful look and pulled her forward.

Olivia led them up past everyone to the front of the line. "Oh, so I guess they think they're *special*," someone in line called out.

Lucy turned. Three girls were glaring at them.

"Oh, honey, it's not that we *think* we are," Liza said. She blew them a kiss off the tip of her middle finger.

At the front of the line, standing next to the box-office scarecrow, was a guy a few years older than them, in a white tank top, all big, square jaw and rippling muscles, and thick, dark hair.

"A pleasure as always, ladies," he said to Olivia and Gil. His voice was so slow and deep it sounded like a recording of a regular person's voice played back at the wrong speed. His eyes settled on Liza. "And you," he said. "Get up in this." He pointed to his massive chest.

Olivia and Gil walked forward, pulling Lucy with them. But she turned back and watched as the guy wrapped his enormous arms around Liza's shoulders and pulled her in for a hug. In his arms, Liza looked positively tiny. "God, I've missed you." He stuck his nose in her hair and smelled it.

"That's Scott," Gil whispered.

"It *is*?" Lucy stared at them. "As in the guy on the phone?" Gil nodded and pulled Lucy forward again.

There was an angry-looking girl in a tiny black dress and turquoise heels guarding the door. Olivia leaned over to whisper something to her. Olivia's white hair brushed against the girl's black locks. Lucy snapped a picture. The girl turned and kissed Olivia on both cheeks, then stepped back to let her inside. She did the same to Liza and Gil. And even Lucy.

They went down a dark hallway that led into a huge room with a high-domed ceiling. It looked like the type of place where you'd go to hear a symphony or an opera except there were no seats. "A lot of famous people sang here back in the twenties when this place was first built," said Olivia. "And lucky us, there's an amazing new singer doing her debut performance here tonight."

"Who?" Lucy looked up at the stage. Thick, red velvet curtains hung from a twenty-foot ceiling. Thousands of pinpoint lights hung from the ceiling on invisible threads, making it look like the room was full of tiny floating stars. The place was empty except for a few guys walking back and forth carrying giant pieces of sound equipment.

And a slow smile spread across Olivia's lips and her tinkling bell laugh rang in Lucy's ears. "You."

Lucy's entire body went cold.

"Welcome to your first show, rainbow cake," said Olivia.

"But how did you even know I . . . ?"

"Remember when you were singing in the car the other day?" Gil said. "You were amazing."

"You guys heard that?" Lucy whispered.

"Nature gave you something precious," Olivia said. "Don't waste it. You were meant to do this. It's only fear that's preventing you."

"I . . . ," said Lucy.

Gil squeezed her hand. ". . . will be wonderful."

"But I can't . . ." Terror tightened around her throat and no more words would come out.

"Don't follow that," Olivia said. She pointed to Lucy's face. "It's fear that separates the Heartbreakers from the heartbroken. It's fear that keeps people from getting"—she gave Lucy a meaningful look—"what they want the most. If you do a good job, we have something very special to show you."

Her meaning was clear. *This was the final step.*

If Lucy wanted their magic, this is what she needed to do. If she wanted Alex back, this is what she needed to do.

So this is what she would do.

Lucy raised her hand to her lips. She didn't even bother to try and smile. "When do I go on?"

"Pete has lived here ever since we've known him," Gil said as the four of them walked across the giant room. "Apparently the place is haunted by the ghost of some magician or something." They went through a side door. "He says sometimes at night he'll hear the sounds of cards shuffling and"—then down a narrow hallway—"sometimes finds aces tucked in between his covers"—and up two sets of stairs.

Finally they popped out into a big room behind the stage that was filled with a crazy mass of wires and cables, laptops, soundboards, and a couple dozen musical instruments.

"I can't believe this is your friend's *house*," Lucy said.

Gil shook her head. "I know, right? That's where he sleeps." She pointed behind a pile of spotlights to a smallish bed covered in a quilt.

"Is sleeping," a muffled, British-accented voice called from under the covers.

Olivia poked at the lump on the bed.

It reached out one arm, hooking Olivia around the waist and pulling her down on top of him.

Pete sat up. He was a few years older than they were. He had this look on his face like a kid who'd done something naughty. Or was just about to. He was still holding on to Olivia. She swatted at his arm, turned her head, and gave him a long kiss on the lips. Her bright white hair pressed against his bright red. He let her go and she stood back up.

"What time is it?"

"Ten," Gil said.

"Hmmm." He rose, shirtless in pin-striped suit pants. "Hand me that, would you, love?" He pointed to Lucy, then to a white button-down shirt hanging on the back of one of the spotlights. She handed it to him. He smiled. "So is this little flower my new singer for the night?"

Lucy nodded.

"Everyone's talking about how incredible you are," he said.

"They *are*?"

"Well, no," he said. "But I'm sure they will be after tonight."

"She's wonderful," Gil said.

Pete nodded. "Good." He finished buttoning his shirt. Tucked it into his pants. Let out a yawn and stretched. "All right, I'm off. It would seem I'm having all my closest friends over for a party tonight so I suppose I ought to attend to some matters of hygiene . . ." He grabbed a green toothbrush out of the top of a giant speaker.

"They're already lined up outside," Gil said.

"Oh, some of them have been here since this morning," said Pete. "Someone posted something on some website that said I'd be closing the door after the first five hundred people or something." He shrugged.

Lucy raised her hand to her mouth. "Five *hundred*?"

"I know, it's very silly," he said. "This place can fit a thousand at least. Especially if you put the people on top of each other, which is how they usually end up." He waggled his eyebrows and stuck his tongue between his teeth. "Now, if you'll excuse me . . ." He disappeared through a door in the back. Two cinnamon-colored cats marched out behind him.

A thousand people. That was more than the entire student population of Van Buren. That was more than three times as many people as would fill the biggest concert hall in town. That was . . . Lucy stuck her hand out for something to grab on to.

"Oh, calm *down*," Liza said. She caught Lucy's wrist. "Making an audience love you is the same as making one person love you, but a bunch of times over. It's honestly not that big a deal."

Lucy sank down onto Pete's bed.

"You could always back out," Olivia said. "But I wouldn't recommend it."

Lucy looked down. Her broken heart thumped.

"So what am I singing?" Lucy asked.

Olivia smiled. "Gilly, deal with our little songbird here, Liza and I have to talk to Pete about something. . . ."

"You're not . . . ," said Gil.

"Not yet," said Olivia. "He's not ready."

"Soon though," said Liza.

Gil led them across the stage behind the curtain into a room on the other side, which contained various complicated-looking pieces of musical equipment, speakers, a keyboard, a guitar, and five laptops.

"You know the boys, of course," said Gil. Standing amongst the laptops were Jack/Bathrobe and B/Lying on the Couch, the two Lucy had stood alone with in the apartment only a few days before, the ones she'd been too scared to talk to. Funny how long ago that seemed.

"Hello," Lucy said.

Jack looked Lucy up and down. Then yanked down his pair of black tuxedo pants to reveal a pair of pastel yellow boxer briefs. "We match," he said.

"Put your pants on, Jack," B said. "You don't want to scare her."

Jack nodded solemnly. "My manhood scares the ladies sometimes. It's a curse."

"It's not your manhood that I'm scared of," Lucy said. "It's the singing in front of a thousand people."

Jack grinned.

"Ah, right, you're our singer tonight," B said, nodding. "A mute singer. Perfect. How very avant-garde. Hope you're better than Jackie here. He just cannot hit those high notes."

Jack nodded. "Again, it's the manhood, I think."

"Too much testosterone and all that, probably," Lucy said. But she was staring at the opening of his shirt and his completely hairless chest.

Gil laughed. "Listen, I have to go make a phone call and I don't get reception back here. Lucy, you'll be okay if I leave you?"

"Of course she will be," said B. He was grinning at her. "She's our brand-new buddy."

Gil kissed Lucy on the cheek. "I'll see you out there, sweetie," she said, then left.

B hit a button on one of the laptops and a heavy bass beat filled the room. Jack hit a button on another laptop and a beepy boopy melody joined in. B flipped on the keyboard and pressed a few keys. There was an airy whistle, and the rich, warm sound of bells, and on top of that a bluesy twang somehow mournful and hopeful at the same time. There was a heartbeat behind all of it, and she could feel it beating with her own heart.

She closed her eyes. She was somewhere else, floating through the air; she could feel the wind rushing past her face. When the song ended she opened her eyes.

"So that was it," said B. "Like it?"

"I completely love it," Lucy said, and meant it.

"Well that is glorious news," said B. He clapped his hands together. "Because that's what you're singing to."

B closed the laptop and Jack took a silver flask out of his hip pocket and took a sip of whatever was inside.

"Aren't we going to practice?" Lucy said.

"That *was* practice," said Jack. "Now shoo, we have manly matters to attend to."

"Wait," Lucy said. "I'm not ready . . ."

But they weren't listening. Jack was leading her out the door, and for a second he stopped. "Oh," he said. "And PS, when you get to the stage, make sure you stand on the X because that's where the spotlight'll be."

"The spotlight?!"

The door shut behind her with a click.

An hour later the place was packed with people. A thousand? Five thousand? A *million*? All Lucy could see in every direction was a blur of bodies—dancing, bouncing, sweating. She had wandered out onto the dance floor to clear her head before going onstage, to try and deal with the hot bile that was working its way up her throat. But now she was trapped.

A giant dude in a black T-shirt stood directly in front of her, blocking her way. His thin brown hair was drenched with sweat. He shook his head in ecstatic dance and little beads of it sprayed around him in a halo.

"Excuse me," she said. She moved right, moved left, but everywhere she tried to go, he already was. "Excuse me, please!" she said again, louder this time. She tapped him on his arm. It was wet and gritty feeling, like he was coated in sand. He looked down at her and blinked. Then just kept right on dancing.

Hot panic shot up the back of her neck. She was supposed to go onstage soon, probably any minute. But if she could not get to the stage in time, she could not go on. And if she did not go on . . .

"Birdie?"

Lucy looked up. Delicate features, dark gray shirt, black pants, hair spiked up slightly. It was Paisley and he was grinning. "Paisley!" she said.

"Hey!" He pulled her in for a hug. His skin was warm and smooth. And Lucy was flooded with relief. A familiar face, even one she'd only seen once was better than nothing. "Aren't you supposed to be in Tokyo?"

"Missed the flight. It's okay though, the guy who was going to fly me in ended up beaming me in as a hologram. I was watching on a webcam. People kept trying to make out with hologram-me and kept being really confused when I wasn't actually there." He laughed. "How are you?" He tipped his head to the side. "You kind of look like you are freaking out. You okay?"

"I'm supposed to be up there." Lucy pointed to the stage.

"Performing tonight? Hey, awesome."

"Olivia just sort of told me I was, so . . ."

"Well, *that* doesn't sound like the Olivia I know." Paisley grinned.

Lucy half laughed. "But I can't get there."

"You, my dear, are lucky I came along. You don't spend half your life in clubs without learning a thing or two about getting through a crowd. My ex used to say watching me get through a crowd was like watching salt get through soup. The sweet boy was never very good at analogies." He shook his head. "Anyway, allow me." Paisley took Lucy's arm and put it around his shoulder. Then leaned in and said: "In all the clubs I've been to I've met a thousand different types of people, but you know the one thing they all have in common? No one wants to get puked on." Paisley leaned over then, put his hand over his mouth, and jerked his shoulders. "OH NO, I THINK I'M GOING TO . . . ," he shouted. Then he winked at her and started lurching forward. Everyone around them started backing up. The backup spread like a ripple through the crowd. People were elbowing each other left and right to get out of his way. Every couple seconds Paisley would shout something like, "I DON'T THINK I CAN MAKE IT TO THE BATHROOM!"

"HOLD ON, PAISLEY!" Lucy shouted. "JUST HOLD ON!"

A minute later they were standing at the side stage door. It opened and she found herself pushed through before she even had a chance to thank him.

Nineteen

*L*ucy stood in the wings, heart thumping along with the music, camera pressed against one wide-open eye. Instead of focusing on the pounding of her heart, she tried to direct all of her attention on what she saw through the lens: Two cabaret girls were out onstage, one playing an old-fashioned harp and the other playing this weird electronic instrument, which sounded like a creepy woman singing and was played simply by touching the air around it. Jack and B were out there too with their laptops, their cymbals, and a giant sousaphone. She took pictures of the coils of wire, of the dusty air, of the bright lights on their faces. When the song ended, she raised her camera and snapped a picture of the cabaret girls as they dragged their instruments into the wings.

Up close they looked like life-sized dolls—bright red Cupid's bow mouths, huge fake spider-leg-looking lashes, faces powdered pale, and a red circle of rouge on the apple of each cheek. They were twins, Lucy realized, identical except for the dark freckle at the corner of one's mouth. Which may have been painted on anyway.

They stopped in front of Lucy. They smelled baby-powder sweet.

Lucy put the camera down and took a deep breath. She stared out at the dark wood on the stage, a glow-in-the-dark X was taped out in the middle. So that's where she'd be standing. That's where she'd be standing when she puked all over herself.

Freckle reached out one tiny hand and squeezed Lucy's arm. "You know what we always think about when we're nervous?" She had a little girl voice, high and breathy.

"The Amazing Arturo!" said the other one, in the exact same voice.

"He was this famous magician back in the twenties, who was killed on that very stage. His assistant accidentally used steel knives instead of rubber in a knife trick."

"She wasn't so smart," Freckle whispered. "But she had perfect aim."

"The moral of the story? No matter what happens to you up there, it won't go as bad as that. . . ."

They giggled. "Probably!"

Freckle grabbed Lucy's camera off the shelf and started poking at it. "Oh, a picture-taker machine. Fun!"

The cheers were dying down and the lights were dimmed except for three blue spotlights on the stage.

"Ready?" Jack was about to walk back onstage.

"Wait!" Lucy's stomach lurched as she realized something. "I don't even know what the lyrics are!"

"Oh right, silly me." Jack pulled a little piece of paper out of the back pocket of his tuxedo pants.

He handed it to Lucy. It was blank.

"But there's nothing on here!" Lucy shouted.

"Well then, you'll just have to make it up," Jack said. He shrugged. And B shrugged. And they both strolled out onstage. B stopped under the spotlight on the row of laptops. Jack stopped behind the keyboards.

There was one blue light left, waiting for Lucy.

Lucy stared. For a moment she could not move at all. *This isn't real,* she tried to tell herself. *Just go, this is only a dream.* But she could not convince her body; she could not convince her pounding heart. She was more awake than she'd ever been. She could not believe what she was about to do.

But that didn't mean she wasn't going to do it.

Lucy's legs were shaking as she stepped out. The stage was hot and dusty. She coughed. She could barely breathe. The lights were directly in her eyes, which was maybe a good thing because it meant that she could not see the crowd out in front of her.

The music started.

The whistle, the beat, the heart.

She squinted out into the crowd. She could not see anyone, but she knew Olivia and Gil and Liza were out there, watching her, judging her. So was everyone.

The music rose, up, up, up. *Sing, Lucy! SING!*

Lucy opened her mouth. Nothing came out but a thin raspy squeak.

The spotlight moved, swirled around. She stared out into the crowd and she could—*oh, please no*—she could suddenly see them. All those people there, waiting for her to go, all of them, staring at her as they danced. Hundreds and hundreds of faces. Hundreds of people with brains and bodies, and hands and hearts. But none of them was the one she wanted.

None of them was Alex.

Her heart squeezed then. A pain shot through her so sharp and hard, she stumbled backwards. If she could do this, just this one last thing, access to the magic would be the reward. And Alex's return would then follow. She closed her eyes and she pictured his lips against hers, breathing his love deep down into her. That was worth all this of course. *That was worth anything.*

So she took one last breath. Filling her lungs down to the pit of her stomach, and then, standing up there in front of a thousand people, Lucy, still absolutely terrified, opened her mouth.

A voice came out.

"OOOOOOOOOOH," the voice sang.

It wasn't even Lucy's voice. Lucy's voice was high and sweet. This was deep and ragged and raw. This was not a note pushed out her open mouth, but something escaping from the split in her heart. She could feel the cry leaving it, vibrating up out of it.

"OOOOOOOOOOH."

When she heard that voice, that rich, strong voice, hers but not hers, something happened and her fear broke like a fever. She opened her mouth up wide and felt the vibration as the sounds left her mouth, more and more and more of them. There was an endless supply.

Was that really her up there? Singing? Howling? Screaming?

She was no longer aware she was up on that stage. She was no longer aware of anything but the feeling of prying apart that crack in her heart, of letting what was inside of it out.

She could not see anything, just the blue light pulsing through her eyelids. And for a moment she did not even know where she was, or who she was, or what she was.

But she didn't care.

And what was she singing up there on the stage that night?

The song she'd written for Alex, of course. The only song that had been in her head for two months. The song she'd sang quietly to herself a thousand times over.

It was the first time she'd sang it in front of anyone at all. Only instead of singing it sweetly the way she'd always practiced, she was screaming it:

I feel you here when you're not

Her voice grew louder and louder.

I see your face in the sky when you're not here

I hear your voice in my head when you're not here

She was really screaming then. And she did not stop.

You're always here, you're always here

You are you are you are

She sang until the singing vibrated down deep within her chest. She sang with all she had. *She just sang everything out.*

And then, when she was empty, when all the blackness had been expelled, she stood there as the beat faded. There was a whirring pulsing, and her voice above it all a final sweet high, clear note. The music stopped. The song was over.

For a brief second there was complete silence.

Lucy opened her eyes as the spotlight circled and went down into the crowd. All those bodies were suddenly frozen. No one was dancing anymore. No one was moving. All she could see was the light reflected off of the two thousand eyeballs that were staring right at her. And in one horrible moment it all came rushing back, where she was, who she was, and what she had just done.

They hated it. They hated her. She'd been so terrible that she'd paralyzed everyone with her terribleness. She felt as though she were standing onstage completely naked. Worse than naked: without her skin.

She gasped.

Then the silence broke. Her gasp was drowned out by a rushing wall of deafening sound, a thousand voices screaming just for her.

Twenty

reathless, Lucy just stood there, staring out at that crowd, completely frozen until her legs decided to walk her offstage. Behind the curtain people hugged her, squeezed her. "AMAZING!" they shouted. "INCREDIBLE!"

She kept going, all the way back, into the hallway, head buzzing. All alone, she leaned against a wall to catch her breath. She brought her hands up to her face. There were tears leaking out of the corners of her eyes. Not of sadness, but of something else:

She'd done it.

She'd gotten up onstage, stood in front of a thousand

people, and sung her heart out, sung her *guts* out. She'd lived through her greatest dream and her very worst nightmare. And survived.

But what exactly had *happened* back there? Why were people reacting this way?

BLAM! The answer exploded in her skull.

Most people spend their entire lives afraid—of looking stupid, of being lonely, of wasting their life, of losing someone they love, of never finding anyone to love at all, of spiders, of drowning, of being burned alive, of bees, of crossing the street, of flying, of fighting, of being hated, of heights, of sharks, of failing, of winning, of elevators, of escalators, of falling, of fire, of getting up in front of a thousand people and singing out loud.

We like to say that love is what unites us; however it's *fear* that we all share.

But standing up there onstage, nakedly, honestly, showing them the real, ragged insides of her ravaged heart, Lucy had appeared entirely fearless. Because in that moment she was. And *in this way she had seduced them all* . . .

Offstage, Lucy still couldn't make her way through the crowd, but this time it wasn't because people didn't see her, *but because they did.*

People called things out to her, stopped their dancing or pulled her in to dance with them. She was passed forward in a daze. Everyone wanted a piece of her. They would not let her go.

Someone may have put a glass of water in her hand. She may have even drunk it. A very tall girl asked for her *autograph* and it was only after she walked away that she realized the girl had not in fact been kidding.

Jack and B were still up onstage; a cello player was out with them now. On the wall behind them was a time-lapse video of flowers blooming, blooming, blooming.

Some people said things to Lucy, about the beauty of her voice, about her dress, her hair, her presence. Some just stared at her in awe, too intimidated to say anything at all.

But through all of this, she kept thinking if only, if only Alex had been there to see her.

She took out her phone and wrote him a text.

Just performed a song in front of a thousand people. Wish you could have been there. X

She hesitated for one second, then hit SEND. She stuck her phone in the little side pocket of her dress.

A moment later Gil flew through the air and attacked her in a hug. She dragged Lucy off to the side. Olivia and Liza were right behind her.

"YOU WERE COMPLETELY INCREDIBLE!" Gil shouted.

Liza was shaking her head. "Damn, girl," was all she said.

Olivia just nodded, looked at Lucy, and let out a laugh.

"I'm not surprised by much," Olivia said. "But *that* surprised *me.*"

Lucy blushed with pleasure.

"And speaking of people who think Lucy's fabulous . . ." Gil was looking at someone behind Lucy. "*There* you are," she said. She reached behind Lucy and pulled him toward her. Tall, square glasses, sweet face, dimples, blue eyes. Colin. "Where have you been?" Gil said. "Did you just get here?"

He shook his head. "I got here a while ago. But it's so crowded and it's so hard to get through a crowd like this. I was over there by the wall. I could still see though."

"Did you get to hear Lucy sing?"

He nodded, then turned toward Lucy. "Hey, you were really . . ." His voice was quiet and Lucy had to lean in to hear him. ". . . watching you up there on that stage. I mean, I've never heard anything . . . you were just—" He took a deep breath. "Luminous."

"Thank you," Lucy said. "That is really nice of you to say."

"How did you do that? How did you just stand up there in front of all these people and sing like that? And radiate that? And look so comfortable?" He blushed then, as though he'd already said more than he meant to. But then he did not stop. "If that had been me up there I would have been so scared . . . mostly of getting shot, because the only way I'd have ended up on that stage in the first place would be if someone was standing behind me with a gun."

Lucy laughed.

But Colin's face got even redder then, as though he had just heard what he'd said and decided it was exactly wrong. He stood there bouncing from foot to foot to foot, vibrating with jangly nerves, just staring down at her with his big, actually rather beautiful eyes open all wide. She could feel the discomfort radiating off of him.

"Colin," she started to say. She wanted to tell him something then. Standing there, in that place with all those people who had just heard her sing, in that hot room filled with music and noise, what she wanted to tell him was something about how he did not have to feel so trapped by his own nerves, trapped in that little box he was in. She wanted to tell him that things are not as set as he might think they are. And that no matter what he believes about himself, one day he just may surprise the hell out of himself by what he is able to do.

But she did not know how to begin that kind of conversation with someone who was practically a stranger, even one who was looking at her the way he was, like he was not any kind of stranger at all. And even if she did know what to say and how to say it, it's not like she could have with Olivia and Liza and Gil standing right there. With Gil, in fact, watching her at that very moment. Gil was nodding and grinning as though she was signaling for Lucy to do something, although Lucy had no idea what this was. Before she could figure it out, someone came up behind her.

"Mmmf, I could just chop you up into little pieces and *sauté* you," a voice said. Lucy turned. There was a man standing in front of her. He was short and broad shouldered, with tattoos covering both his arms and a face like chewed-up meat. He was old, not quite parent-age but close. He licked his lips, then *mmmf*-ed one more time before he started walking away.

When Lucy turned back, Colin had moved a few feet away, was standing with Gil. It was as though he'd felt like he was intruding, as though he thought Lucy and Chewed-up-Meat-face might want to be alone.

"Colin is going home now, Lu," Gil said. She looked disappointed. Her little arm was linked through his. "I tried to convince him to stay, but he won't."

"I'm sorry," Colin said. "I just . . . need to."

"Colin, why don't you give Lucy your number so she can call you?"

Colin blushed even more.

"Uh," he said.

"Lucy wants it, right, Lucy?" Gil looked up at her. "She already has her phone out."

Lucy nodded quickly. "Yes," she said. "Of course."

She handed her phone to Colin.

Gil winked and walked off.

Colin was looking down at her phone, punching numbers slowly, like he was trying to avoid having to look at her as he said whatever he was about to say. "I would love to hang out more. It's just that big crowds like this are not so much my thing . . ." He chewed his lower lip. "I guess maybe you noticed yesterday. I'm sorry about running out so fast. But I'm glad I got to hear you." He handed her the phone. "You were amazing."

He turned to leave, started trying to work his way through the crowd. Then stopped, turned back. "Um, bye!" He reached his arms out and pulled her toward him into a hug.

His body did not feel like she would have guessed it would. There were strong muscles in his arms, in his chest, in his back. She could feel them through his thin gray shirt. This was not the tentative hug she would have expected from him. This was something else. . . . She leaned against him. She felt his arms around her waist, his strong hands pressing against her lower back, pulling her now more firmly toward him. She felt his stomach against hers as their entire bodies lined up. She leaned her head on his shoulder. She could smell him— he smelled like clean, sweet sweat.

Lucy sighed. She closed her eyes. She felt some part of herself melting, the harsh edges being softened. She hadn't been hugged like this in so long, held like this in so long. The last time was the day before Alex left.

Alex.

Lucy's eyes popped open. She pulled back. She shook her head.

Colin was staring at her. His face was flushed.

"I really hope you call me." He had a glassy look in his eyes, as though the hug was a drug and he'd been suddenly made braver by it. "I mean, I don't mean to make that sound weird and pressure-y or anything. I just . . . hope that you do." He smiled one last time, a big full smile. A dimple dimpled deeply in each cheek.

Then he turned and slipped off into the crowd.

But when he was gone, and no one was looking at her, Lucy felt the empty space in her heart all the more deeply. Lucy looked down at her phone.

No text.

Well, really that didn't mean anything. Alex just wasn't a quick text-backer. The night before had just been a fluke.

So no, she could not expect one back yet. No, she would just be calm. She would wait.

Except her stomach started to churn. *Where was he?* It was just before midnight. What was he doing? Where would he be when he received the message? Would he be excited when he saw her name flashing there? Well, assuming she was still in his phone . . . And *was she* still in his phone?

But then, suddenly, her phone *did* vibrate with a text, as though she had brought it forth by the force of her wanting it.

She held her breath and looked down.

**Hope ice-cream night is going well, bud. If you run
out of mint chip, let me know!**

Lucy's heart popped. The pieces flew everywhere.

She stood squeezing her phone until she felt a hand on her
shoulder. There was Olivia, standing alone.

"All right, my little bean cake," Olivia said. "You come
with me now. I have something to show you. Something
you've earned the right to see"—she took Lucy by the arm—
"finally. We never show this to people who aren't one of us.
But I suspect you will be soon enough." She gave Lucy a sly
smile and pulled her into the crowd.

Lucy could barely breathe.

This was it.

Olivia pulled Lucy through a door, down a narrow hallway, into a back room. They walked until the booming
music faded into a faint pounding. They went through one
last door and there, straight ahead, was a tall metal ladder
stretching twenty feet into the air and leading to a hatch in
the ceiling.

Without speaking, Olivia started to climb, her smooth calf
muscles barely flexing with each step. A few moments later,
she vanished up into the hatch.

Lucy gripped the ladder's thin metal sides, and waited for
the familiar tight fist of fear to clench her stomach. This was
a ladder after all, leaning against nothing, leading straight up

into the sky. But the clench did not come.

Lucy climbed. As the floor got farther and farther away, all she could do was smile a tiny and bewildered smile at what she knew was waiting for her up at the top. At what she was leaving down below her.

Four days ago, Lucy was a scared little girl sobbing broken-heartedly in the bathroom, and now here she was, having just sung in front of a thousand people, on her way up a ladder about to be taught how to do *magic* that she would then use to get back her lost love.

Life is nothing if not surprising.

Lucy entered a warm dark room. Olivia flipped on the light.

In the center of the room there was a big metal desk facing a wall with nine flat-screen monitors stacked in a square.

"Where are we?"

"Pete's surveillance room." Olivia sat down in a fancy leather desk chair and motioned for Lucy to sit in one beside her. "He had this stuff installed last year when he thought someone was stealing from him. Turns out he'd just forgotten he'd put a big stack of cash under his bed to keep anyone from stealing it. He ended up keeping the cameras." Olivia grinned. "Because in addition to being kind of forgetful, he's also kind of a perv." She pointed to the monitor on the bottom right corner, which showed a couple in a hallway heavily making out. "But I didn't bring you up here for *that*," Olivia said. "I brought you here . . ."

Lucy held her breath.

". . . for this."

Olivia twisted a few knobs on the control panel, then raised her finger to her lips. "It looks like she's already started." Olivia tapped the monitor in the middle and flipped a switch. Liza's voice came crackling through the speakers.

". . . we are done now," Liza said.

On the screen, Liza was sitting at a picnic table in an outdoor courtyard. Across from her was a guy with short brown hair in a black T-shirt, his back to the camera. His shoulders were hunched and he was leaning his head against his hands.

"But there must be a reason," the boy said. "Please"—his voice cracked—"whatever it is you can tell me . . ."

"That's Max," Olivia said. "He really loves Liza. It's quite sweet."

"Okay? You want reasons? Do you have a pen? A notebook? This might take a while." Liza laughed. "Number one, your voice is too soft. Two, you always look like you need lip balm even after you've just put on lip balm. Is there something wrong with your mouth? Do you have a mouth disease? And three, the lip balm you use smells bad, like medicine. Which was only one of the many things wrong with kissing you by the way, which we will discuss more extensively when we get to items eleven through twenty-five. Number four, every time you told a joke you'd look at me after, like checking to see if I thought it was funny. Five, you have freckles."

"Wait," Lucy said. "Why are we watching this?"

"This is your prize! You get to watch Liza break a heart."

"But I don't . . . ," Lucy started.

"Ssh," Olivia said. And she pointed toward the screen.

"But . . ." Max said. His voice sounded strange, shaky. "You told me you liked them."

"Well, I don't. Six, you gave me too many presents. Seven, I hate your belt. Eight, you're allergic to lemons. . . ."

Lucy stared at the screen where Liza was still listing and Max now seemed to be crying. A cold heavy weight sank in Lucy's gut. These girls broke hearts, she *knew* that. She'd seen Ethan post-heartbreak and had felt, if not good about it, at least generally okay. Ethan was strong and a jerk and Lucy could see how his broken heart might help both him and the world. But this was different. All Lucy needed to know about Max she already knew—he was sweet and he was weak. And Liza was shredding him to pieces. And nothing about it was okay.

Lucy couldn't watch any more. She had to turn away.

Olivia was leaning back in the chair with her legs up, smiling at the screen as though she were watching a favorite TV show.

"Why doesn't she stop now?" Lucy said. "He's obviously already crying. Why doesn't she just take his tear and go?"

"What'd be the fun in that? Now, ssh. My favorite part is coming."

Lucy felt hot chills run up the back of her neck.

Olivia held one finger to her lips and pointed to the screen.

". . . change," Max was saying, "if you'll just give me a chance, just a couple of weeks, I think I can. I promise I will . . ."

Liza let out a cruel laugh. "Do you even know how pathetic you sound right now?" She tipped her head to the side. "I don't mean that rhetorically. Like, this is an actual question. Do you?"

Max stopped moving.

"Because if you doooon't"—Liza stretched the word out, grinning—"I could just show you the video." Then she leaned over and whispered something to Max, who jolted upright. She pointed directly at the camera. "See it up there? Wave to the camera, Maxie." Max turned toward it, his hands over his mouth, his warm brown eyes full of pain. He turned quickly away.

"You're taping this?" He sounded scared.

"Yup! But not just this, honey. If you want something to cry to later, let me know and I'll send you some files. I've recorded everything we've ever done together."

"Everything? Wait . . ."

"Yes, Max, even *that*. Really powerful cameras come really

small these days. You'd be surprised at some of the places a person can hide one. They're quite expensive but well worth the price, I've found. Speaking of expenses, how much do you think those rich parents of yours would be willing to give you to, say, keep this tape or some of your other greatest hits from accidently being played at the next Van Buren school-wide assembly?"

"You wouldn't actually do that." His voice was shaking. "You're not that cruel."

Liza laughed, then reached out and stroked his hair. "Oh, lover, I don't think *either* of us believes *that*."

Lucy turned toward Olivia. "She's not serious, is she?"

"Well, of course she is," Olivia said. "Don't look so surprised, sweet cakes. There are many benefits to being a Heartbreaker—making magic is only one of them." Olivia shrugged. "We do this to pretty much all of our targets."

Lucy's entire body was suddenly ice cold.

"You do? All of you?"

Olivia nodded.

"Even Gil?" Lucy pressed one hand to her lips and another to her belly.

"Of course. You should watch the recording of this one she did six months ago. The guy basically went insane, threatened to *kill himself.* I mean, of course he didn't, but still, it was amazing. Gilly was the one who figured out how to hook up our newest camera so it streams to the internet. That way

Jack and B and our other friends can watch from home. I mean we don't tell them what we use the tears for obviously, but it would be a crime to let all *that* go to waste." She pointed toward the screen again where Max was hunched over the table crying into his hands. "That's some high-quality reality TV right there."

Liza was standing over him, staring into the camera. She made a mock frowny face. Then she winked at the camera, then mimed kicking Max in the butt.

Olivia began to laugh and it was not the tinkling of bells but something louder, harsher. Lucy looked at her. Gone was the cool and calm, wise and otherworldly Olivia that Lucy had known. In her place was a beast, red faced, head tipped back: a hiccupping, high-pitched hyena wail emerging from her wide-open mouth. There was nothing beautiful about her now.

Hot acid flooded Lucy's insides. She shook her head.

"But you said that when you break hearts you're doing a good thing, giving a gift. How can that . . ." Lucy pointed to the screen, to where Max's shoulders were shaking. "How can that be a good thing? How is that a gift to him?"

"Weeell, yeah about that." Olivia laughed again. "I guess that's all sort of subjective, isn't it? But, look at it this way, it'll definitely be a gift to our wallets! And we will be helping support the local economy when we spend Max's parents' money."

Lucy's heart was pounding so hard she could feel it in her teeth.

"Hey," Olivia said. She gave Lucy a nudge. "You know what would be funny? If someone came into the courtyard right now and 'discovered' this little scene. You should do it, fruit tart. Just go back through the main room through an orange door off to the side." Olivia was nodding. "Oh, poor Maxie, he'll probably die of embarrassment. It'll be so awesome."

Lucy pressed one hand against her stomach.

"Go on then," Olivia said. She was no longer smiling. "Surprise the little loser. And then come back here and we will finally give you everything you've been waiting for."

"Everything?" said Lucy. Her voice sounded hollow.

"Yes," Olivia said. "Everything." She looked up and their eyes met. "And just so there's no mistake. That means the magic."

Lucy's heart was hammering as she stood. She walked toward the ladder and began the long climb down. She could not believe what she was about to do. She knew she had no choice. She walked through the main room. She stopped outside the orange door. She could hear muffled voices coming from inside. Across from the door was a white cement beam. Lucy reached into her bag for something to write with, and closed her fist around a marker: the green Sharpie she'd gotten for her game with Alex.

She uncapped it, and onto the white cement she scribbled out a message.

It's going to be all right.

She stopped and looked at those letters. Max would see this when he came in from the courtyard, heart wrecked, feeling all alone. And maybe, for a moment, just a moment, some tiny part of him would be able to believe it.

Lucy pressed her fist to her heart.

Then at least someone would.

She walked out into the night without looking back.

Twenty-One

*I*t was only when she was halfway down the street that Lucy's heart and brain stopped racing enough for her to realize that she was out in the middle of nowhere, and there was not a single person she could call to come and pick her up. Tristan thought she was at home. Her parents were still out of town. And she didn't have enough money with her for a cab. And that left who? *Alex?*

Lucy shook her head.

No, she would walk. According to her phone, it would take her a little over five hours to do it. Fine, so that's what she'd do.

Lucy kept going, all alone through that dark night, too angry to feel afraid.

Her phone vibrated with calls from Olivia. But there was not a single thing Lucy could imagine wanting to say to her right then. Or ever again.

Lucy shut her phone off. She walked on dark quiet roads, the only sounds an occasional car passing in the distance, the occasional hoot of an owl. But all the while she could not get the sound of Max's ragged cries out of her ears, and she could not get her ache for him out of her heart.

Twenty-
Two

round nine Lucy woke enough to register her parents pulling into the driveway, back from their trip upstate. Then she was pulled back into the same dream she'd been having all night in which a conveyor belt made of old, scratched leather carried a parade of bloody hearts toward a set of giant copper gears. Each heart had a bomb inside. *TICK TICKTICK.* In the dream Lucy knew there was a message for her, from Alex, in one of those ticking bomb hearts. The message was something he desperately needed to tell her, but the only way for her to get it was to stand there and wait for each heart to explode.

BOOM BOOMBOOM. The hearts blew, covering Lucy with their blood.

Boom boomboom. Lucy's mother was knocking on her door. "Are you in there, honey? It's almost noon."

It was only then that Lucy opened her eyes. Sat up with a start. She grabbed her phone before she even took a breath. She turned it on.

Nothing but texts from Olivia. DELETE, DELETE, DELETE, DELETE.

"YES!" Lucy shouted. "Getting up now!"

She felt as if she hadn't slept at all.

Downstairs, her dad was standing at the stove. Her mom was next to him holding a plate of grilled cheeses. "There's our girl!" her mom said, enveloping Lucy in a cheddar-scented hug.

Her dad waved his spatula. "Hope you're hungry."

"We went a little bit overboard at the farmers' market near our bed-and-breakfast this morning." Lucy's mom motioned toward a stack of paper-wrapped chunks of cheese, huge loaves of bread dusted in flour, piles of peaches and radishes and tomatoes and cucumbers. "We had such a lovely time I guess we just wanted to bring it back with us."

"I think we are probably breaking some important fancy food rule frying up all these *artisanal* cheeses, though," her dad said. "I'm so ashamed." He was grinning.

"Well, call us a couple of crazy rule-breakers then!" her

mom said. She bumped Lucy's father with her hip, and he kissed her on the cheek.

Lucy tried to force a smile.

Every so often, usually right after a vacation or a holiday, her parents did this happy couple thing. They would make jokes and cook together and kiss each other when they thought no one was looking and giggle if anyone was. But it was not to be trusted. The happy couple thing was always followed by the angry couple thing, which was then followed by months of barely speaking, which always culminated in the announcement that they were getting a divorce. Which they never did, because then the cycle would start all over. This was just how it was—always changing, nothing ever solid. Ordinarily, seeing them so giddy would fill Lucy with a particular pang in her chest. But in that moment, Lucy felt nothing but a sickness in her stomach over what she'd seen the night before and the ever-present emptiness of missing Alex.

Lucy's father looked up. "So I guess you were partying it up pretty hard while we were gone, huh? Sleeping until noon? Wooweee!" He was smiling, kidding.

"Ha-ha, you know me," Lucy said. Only the thing was, they didn't, and they hadn't in an awfully long time. "Did you have fun?"

"Oh yes," her father said. "Except for the two-hour drive home in a car that smelled like ripe Brie!"

"And we missed you, of course," said Lucy's mother. "Are you feeling better, honey?"

"I'm . . . ," Lucy said. She stopped. How did her mother know?

Her mother smiled expectantly.

It was then that Lucy remembered her fake stomachache. *That's* what her mother was referring to. That's all she knew about. Stomachaches and small talk, that was the extent of their conversations now.

When Lucy was younger she and her mom had been close, but lately things had changed. When Lucy first started dating Alex, her parents had been talking about divorce, radiating miserable gray clouds, and it just felt unfair to bring her manic giddiness into a house that felt like that. Besides, it was private and precious and there was part of her that had wanted to keep all of it just for herself.

And now she would keep her pain to herself too.

Lucy looked up at her parents. They were staring at her, identical grins plastered on their faces.

"Yes," Lucy forced herself to say. "I sure am."

A little while later, Lucy and Tristan were at Uncle Smooth's, the smoothie place they often went on Sunday afternoons.

"Are you sure you're okay?" Tristan said again. "I'm not trying to be pushy here, kid. But I thought a night of ice cream was supposed to make a person feel *better* not worse. Unless they have lactose issues. And you kind of look like crap . . ."

"Thanks," she said.

"The prettiest crap!"

Lucy tried to stick out her tongue. Oh, if only she could tell him all of it.

"Maybe you're suffering from a lack of banana blueberry peach protein?" He stuck out his cup.

Her phone buzzed. Another text from Olivia, the third she'd gotten in the last hour.

DELETE.

"Looks like you've got yourself a very persistent suitor, Ms. Wrenn. One of the guys from the other night?"

Lucy shook her head. "Olivia," she said. And she shook her head again.

"Dear Lucy," Tristan said in a jokey high-pitched voice. "Pillow fight later? Make sure you invite your hot friend Tristan!"

Lucy shook her head.

"They're . . . I don't think I'm going to be hanging out with them anymore."

"What happened?"

Lucy pressed her lips together. "I just don't want to be friends with them anymore is all."

Lucy's phone buzzed again. She clenched her teeth. "I wish they'd leave me *alone*!"

It was then that she looked down, her finger on the DELETE

button, but her heart exploded when she saw what it was. Lucy raised her hand to her lips.

Did anyone make a recording last night? I need a copy of that.

It was from a number she didn't recognize.

"What's in there?" Tristan said. He pointed to her phone, which she was trying to hide in her lap. "Those girls begging you to come back?"

"Not sure," Lucy said. She tried to shrug. But she was sure. She was so sure her hands were shaking.

"Speaking of people, y'know, doing things. So, that girl Janice from last night?"

A second later, her phone buzzed again.

Btw finally caved and got a new phone, new #.keysarehardtotexton

Her entire body was tingling. This message was from Alex. It had to be.

PS Ur my 1st text

The hammering in her chest was almost unbearable. It felt like her heart was about to crack clean through her ribs.

Lucy typed, *I'm honored!!* But then deleted it before she hit SEND. That's what the old Lucy would write. She was not welcome here anymore.

"Go on, Tristy," Lucy said.

The new Lucy typed.

Not sure about recording. Things got kind of crazy afterward . . .

Lucy hit SEND. Tristan was still staring at her.

"I'm listening," Lucy said.

". . . so I get to her house," Tristan was saying. "And . . ."

Lucy nodded. She squeezed her phone. New message.

So what are you up to? Maybe you could sing something for me? Are you around next weekend?

Lucy felt her face burn and her mouth spread into a smile. She was so happy and relieved, she thought she would cry. But no.

Lucy shook her head and took a deep breath. Maybe he wasn't trying to be flirty. Maybe he just felt sorry for her. Or maybe this was his way of trying to be her friend. . . .

So then, how should she respond? Liza would probably write something flirty and mean, like, *Only in your dreams . . . the dirty ones.* But more clever than that. And Gil would probably just write back a smiley face. And Olivia would write . . . what *would* she write?

It didn't matter what those girls would do. They were evil. And she was done with them.

". . . so then she's just standing there about to, I don't know, perform this dance number, I guess," Tristan continued.

Lucy stared down at her phone. She had to text back fast, while he was still in whatever mood he was in that made him send that text message in the first place, which must be a weird one since it honestly didn't even sound much like him. But what to say?

". . . and I didn't want to hurt her feelings but . . ."

Lucky you, I think I am . . . , she typed back.

A second later: *Lucky me indeed. Friday night? ;)*

Lucy's mouth dropped open into an O and she brought her hand up to her lips. She gasped.

". . . I feel like maybe she read one too many of those magazines that tell girls all guys love spontaneity or something," Tristan went on, "because when she was done . . . Lucy, are you okay?"

Lucy couldn't hold it in any more.

"Alex just asked me out for Friday." she blurted out in one breath. "Look!" She held her phone out so Tristan could see.

"This is from him?" He sounded confused.

Lucy nodded.

"And you asked him to meet us here?"

"No. . . . What are you talking about?"

Tristan pointed. Lucy turned. There he was, Alex—her love, her heart, her everything, walking right into Uncle Smooth's. Was he looking for *her*?

Turn around . . .

She clicked SEND, licked her lips, and tried to force herself to take a deep breath.

She stared at the back of Alex's head, waiting for him to turn. He was up at the front talking to one of the guys at the counter. He reached for his wallet.

Tristan was staring at her. "Wait, so you're dating again? When did that happen?"

Lucy's phone buzzed. *Why?*

i'm sitting right behind you . . .

Lucy waited, staring at the back of his head. He didn't turn.

Lucy stood.

Tristan raised his eyebrows.

Up at the counter Alex was paying for a big smoothie. Then he turned and started walking toward the door. As he passed their table, Lucy poked him in the side.

"I'm right here!" she said.

Alex looked down. "Oh, hi, Lucy." He looked up at Tristan. "Hey man."

Tristan nodded. "Hey."

Alex stood there, just sucking on his smoothie.

"Oh, hey, I got your text about the concert last night," he said easily. "I was on the phone though, so I didn't see it until this morning." He held up his phone.

Lucy stared at it. The green packing tape, the Sharpied-on numbers. "But I thought you just got a new . . ." She stopped as *clickity-clickity-click* the pieces joined together in her head.

Her phone vibrated again.

I am looking and looking but I don't see you . . .

Lucy raised her hand to her lips. *Oh no.*

"So." He turned toward Tristan. "How was she? I kind of can't imagine her doing something like that."

"Well . . ." Tristan paused. "I'm sure she was amazing at whatever it was she was doing, but I have no idea what you're talking about."

"He wasn't there," Lucy said quietly. And then, quickly, "So, um, what are you up to today?" Her voice was too high. She coughed.

"I'm talking about the performance last night," Alex said. He looked confused, then suspicious. "You know, the thousand-person concert? You weren't one of those thousand people?"

"No," Tristan said. "I wasn't." His face was toward Lucy, but he wasn't looking at her. He wasn't looking at anything.

"Weird, man." Alex turned to Lucy. He tipped his head to the side. "Where did you say this concert was again?"

"Just this place, this old theater, some guy lives there." Lucy bit her lip. "It didn't have a name."

"Okaaaaaay," Alex said. He stretched out the word and let it dissolve into nothing. He gave her this look, *this look*. And despite her inability to decode most of the facial expressions he made during the entire course of their relationship, the meaning of this one was clear: he thought she was lying. For a moment he looked like he actually felt sorry for her. Then shrugged. "Well," he said. "I'm off. Going to the darkroom to develop some rolls of film so . . ."

Tristan was looking down, and Alex was looking away. Lucy was drowning. "Wait," Lucy said. "Wait!" She reached into her bag and pulled out a black canister. The film from last night. "There are photos in here. From the concert. Can you throw them in with yours? I have some pictures in there that I want to work on in class tomorrow so . . ." He would see the pictures. He would see the pictures and he would know the truth.

"Um, sure," Alex said. He shrugged one more time. "See you guys later."

Hot, sick, liquid panic rose up the back of Lucy's neck. Her hands were shaking. Her phone vibrated and she left it alone.

"I don't understand," said Tristan. It sounded like his throat had shrunk and there was only a tiny opening for the words to get through. "What was he talking about?"

There was so much she wanted to say right then. *So much* but she couldn't.

Lucy just shook her head.

"Oh wait, I get it. You were making that up and I was supposed to go along with it. Sorry, I didn't realize, bud!" Tristan sounded so hopeful then, so happy with that explanation.

Lucy's heart squeezed. "I wasn't."

The muscles in Tristan's face twitched and something was happening around his eyes. She could barely look at him. But she couldn't look away.

"I didn't know I was going to," she said. "Be performing, I mean. Those girls just told me I was going to, so there wasn't really any time to . . ."

"Home alone all night, eh?"

Lucy opened her mouth. But there was not a single thing she could think to say.

"I should probably take you home now," Tristan said. He stood up awkwardly.

Her stomach twisted.

Tristan started walking toward the door, doubled back, threw the smoothie out in the trash.

"I'll be outside," he said.

It was then Lucy remembered her phone, the message waiting inside.

She flipped it open to see a new text. It could only be Paisley.

All I see behind me are an incredibly cute guy and a middle-aged punk lady. Did u turn urself into some1 else?:p

If only, Lucy thought. *If only I could.*

Twenty-
Three

When Lucy got home, she mumbled something to her mother about feeling sick again and dragged her body up the stairs. She was suddenly so, so tired. She collapsed on top of her bed, felt herself yanked down into a heavy sleep. She dreamt of only blackness and a sound: *tick tick tick.*

Hours later, Lucy was smashed back into consciousness by a crashing sound outside and a buzzing next to her head.

She sat up, heart pounding. It was dark. Through her window the sky flashed. The rain was coming down so hard, it didn't even seem real. Lucy was not entirely sure she was not still sleeping.

Her phone kept buzzing next to her head. She reached for it without thinking.

"Well, if it isn't my tiny cake wad."

Thunder shook the house and the windows chattered like teeth.

Adrenaline shot through her veins. She was suddenly wide awake.

"I am not your cake wad," Lucy said. Her voice was tight and flat. "I'm not your honey pie or your sugar face or your fish stick marzipan banana bread lasagna." She felt the anger bubbling up, pushing like steam against her lips.

"Well, well, well," Olivia said. She laughed lightly. "What do we have here?"

During her long walk home the night before, Lucy had thought she never wanted to talk to Olivia or any of those girls ever again. With every step she told herself she was walking farther and farther away from them. But in that moment Lucy realized there were, in fact, a lot of things Olivia needed to hear. And some strong hard place inside Lucy, a place she didn't even know she *had*, told Lucy she was the one who needed to say them.

"We have someone who knows what you are now," Lucy said. "And needs to talk to you. Face-to-face."

"Good," Olivia said. "Because I need to talk to you too."

"Meet me outside at midnight," Lucy said.

"Okay, Lucy," Olivia said. And then they hung up.

Lucy sat there, trying to slow her breathing. She'd see Olivia one last time. She would tell her what she needed to tell her. And then that would be it. Lucy would go back to the regular magic-less world, where Tristan was mad at her and Alex didn't love her. And somehow she would manage to survive, just survive. It was all she could hope to do.

Twenty-
Four

*L*ucy had told herself she wasn't going to be afraid anymore, but when Olivia pulled up at midnight that night she felt that familiar fizzle of fear deep in her gut. And when their eyes met by the light of the cloud-covered moon, Lucy's hands began to shake. *Well, let them shake,* Lucy thought. And she balled them into fists.

"You and your friends are monsters," Lucy said. She took a breath. Her entire body was trembling now, even her heart inside her chest. But it didn't matter.

Olivia tipped her head to the side, curious. "Go on."

"When you first explained heartbreaking to me, I thought I could maybe see how it was okay somehow. But everything you told me about what you do is a lie. Max did not need to have his heart broken. He did not need to be *humbled* or *opened up*. And I don't need any kind of magic to know that.

"What Liza did last night was disgusting and evil. And from now on I'm going to do everything I possibly can to stop you guys from hurting a single other person. And yes, you are powerful. And yes, I'm just some sad, pathetic, heartbroken girl with no boyfriend and no friends and no magic. But if you think that will stop me . . . just you wait."

Lucy stopped. A wave of calm washed over her.

"That's it," Lucy said. "You can go now."

She looked Olivia straight in the eye and felt nothing but relief.

And then Olivia smiled. She brought her hands up and started a slow clap. "Bravo, Lucy." The sound of her claps echoed off the trees. "You've passed. The magic is yours."

"I don't want it," Lucy said.

Of course she did. But not from them. Not like this.

Olivia reached out for her. Lucy stepped back.

"Lucy," Olivia said. "What you saw last night, what I showed you on the cameras at Pete's. That wasn't real."

"Whatever you're going to say now? Don't bother. I won't believe you."

Olivia shook her head. "Magic is power. Power beyond what most people are capable of handling. We needed to know you had the moral center required not to abuse it. And the balls to stop anyone who doesn't. Last night was a test. The guy you saw? Max? There is no such person." Olivia held out her phone. On the screen was a photo of Max from the back. Olivia scrolled to the next picture—a three-quarter view. Then a side view. Max was starting to look familiar. Olivia flipped to the next shot and then there was a photograph of Gil. Narrow-hipped Gil with her short pixie haircut slicked down. She was standing next to Lucy's green Sharpie message—*It's going to be all right.* She had one hand pointing at the camera, the other pointing at her heart.

Lucy wasn't sure whether to laugh or cry or turn back and run or just start screaming. "But *why?*"

"Before we could give you magic to use on your own, we needed to test you. When I gave you the scarf in the bathroom that was the first test. Your tears activated the ink. That meant that you had the potential to become a Heartbreaker. Last night was the second test. But it was only a test." She paused. "We needed to know you could handle the magic." Olivia smiled. "And you can." She held out a little vial. "So here."

The vial was a bit larger than a perfume sample. There was silvery-gold liquid swirling inside.

"Please take it," Olivia said. "Okay? Just hold it and look at it? Can you at least do that?" Her voice sounded different then, pleading.

"Fine." Lucy took it. The swirling slowed, and in that heavy, shimmering silver-gold, Alex's face appeared: the curve of his cheek, the hollow of his eye. The face blew her a kiss.

"What is it?" Lucy whispered.

"Drink it," Olivia said. "And then you'll see. Then you'll see everything."

"You think I'm going to drink something because you said to?"

"Please, just drink it. It won't hurt you."

"And why should I believe you? How do I know it's not poison?"

"Because if I am ever planning to poison you . . ." Olivia smiled then, just ever so slightly. "I won't say please."

"Well . . ." Lucy said. "That's . . ." But crazy as it sounded, for some odd reason, Lucy believed her.

And besides, now she had nothing to lose.

Lucy raised the vial toward the sky like she was making a toast to Alex, to herself, to their future, whatever that was going to be. She tossed it back.

The liquid slid over her tongue and down her throat. It was freezing cold and chilled her insides.

She felt suddenly dizzy. There was an aching in her head, in her arms and legs. All her muscles contracted at once. She could feel the earth rotating under her, and for a second, just a second, she did not rotate.

"Open your eyes," Olivia said.

Lucy felt her eyes open.

Tiny flashes of light glittered all around her; sparks sparkled. She heard a soft but many-layered hum, as though everything around her was vibrating its own note. She listened to the trees, to the moon, to the blades of grass.

It was funny that she'd ever existed in this world and not known about the magic. Because now that she could see it, she knew this: *it was everywhere.*

She looked down at her own hand. Shimmering pink light was coming off of her skin.

"Oh my God," Lucy said.

"Oh my *Goddess,*" said Olivia. She laughed gold glitter bubbles. "Don't worry. It'll fade in a couple of minutes."

The air was filled with thousands of tiny fireflies.

Olivia said, "Just breathe."

Lucy breathed in and watched swirls of liquid floating through the air.

"But what *are* those?" Lucy said. She tried to point at one.

"Currents of energy," Olivia said. "Visible to you because of the Magic Magnet."

"The what?"

"What you just drank. It was a liquid Magic Magnet. It makes you able to see more of the magic in the world, including some not usually visible to the human eye. Although only temporarily. And that part is more like a side effect. Its real purpose is to protect us and you."

Lucy blinked. "From what?" Her voice sounded funny, like

she was very, very far away.

"Well, imagine what would happen if people found out about our powers, about what we can do?"

Lucy blinked again. Each time she opened her eyes the sparks were dimmer.

"It's only active so long as your heart is in the first seven days of being broken, which means it will seep into you over the next two days. If you don't break a heart by then, it will gather all your magical memories and pass them back into the air."

"But what does that mean?" Lucy blinked one more time. The sparks faded until they were gone.

"It means that if you don't become one of us, you won't remember any of this. Right now, this moment, this conversation, it will not exist to you three days from now." Olivia reached down her shirt and pulled something out. "And it means that what I am about to give to you, you will have no memory of ever having gotten."

"Wait," Lucy said. "You'll take my memories?"

"Don't worry," Olivia said. "The memories the magnet will suck up aren't memories you'd want to have if you aren't a Heartbreaker. To know for sure that the world is filled with magic that you cannot see and cannot ever touch is far worse than not knowing there is any magic at all. . . . Now, will you get in the car, please. I have something for you."

Lucy got in.

Olivia opened her fist and revealed a tiny eyedropper and two foil packets, one silver, one gold.

"Don't look like much, do they?" said Olivia. "Funny to think how many people there are out there who would do absolutely anything to get at these little things."

"What are they?"

She pinched the silver foil. "This is Empathy Cream. If you rub it on your skin and then touch someone else's, you'll feel their feelings instead of your own for the entire time you're touching them. That means instead of believing someone when they say they're fine, you'll know whether they're fine or not. You'll know if a guy is scared even if he's pretending to be big and tough. It's useful for calling people out on their bullshit. If you can figure out what a person is feeling and put it into words even if they themselves aren't able to, it will give them the impression that only *you* get them. That only you can truly understand them."

Lucy stared at the packet. If only she'd had that while Alex was still her boyfriend. If only she'd had gallons of it to slather all over herself.

"The only caveat I'll give you with this is that we had a bad batch of tears once. Tears that we thought were heartbreak tears but were just cried by a really good actor. And they got mixed in with the tears we were using when we made our last batch of this stuff. So there are a couple packets that don't have any magic in them. Chances are you didn't get one. But if you did, it still makes a really good cuticle cream." Olivia winked. "There's sweet almond oil in it."

Lucy just nodded.

"It can also be useful in some more, how shall we say, *recreational* settings." Olivia paused. "But in your case, it will help you know the exact right moment to strike. And in three minutes I am going to tell you what I mean by that. However, first . . ." She held up the eyedropper. It was amber colored with a black rubber top. "This is something I've thought you needed since the first second I saw you all crumple-faced in that bathroom, honey pie." She unscrewed the top and held up the dropper. "Tip your head back." She touched Lucy's forehead, chin, eyelids, and cheeks with the tip. Lucy's skin began to tingle.

"Your face is too expressive," Olivia said. "It's sweet really. But it's not very useful. So now for the next forty-eight hours or so you'll be able to make your face do or not do anything you want." She held up the tiny vial and tucked it into her purse. "The stuff I put on your face is called Involuntary Muscle Control Serum. Basically what it does is slow down all the involuntary muscles in your face, the ones that react before you even know you're doing anything. And gives you control over them."

Lucy felt her face start to register surprise: Her eyebrows began to lift; her mouth began to open slightly. But then instead of letting her face follow through with it, she stopped herself. And decided to look not impressed at all.

"Gil calls them Oscar Drops because it makes people into such good actors; it's like anyone who uses it could win an Oscar."

Or their boyfriend back, Lucy thought.

"Thank you," said Lucy.

Olivia smiled. "Now, see even I can't tell if you're honestly grateful or are pretending to be. That's how well this stuff works." Olivia held out her hand. The last packet lay flat on her palm.

"What you're looking at right now is so valuable and so rare that Gil and Liza have never even seen it or even know for sure it exists. And of course it goes without saying that you will never, *ever* tell them that I gave this to you. . . ."

Lucy stared at the packet.

"My grandmother made this a long time ago," Olivia said. The packet glittered in the moonlight.

Lucy reached out, her heart bubbling, her stomach bubbling. She held it in her hands.

"Remember when we told you a Heartbreaker can't use magic to make someone love them?"

Lucy nodded.

"Well, that's not *entirely* true. You can't use magic to make someone love you who isn't already *on their way*. But using what I just gave you, you can take someone who's close and push them right over the edge."

"How?"

"Those are called Sparks. To you they look like glittery bits, but that's only because you've taken the Magic Magnet. To anyone else, they're invisible. Olivia leaned in close. "Sprinkle them on your palm, and blow them at your target." Olivia blew Lucy a kiss. "And then . . ." She poked a finger gun into Lucy's chest and pulled the trigger. She leaned in and whispered, *"Kapow."*

"Wait, I don't understand, they'll *kill* someone?"

Olivia let out a silvery laugh. "No, doll cakes, they give you a direct line to someone's heart. The Sparks take whatever someone is feeling about you at the moment at which they inhale them, and amplify it, and make that feeling last for a day, a week, maybe more. Be careful, they can be dangerous. If someone is angry at you, these will make them furious. And if that happens you better watch out. Remember Ricky back at the party the other night? Sparks gone wrong." She shook her head. "But if someone likes you a lot, they care about you a lot but aren't *quite there* yet, these, well, these will make them love you, really and truly and deeply. Maybe not for forever, but definitely for long enough to break their heart. The thing is, people's feelings about each other fluctuate a lot, sometimes from moment to moment. You walk into a room looking hot and he suddenly feels a rush of lust. A minute later you take out a pack of gum and don't offer him any and he feels hurt. So you have to time it all *just right . . .*"

". . . and that's where the Empathy Cream comes in?"

"Exactly."

Lucy felt the color rising in her cheeks again. *This was what was going to save her.*

Maybe Alex had never *loved* her, but he'd definitely liked her at some point, and that was before she knew what he really wanted. But now she did and her next steps were crystal clear—all she had to do was everything they'd taught her, pick the right moment, use the Sparks, and then . . . Alex would fall in love with her. And this time she'd do everything right, so even after the Sparks faded he still would. For real this time.

And then, and this was the especially wonderful part: *She would be able to forget what she'd done.* The Magic Magnet would take effect, and she would not know how she and Alex had ended up back together. She would never have to deal with the guilt of knowing and not telling, never have to wonder if it was wrong to use magic to make someone love you, because she would forget that she'd done it.

The only magic she would know would be the magic of love. Which would be more than she'd ever need.

She felt such relief then, that the tears did start coming. She did not try to stop them. They dripped down onto her cheeks. She looked up. Olivia was staring at her. But Lucy could not look her in the eye. She looked, instead, right past her, to the trees, which were still ever-so-slightly shimmering.

"Thank you," Lucy said. Even though she knew Olivia had no idea what she was actually thanking her for.

"Maybe one day you'll have a chance to repay us," said Olivia.

Lucy got out of the car, holding on to those two tiny packets.

"Good luck," Olivia said. "Your training is complete, so for now at least, this is good-bye." She pointed to Lucy's fist. "And be careful, sugar pie," Olivia said. "Don't waste that. It's more valuable than you even know. And it's all you're getting until you're one of us."

"But what if it doesn't work?"

"Well then"—Olivia shrugged—"I guess that's all you'll ever get."

Lucy nodded.

Olivia drove off then into the night, but Lucy swore she could hear the tinkling bells of Olivia's laugh echoing long after she was gone.

On the morning of the sixth day, there was Lucy walking down the hallway with a blank face, a bubbling stomach, and two very special somethings hidden in her pocket.

She stared at each person as she passed. Two girls laughing at something a third girl had said. Two guys who looked bored. A couple who were having a fight. People were fixing their hair and putting on lip balm and sending secret text messages and hurrying to class. They thought the world was just what they saw, the way she always had. The way she always used to. They had no idea that they only saw the top layer, like the thin skin of ice on top of a deep lake at first freeze—everything that really mattered, everything that made a lake a lake was trapped down below. All it took to get to it was one tiny poke.

Around the corner from the photo lab, Lucy slipped the silver packet out of her pocket and was about to unwrap it when Gil appeared right in front of her, a giant smile on her sweet face.

"Don't worry," Gil said. She glanced down at the packet, then back up at Lucy. "I'm not going to ask you anything about what happened yesterday, I know that's private. I just wanted to say that I'm excited, that's all." She reached out and pulled Lucy in for a hug. "I'm so sorry we had to trick you. I promise we'll never do it again."

Lucy swallowed hard.

This was the kind of hug you can feel all the way into your heart. There was so much love in it that for a moment Lucy wanted to cry. Not because Gil had tricked her but because *she* was tricking Gil. And for what?

The answer came walking right toward her.

Over Gil's shoulder there was Alex.

For what?

For his sweet ears, for the tiny adorable space between his teeth that she wished she could climb into, for his freckles, for the way he looked at her when he was taking her picture, for the way he walked, for that calm that was radiating off of him. For the flash of recognition her heart gave still, even at that moment as their eyes met over Gil's shoulder.

He was who she was doing this for. But that didn't mean she didn't feel bad about it.

Lucy pulled away from Gil. She shook her head. She had to keep focused; all she wanted was so close now.

"See you later," Gil whispered.

Lucy nodded. When Gil was gone she peeled open the packet, rubbed the swirl of cream between her fingers, and smoothed it out on her palm. It felt cool on her skin.

She took a deep breath. She followed Alex inside.

The photo lab was buzzing. A guy was at the paper cutter slicing the border off a photo of himself posing in a fancy car. A girl Lucy had never even seen before was holding up a contact sheet covered in photo after photo of her own leotard-clad ass. But Lucy did not stop to think about any of these things, to appreciate the oddness the way she normally might have.

She could feel him behind her before she saw him. She turned. Alex was holding a sheet of negatives in a negative sleeve, and a contact sheet that he'd made for her. He handed them to her and walked into the darkroom. He hadn't even said hello.

Wait! Wait!

She hurried to one of the enlargers. Grabbed a random negative from her sheet of negatives and stuck it in. Her hands were shaking a little as she put her photo paper underneath it and flipped on the light.

She brought the photo paper over to the chemical baths. Alex was swirling a photo around in the stop bath with a pair of rubber-tipped tongs.

She reached out and touched the back of his hand. "Can I borrow those tongs when you're done?" she said. She held her hand against his. She waited. Her mouth tried to open in a gasp of love, but she would not let it. Her eyes began to water, but she sucked her tears back in.

"You have to get a new pair," Alex said slowly. "Otherwise you'll get the chemicals mixed together. There's supposed to be a set of tongs in each container." There was something in his voice, his tone, scolding almost, as though he felt like maybe she was up to something, but had no idea what it might be.

She held her hand against his a second longer. But all she felt was a surge of desperate love, and this time, the squeezing desperation of a longing unmet. Her own feelings.

The Empathy Cream wasn't working.

"Right," Lucy said. "The tongs." And what else could she do then? She got her own set of tongs, and fished the photo out of the first chemical bath into the second and the third.

When she was done she went back out to the light side and saw what she'd printed: a picture of Jack that she'd taken right before she went onstage, his face dotted with sweat, eyes closed, mouth frozen open. Behind him were the fuzzy, unfocused figures of the cabaret twins; the bright stage lights shone down from above.

Mr. Wexler tapped her photo with a thick, nicotine-stained finger. She felt her stomach tighten. He did not look at her, just stuck his pinky and thumb of his other hand in his mouth and let out a piercing whistle.

"Look over here for a second, people," he said. He snatched her photo and held it up in the air. "This is what I was talking about when I was explaining about capturing energy, capturing a feeling and a moment."

He turned to Lucy. "Nicely done, Miss Wrenn." He paused and stared at it again for another minute before clipping it to the drying line and walking off.

Lucy felt a blush trying to rise in her cheeks but she pushed it back. Her whole body was suddenly tingling. She felt something pressed against her shoulder. It was Alex, his warm shoulder pressing against hers, only the thin fabric of his T-shirt separating their skin.

She turned toward him. He was looking at her. Not smiling. Just looking, really looking.

"I didn't believe you," Alex said. "When you told me about the concert and gave me the pictures, I honestly thought the photos were going to be all black or something and you'd say it was a mistake. Or, I don't know what . . ." He stared down at her contact sheet. She looked down too: there was

Jack singing, the line of partygoers waiting outside in the moonlight, Tristan staring back at her, his mouth bulging with her pancake, syrup caught somewhere between his chin and the table.

"I didn't know you knew how to take pictures like that," he said. His voice was quiet, different than she'd ever heard it.

There was a thud inside her chest but Lucy did not show it on her face. She shrugged one shoulder. She wondered if maybe it was time now. She reached out and put her hand on his arm again. But still nothing except her own feelings. It wasn't working. *It wasn't working.* She'd gotten one of the defective packets.

She felt her heart sink down, down. But she kept her face calm.

Without the Empathy Cream, she'd have to guess when the moment was right. If there was indeed a right moment at all. But if she'd understood Alex well enough to guess what he was feeling, maybe he'd never have left her in the first place. Maybe she'd have been who he wanted all along.

She looked up at him, standing there. But he had a funny look on his face then, and she knew it was not time.

She turned and forced herself to walk back into the darkroom.

She slipped another random negative into the enlarger, put the photo paper down below it. She flipped the light on. Her heart was pounding so hard. She barely registered the image that appeared on the paper. She barely registered *being in that room*.

As she swished the photo paper around in the chemicals a photo appeared. But it wasn't until the photo was rinsing in the water, back out in the light half of the room that she saw what was in the picture.

Or rather who:

It was Lucy, only a Lucy she'd never seen before. A Lucy *no one* had seen except for a thousand of her new friends.

There was little Lucy, onstage. Eyes closed, mouth opened, head tilted ever-so-slightly back, fist clenched around the microphone. The edges of the photo bled off into the white. She was glowing.

"It looks like something out of a dream." That was Alex. He was standing next to Lucy again. "My God," he whispered.

He exhaled and looked at her. Really looked at her the way he had the very first time he took her picture. Except this time there was no camera between them. There was nothing but a few inches of air.

"How is this you?" he said. "How is this the same person that I . . ." He trailed off.

"I guess there's a lot you don't know about me," Lucy said. She let one corner of her mouth inch up into the perfect sexy smirk.

"Apparently so," Alex said. But he was not smirking back.

"Guess I should get back to my own photos," he said.

"Looks like I have some competition now." He smiled, only he suddenly looked very sad. Lucy had no idea why.

But she did know one thing: if there had been a right time to use the Sparks, she had missed it.

She just hoped there'd be another one. . . .

Twenty-
Six

What did Lucy do then? Well, what could she do then, really? When homeroom ended, she headed to bio. When she walked into the lab, the sickening scent of formaldehyde filled her nostrils. Dozens of fetal pigs lay in trays up at the front of the room, pale and soft and small, like loaves of unbaked bread.

Lab partners were assigned: Lucy was paired up with Lee Green, a stocky junior with dry-looking lips.

Lucy walked over to their lab station, where he was waiting with their pig. As she walked, she could hear some of the other students naming theirs, laughing—Bacon, Sleepy, McRib, Charlotte. Lucy did not like it one bit.

"Hi, Lucy," Lee said. He waved even though she was now standing right next to him. "This is super cool, isn't it?"

Lucy stared down into the tray, at bleached pink flesh, at those little bulging eyelids trapping tiny eyeballs that had never gotten a chance to see anything and never would. Lucy felt a wave of sadness and revulsion.

Lucy tried to convince herself that it was rubber, not real, but it was near impossible because of that smell and those tiny colorless whiskers sprouting out from its tiny chin. And all she could think was that there was a tiny heart trapped inside that body that had long since stopped beating.

She felt her throat closing, and dizziness setting in. She stumbled sideways, reached out for something to hold on to. Lee was studying the list of dissection instructions. She grabbed his forearm to steady herself.

And suddenly the dizziness, sadness, and revulsion were replaced by something else totally—a whoosh of excitement, a rush of adrenaline. And a thrill at knowing that in a few moments she'd be looking at something that no one on earth had ever seen before. It was like a treasure chest; this animal would be cracked open for the first time, filled with tiny lungs, liver, heart, where the gold and diamonds would be.

What the hell was going on?

She turned toward Lee. He was staring down at the tiny pig. "Isn't this the awesomest thing you've ever seen?" He looked excited and happy, like a kid playing his favorite video game.

Lucy looked down. Her hand was still touching his skin. Her hand. His skin.

The Empathy Cream was working.

That meant it had been working earlier when she touched Alex. Which meant the feelings she'd felt earlier when she'd touched his hand, the surge of love, of longing, of everything—those were not her feelings.

They were his. Which meant: *Alex felt just like she did.*

Lucy stared at Lee as he raised his scalpel and made the first cut.

Lucy turned away and closed her eyes. She could feel the joy bubbles rising up in her.

She tried to keep calm, not to jump to conclusions, to be reasonable. *Be reasonable, Lucy!*

But she wasn't even sure what that word meant anymore.

She was so close now. So close to getting everything she wanted.

She reached in her pocket for the Sparks. The tiny packet that was going to fix everything, that was going to change the rest of her life. . . .

Lucy opened her mouth into a little O. And then a bigger O. And put her hand over her mouth to keep from screaming. *Her pocket was empty.*

She checked again. But all she felt was fabric, smooth

cotton, and empty space where things had been before. And now nothing was.

Lucy's heart hammered. She checked her pockets again and again. She turned around, looked at the floor, on her desk, on her workstation, in her bag, *she even looked inside the pig.*

"Lee, I'm sorry," Lucy said. "But I have to go. I feel . . . sick. If anyone wonders where I am, can you tell them I've gone to the nurse? I think I'm going to barf. . . ." And then Lucy put her hand over her mouth and ran out of the room.

She ran back to the photo lab. There was another class in there, but she didn't care. She checked every foot of that space, every inch, every centimeter, looking for that tiny gold packet.

But she did not find it.

She had had her chance and she'd blown it.

She had had her access to the magic, but now there was no more.

No more.

Tick tick tick.

Her time was almost up.

She leaned her back against the wall, closed her eyes.

And then she opened them—stared at the wall where some student photos had been hung up: faces, and feet, a close-up of an eye, someone's dog, someone's cat, and right in the center, was a photo of a door with a sign on it—EXIT.

A closed door.

A way out . . .

Then something spectacular happened. Lucy had been paying so much attention to her heart, she'd forgotten that she had a brain too.

Three separate thoughts that had been lodged in three different spots in there, thoughts so tiny she'd barely even been aware of having them, flung themselves together with an imperceptible click. But all Lucy understood was the feeling of remembering something, and understanding something, and suddenly knowing exactly what she needed to do.

Twenty-Seven

At lunchtime, Olivia was sitting by herself, eating green olives, and reading a black leather book.

Lucy stood in front of her with a sesame bagel and a plastic cup of grapes balanced on a blue tray. She was squeezing the tray tight to keep her hands from shaking. Before she could say anything, Olivia looked up. She smiled, but she was not the Olivia of the night before. This Olivia was not her friend. And that made it both harder and easier to do what she had to do.

"We started doing dissections in bio," Lucy said. "It's gross."

Olivia smirked, raised her eyebrows. "Sure, Lucy," she said. She looked back down at her book.

Lucy was still standing there, hovering.

"You're still here . . ." Olivia looked mildly amused. "Do you want to sit?" She motioned toward the seat in front of her.

Lucy sat. She took a deep breath.

"This afternoon," Lucy said. "Can I come over?"

"Training time is done. I thought I was clear."

"I wanted to invite Colin over, I mean."

At the mention of his name, Olivia's face changed.

"And maybe some other people could come too?" Lucy said. "A little group maybe?" She paused. "I have a plan."

Olivia smiled halfway. "Sure," she said slowly. "Okay. Tell Gil. She'll invite the boys."

Lucy nodded. "Thank you," she said. She nodded again. And Olivia went back to her book.

Lucy sighed the tiniest little sigh. But only the easy part was over.

Lucy picked at her bagel. She watched Olivia suck the pimentos from the olives.

When the moment was just right, Lucy knocked over her cup of grapes. "Oops," she said quietly. They rolled everywhere.

Lucy got down on the floor. And there was Olivia's burgundy leather bag right there under the table. That dark heavy sack filled with secret things, like a womb from which who knows what might be born.

Lucy reached into the small front pocket. It was in there. Her fingertips tapped cool metal. That key, the one that had been on a chain around Olivia's neck, that Lucy had picked up at the party and Liza had snatched from her, *it was still there*. Lucy wrapped her fist around it. She pressed her lips together so she would not gasp.

"Lucy?" Olivia's face appeared, down under the table.

"What are you *doing* down there?" She glanced at her bag and back at Lucy.

"I dropped my grapes," Lucy said.

Olivia narrowed her eyes, just ever so slightly, the ice-blue growing colder and bluer.

Lucy sat back up. The cup was pinched between two of her fingers. She waved it around like a flag.

Olivia stared at Lucy's hands, empty save for the cup.

Olivia blinked. Looked back at Lucy's face again.

Poor Lucy's heart was pounding, pounding, pounding.

But Olivia never saw the small stolen key.

Why? Tristan's trick of course. That corny magician's party trick that Lucy had seen him do a thousand times had finally come in handy. She didn't have to hide the key. She'd simply made it disappear.

Olivia shrugged and went back to reading her book.

When Lucy was sure Olivia wasn't looking, she lowered her other hand, slipped that key into her pocket.

Then she sat there, stomach churning, tearing off bits of

dry bagel, forcing herself to swallow them, one by one by
one, until the whole thing was gone. She could not believe
what she'd just done and whom she'd done it to.

"Well," Lucy said. "I guess I'm going to go now."

"Right," said Olivia.

Lucy stood. "So I'll see you after school then," she said.

Olivia nodded. She didn't even look up.

Twenty-Eight

*S*urrounded by scents of green ivy and the muted crispness of early autumn leaves, they sat out there in Olivia's backyard: Olivia, Liza, Gil, Pete, B, Jack, Lucy. And Colin.

Oh, Colin, dear precious earnest boy, they all glowed under that slanting yellow sun, but that day he glowed the brightest. When Lucy called him to ask him over to Olivia's house that afternoon, he sounded so nakedly excited with his, "Oh!" and "Oh yes!" and "I would really love to!" that it made Lucy's heart hurt.

And now, watching him awkwardly sip from that green glass bottle of Jack's homemade honey-wine, hands shaking ever so slightly, long legs pulled up, elbows on his knees, trying so hard to look comfortable, she could not shake the guilt that had latched onto the back of her neck and sunk its claws in deep. Behind the yellow-green wall of his anxiousness was something else. And *that* was what was hurting her so much—that glow of pure shivering joy, and fragile teetering hope that she herself knew all too well.

The poor boy had no idea she was using him.

She needed a reason to be at Olivia's. He was her cover. What other choice did she have?

He passed her the bottle, gave her a nervous smile. She smiled back, turned away quickly.

"What's the verdict, Lucifer?" Jack asked. "Lucy?"

She barely registered hearing her name, barely registered raising the bottle to her lips.

Was it time yet?

She looked around.

No.

"You like the wine?" he asked.

Jack was staring at her, waiting for her to say something.

"You can really taste all those bees' hard work," she said finally, although she hadn't remembered tasting it at all.

"Yeah, it's like bee sweat," B said.

Jack made a mock hurt face. Everyone laughed.

Lucy passed the bottle to Pete, who was sitting behind her, Liza's feet in his lap.

"Thanks, gorgeous," he said. He tipped the bottle toward her before he took a drink. The green glass glinted in the fading sun.

Now was it time?

Lucy looked around her, at Olivia and Gil who both smiled at her when they caught her eye, at Jack and B, whose effortless cool didn't intimidate her the way they once had, at the ivy climbing the walls of the gazebo, at the sunlight filtering through, and realized in a funny way she was going to miss all this.

She couldn't think about this now. She reached into her pocket and squeezed that key.

Pete started telling a story about a recent trip he'd taken back home to visit his parents' farm in England. "My father talks to the goats," Pete said. "When he thinks no one can hear him, he actually bleats at them." And everyone was laughing, settling into the giant silk pillows that Olivia had tossed around the gazebo, settling into each other. Even nervous Colin, who had been sitting next to her, basically mute the entire time, seemed to be relaxing. His arm brushed against her arm.

Now was it time?

The bright sun was dragged down by its own weight; the ground rose up to meet it.

She turned toward Colin who was staring at her, a slightly bewildered expression on his sweet face. He was blushing a little as he moved his hand so that one of his fingers was touching one of hers. He left it there.

It was time.

Lucy stood. "I'm going inside for a minute." She twisted her face into a slight grimace and placed her hand on her stomach. "I'm suddenly not feeling so great."

"I followed the instructions from the website perfectly," said Jack. "There's nothing wrong with my mead!"

"Of course not," Lucy said. She forced a smirk. "I'm sure I'm supposed to feel like this."

Colin was staring up at her. He brushed his fingers against her ankle, tentatively, like he was scared to but could not resist. He left his fingers there, barely touching her. "Do you want me to come with you?"

Lucy smiled, shook her head. "I'll only be a minute," she said.

Twenty-Nine

*L*ucy walked into the house, through the giant ballroom, to that big creaky staircase. She breathed in. Felt the house breathe around her.

Up the stairs she went.

She walked into the giant lavish bathroom and turned on the light and the faucet. Then, quickly, quickly, she walked back out into the hall, to the room with the wrought-iron doorknob, holding the key Liza said she'd never have the balls to steal. Well, she had them now.

Her heart was pounding. The thump thumpthump of it, so loud she was sure someone would be able to hear it all the way downstairs, all the way outside.

Amazing how loud a broken heart can beat.

She slipped the key into the lock. And with a swift turn the door opened.

Yes.

The room was lit only by the light coming in from the hallway. Lucy tried to find a switch but couldn't.

In the dim light she could see that the walls were lined with shelves on which were rows and rows of little jars containing what exactly Lucy had no idea. She silently begged the universe to lead her to the right charm or pill or potion. And then she grabbed a few jars—she would look at them later. She turned to go. She reached out her arm and felt not cool wall but warm flesh.

A hand closed over her mouth before she could scream.

"It's okay," a voice whispered. "It's just me."

Gil. She let go of Lucy's mouth.

"I . . ." Lucy started to say. She stood there, staring at the outline of Gil standing in the doorway, but her memory filled in what she couldn't see—Gil's sweet face, her big trusting eyes. The lies Lucy could have told swirled in her mouth and lay there behind her lips, bubbling. "I . . ." Lucy looked down at the floor. "Should probably try to come up with a good excuse for why I'm here. But I can't."

Gil walked forward into the room and shut the door behind her. Lucy heard her moving along the wall. A moment later a warm red light filled the room. Gil looked up at Lucy and smiled.

"I believe in love, Lu" Gil said. "I've never regretted my choice to become what I am now, and in many ways I'm grateful to Will for breaking my heart so I could make it. But still, despite all that, I believe in it." Her eyes locked on Lucy's. "Real love, the pure and true kind that comes along so rarely, is the greatest magic there is. It is the art and the drug and the story." Gil paused. "I know what you've been trying to do. I figured it out."

Lucy raised her hand to her lips.

"I didn't come here to stop you. I came here to help." She pointed to the three glass jars Lucy held. "But those won't do anything. There's no magic in them," Gil said. "That's just the base—art supplies, herbs, perfume from faraway places. You're taking bio, right? The trick is adding the catalyst. Tears are the active ingredient that gets it all going. And we don't add those until the last minute. The magic is strong, but tears are unstable. We keep them locked in here."

Gil knelt down and moved a panel of wood revealing a safe locked with a big metal lock. Then she reached in her back pocket and pulled out what looked like two bent hairpins. She stuck one into the keyhole of the lock and held it there, then poked around with the other one. "My grandfather on my mother's side, the one who taught me to pick pockets, he also taught me some other things about the, um"—she was squinting at the lock, the tip of her tongue was poking out of the side of her mouth—"criminal arts. He always said I was sort of . . ." The lock popped. "A natural."

Gil smiled as she opened the safe.

Inside were dozens and dozens of amber glass vials. Each one was labeled with a name.

Gil plucked a vial from the pile. On the label was printed: ETHAN SLOANE/WRIGLEY. "I'm not that powerful, not yet anyway. The charms and potions I can make myself now just reveal things. They can't change things so much as help the truth come out, and help you see it. I'll do what I can."

"Won't you get in trouble?"

"Maybe," she said. "But some things are worth getting in trouble for."

Ten minutes later, Lucy and Gil were heading back down the long staircase together, two tiny packages hidden inside Lucy's pocket. "Oh, Lu," Gil said loudly. "I guess mead doesn't agree with some people." She leaned forward, and whispered so quietly that Lucy could barely hear her. "Sometimes you find magic," Gil said, "and sometimes magic finds you."

"Th—" Lucy started to say.

"Don't," Gil whispered. She shook her head. "You don't

need to thank me. This is the right thing to do." She stopped on the stairs, turned toward Lucy. "But tomorrow's the seventh day. Which means . . ."

Lucy nodded.

"Whatever happens"—Gil reached out and pulled Lucy close—"just know I already considered you my sister."

Thirty

On the seventh day of her sophomore year, Lucy Wrenn stood out in front of her school leaning coolly against a fence, a little shard of hard pink sugar dissolving slowly behind her gloss-slicked lips. It had only been seven days since the last time she'd stood there waiting for Alex but much had changed. The entire *world* had changed, or at least her understanding of it.

On the outside, things were very different. Gone were her loose denim shorts, pink tank top, yellow flip-flops, toast brown hair pulled back into a low ponytail.

Now she was all jangly Chinese bangles, and an Indian print scarf flecked with gold hummingbird feathers dangling from each ear. She was wearing a sleeveless white cotton dress, turquoise thong sandals. She'd dabbed jasmine behind both her ears and ginger on her wrists, and rubbed a vanilla bean down over her heart. She was wearing the gold tear-catcher vial around her neck because it was beautiful, not because she actually planned to use it. She wore a dot of liquid gold on the outside corners of each of her eyes. Her dark hair hung loose.

But underneath, inside, there were some things that were not so different. Lucy was still a sack of blood and liver and bladder and gallbladder. Appendix. Pancreas. Stomach. Her heart still pounded painfully. Her lungs still caught breath when she saw Alex walking up toward school looking exactly like he always had, looking like nothing had changed at all.

Her week had been a lifetime. His was just seven days.

She watched him walk and imagined the old Lucy watching the new Lucy watch him now. She was not hopping up and down or waving wildly. She was just leaning, coolly, face calm.

And when their eyes finally met, she allowed the corners of her lips to curl up to the tiniest hint of a feline smile as the last bit of the It's In His Kiss drop dissolved against her tongue.

"Hey, stranger," Lucy said.

He smiled. His eyes were heavy with an emotion she could not place.

She walked closer, closer, until she could smell the warm scent of him. *It's now or never. TICK TICKTICK.*

She slipped her hands onto the back of his neck and leaned in. Her heart was pounding as her body pressed against his. Their lips touched.

And the ticking finally stopped.

She melted against him and sighed into his mouth. And then she waited, for that tingle of hot spicy cinnamon that Gil said she'd taste and feel if he loved her. She waited. She waited.

But she did not feel it. And she did not taste it.

Instead, she tasted vinegar and salt, the chips he sometimes ate for breakfast.

She felt the tears coming.

Well, screw the stupid candy.

It was just wrong then, it had to be. Love was the strongest magic there was and she could *feel* him loving her. Or at the very least she could feel herself loving him. And that was enough, wasn't it? *She loved him enough for both of them.*

She pulled him more tightly to her.

It didn't matter. Nothing mattered but this. This moment in which she would have been happy living the entire rest of her life.

But he was pushing against her. He was pushing her away.

Lucy stumbled backwards.

"What the hell? STOP IT! I BROKE UP WITH YOU!"

What happened next? Well, of course, the tears came. She could have stopped them but why even bother? She knew it didn't matter if she held it together or not, because this time

Alex did not even wait to watch her walk away.

Drippity drippity drip, down her face they went. She thought about erosion, how over time water cuts through stone and steel. She thought about the twin tear tracks that she'd soon have carved into her cheeks.

Alex did not love her. He never had and he never would. She knew that now with a gut-socking certainty.

Alex broke up with her because he did not want to be with her. It was not a fluke. It was not a mistake. It was quite simple, really. She knew all she needed to know now.

But she felt the Fantasy Lens bulging in her pocket and she knew Alex was behind her, walking away forever. And she just could not resist. She held it up to her eye and turned around.

There, hovering above him in the air, was a hazy scene: Alex and a girl on what looked like a boat, a pirate ship actually. He was wearing a pirate shirt and leather pants. A sword was strapped around his waist. And she was all dressed up like a pirate wench, long hair a-flowing, heaving bodice barely contained in a white off-the-shoulder top, long rust-colored dress and leather waist-cincher. Her feet were bare and she was wearing an anklet made of flat, circular beads covered in ancient-looking carvings. Her back was pressed up against the mast of the boat and they were kissing passionately while being sprayed with the sea.

This was his deepest fantasy.

If Lucy weren't so horrified, she might have laughed at the sheer corniness of it. Laughed at the fact that the deepest fantasy of someone who prided himself on being so *worldly* and *unique* and *artistic* was a scene out of a PG romance novel set at Disney World.

But there was something about this pirate wench that was familiar. Not the long hair, streaked by the sun, the surfer body. But that anklet—the flat, circular beads, the ancient-looking carvings. Lucy had seen that anklet before.

And she knew exactly where.

Lucy felt a hand on her shoulder. "I just wanted to see how everything was going but . . ." It was Gil.

Lucy turned, a fresh batch of tears ready to fall.

"Oh, sweetie." Gil shook her head. She reached out and hugged Lucy close. "I'm so sorry."

"It's not me that he wants," said Lucy.

"Who is it then?"

"I'm not sure," said Lucy. "But I'm about to go find out."

The darkroom was empty when Lucy reached it. She flung open the gray portfolio closet filled with its photo-chemical smells, and went inside. She looked through the stacks of student folders until she found the one with Alex's name on it written in his giant messy print. She opened the folder, grabbed all the photographs he'd developed so far this year, the paper slick under her thumbs. She flipped through them, her stomach turning. There was that lake, that canoe, those legs around a campfire. And then . . . there was the girl the anklet belonged to.

That girl, long hair, streaked, wide face, her wrists wrapped in thick string bracelets, her body tan and strong looking, bare feet with short little toenails, and the anklet. That anklet.

Lucy wanted to stop moving. She wanted to run. She wanted to stop looking.

But she couldn't stop.

And there she was in picture after picture. The girl on a horse. The girl in a canoe. The girl at night carrying an armful of sticks to a campfire. It was like a magazine spread about rustic summer activities with this girl as the only model. But there was something in the way the girl looked at the camera, as though *she knew things* about the person behind it.

Still, a fantasy didn't mean anything. A fantasy was only thoughts. . . .

But then Lucy got to the next picture. Printed perfectly. It felt hot in her hand.

A big bed, this girl in it, thin, white sheet barely covering her chest, bare shoulders, tangled hair.

She was laughing, holding one hand out toward the camera as if to say, *Don't take a picture of me,* but her big smile and the look in her eyes say, *Do.* Alex loved her—Lucy knew that now. It wasn't magic that told her that, no, it was the photo.

This was maybe the only really truly good picture Alex had ever taken.

And suddenly Lucy realized something: when she'd told Alex she was ready for them to lose their virginities together and he'd told her "I can't." It was because he no longer had his to lose.

Because he already lost it to her.

While Lucy was thinking of him every second all summer long, imagining him imagining her, he'd been busy having sex with this girl.

The sudden intensity of that thought slammed Lucy like a brick between the eyes.

Her brain stopped. Her heart stopped. Fury poured out of every organ in her body. When she'd asked him why he was dumping her, he said he couldn't explain it. But he could have. *He just didn't want to.*

All summer long she'd sent him those letters, the emails, the presents. *Why did he let her go on with it? Why hadn't he stopped her?* Had he and this girl *laughed* at Lucy? Or even worse, felt sorry for her? For the pathetic little girl back home who didn't realize that while she was embroidering eyes onto a sock for the person she thought was her boyfriend, he was having ACTUAL SEX with someone else entirely?

She'd written a goddamn hangman game on her own goddamn stomach for him!

Lucy realized in that moment standing there in the photo

lab, she'd solved her own puzzle wrong, her own puzzle on her own stomach wrong not once, but twice.

She'd thought the answer was *I'm ready.*

And that was wrong.

And she'd thought the answer was *I = Idiot.*

And that was wrong too.

No, what should have filled those seven spaces on Lucy's belly, the message she should have given Alex six days ago?

F

U

C

K

Y

O

U

"Fuck you," she whispered.

In her entire life, it was the very first time she'd said those words out loud.

She did not yell, she did not shout, she simply whispered, *"Fuck you, Alex,"* as she shoved his photos in his portfolio, as she took out the photo of the girl and then tossed the portfolio back on the shelf, as she walked out into the hall.

"Fuck you, fuck you, fuck you . . ."

Her fingers tingled; her scalp tingled. Her *soul* tingled with a fierce and sudden longing for what she should have wanted all along. Not Alex. Not love. But the chance to be free of all of this. To join a sisterhood. To be a Heartbreaker.

She wanted *that* more than she'd ever wanted anything before, more than she'd even known it was possible to want.

But wasn't it too late now? She had had her chance, and wasted it all on Alex. Wasted everything on someone who deserved nothing.

Wasn't it too late now?

Lucy stared down at the photo of the girl, rolled it up, and started to put it in her pocket.

But something was already in her pocket, a tiny little thing.

Sometimes you find the magic. Sometimes the magic finds you. . . .

She took it out, and held it up to the light. The bit of gold shimmered.

Thirty-One

She told him to meet her out on the street behind Van Buren and by the time the final bell rang, she was already halfway across the back lawn. She squeezed through the hole in the fence, made her way through the woods, every breath pure focus, like a huntress out for the hunt.

She'd taken the gold vial from around her neck and wrapped the chain around her wrist three times. She'd tucked the Sparks into her bra, a flesh-inch away from her pounding broken heart.

I am calm, she thought. *I am ready,* she thought. *It's time.*

When Lucy got to the edge of the woods, she saw him.

On top of a green box of a car, knees up, forearms resting awkwardly on them. Sweet Colin was a flurry of tiny nervous movements—glancing at that red plastic watch, tapping his feet against the hood, chewing on his thumbnail, anxious eyes darting in every direction.

She stood for a moment a few steps back from the road, just watching him.

"Hey, Lucy!" he called out. He hopped off the hood and started making his way toward her, walking like someone who wanted to run but was trying so hard not to.

He reached out awkwardly and pulled her toward him in a half hug. She felt his face brush against the top of her head, very quickly, like he was smelling her hair, but didn't want her to know.

"I was so glad when you called. I had been going to call you to see how you were feeling. Because I know you said your stomach hurt at Olivia's yesterday. But I wasn't sure when you got out of class. But, anyway, are you feeling better?" His face was flushed. She could not meet his gaze.

"I will be," she said. "Soon."

She climbed up on the car, aware of his eyes on her as she arranged herself cross-legged on his trunk. He walked over so he was standing right in front of her, facing her. Like that they were almost the same height.

"I was hoping if it's okay with you that I could take you somewhere," he said. "Like on a proper date. Out for ice cream or something maybe?"

"Let's stay here for a bit," she said. "It's a beautiful day." And she knew she had to do this quickly. She had to do this before she changed her mind. "So," she said. She reached down the front of her dress as though she had an itch. "How do you know Olivia and all them?" Amazing that she could sound so calm when her heart was pounding so hard. "I just realized I never asked you that." She felt the tiny packet there pressed against her heart. She slipped it out, held it in her lap in cupped hands.

"It was such a funny thing," he said. "Such a random thing. I was at this party a couple weeks ago, I don't usually go to parties that much. But I went to this one. And Gil just came up to me. She was so friendly. . . ."

Lucy nodded. Careful not to look directly at him.

"She said she had someone she wanted me to meet but that someone wasn't there just then."

"Uh-huh." Lucy tore open the packet.

"And that someone was you," Colin said. He blushed again. "The craziest thing is, I wasn't even going to *go* to that party but . . ."

Lucy dumped the grains out in her hand. She could feel them tickling her palm. "A few weeks ago?" she said. "I don't know, it probably wasn't me she meant . . ."

"She must have meant you because as soon as I met you I . . ."

Lucy closed her eyes. She took a deep breath, lifted her hand up to her mouth, fingers curled.

She breathed out.

The Sparks lifted up with her breath, hung in the air glittering. Time slowed down. For a moment nothing happened. Then something did.

Colin inhaled.

He stumbled back.

"I felt like I'd been waiting my entire life for you," he said.

He reached out and ever so gently rested the tips of his fingers on the bare skin of her knees. He looked down at his hand, like he could not believe he was really doing this, then started to lean in, slowly. His face was only inches away. Three. Two. One. The air between them melted.

She felt the soft skin of his lips against the soft skin of hers. Her lips began to tingle. She tasted cinnamon until she pulled away.

His eyes were closed and he kept them closed for a second too long, smiling slightly as if replaying the moment they'd just finished having. He opened them finally. She could not meet his gaze.

"Lucy," he said. "You're so . . ."

She raised her finger and pressed it against his lips. "Ssh."

She stared at his chest; through the layers of gray T-shirt, skin, muscle, and bone was his heart. Thump, thump, thumping.

One slice. One swift cut was all it would take.

"Colin," she said. "I don't . . ."

But Lucy made a mistake then, she looked at him. She looked him right in the eye.

And there it was: the love. Naïve, guileless, and earnest. That pure kind of love that asks no questions and wants no answers. A love that leaks out onto everything, carries along with it the belief that people, the world, life is magical. And she knew then without a doubt that he had never had his heart broken before. That sweet Colin had never felt that pain. And that she could not be the one to make him feel it.

Lucy felt her own broken bitter heart heavy in her chest. She pushed herself off the hood. "I just remembered something I forgot to do," she said. "Something back at school."

"I'll wait for you," Colin said. "I don't mind."

"No," Lucy said. "You should go home."

He looked so confused. "I'm sorry, did I do something wrong?"

Lucy shook her head. "No, no," she said. "You're perfect." She was backing up. "You are completely perfect and don't ever change."

"Can I . . . can I see you this weekend, then?"

"I don't know," said Lucy. His face fell. "I mean sure," she said. "Sounds like fun."

And then she turned and walked back toward the woods.

She had made her choice. It was too late now. She looked back and he was watching her. He waved. She knew this would be the last time she'd ever see him. If she weren't already so broken, she might have even felt a twinge of sadness about that, of concern about that. But her heart was too heavy to carry anything else.

Thirty-Two

At the end, there she was, Lucy Wrenn sitting on her bed, knees pulled up to her chest, staring at her own reflection in the window. That damn clock was ticking so loud now.

TICK TICK TICK

But in fifty-nine minutes it would finally stop.

It was fifty-nine minutes until midnight, fifty-nine minutes until the Magic Magnet took her memories away. She wondered if it would hurt when it happened. She kind of hoped it did.

Fifty-nine minutes. One class period. The length of a nap.

Half a movie. That was all that was left until she was sucked headfirst through the door at the edge of the shimmering, glittering magical world she'd only just begun to know, thrust back into the flat, black place that was waiting for her. And the door would be shut and locked behind her. And then disappear entirely.

Fifty-eight minutes.

Fifty-seven.

TICK TICK TICK

Lucy lay back on her bed.

The worst part wasn't the fact that Alex was not hers and he never would be now. The worst part was that she didn't even want him anymore.

A week ago before she knew about the existence of magic or the Secret Sisterhood of Heartbreakers or *anything,* in those first terrifying moments right after Alex had dumped her, she had at least had something to cling to, the teeny-tiny possibility of one day maybe having Alex back. But the worst pain, she realized then, is not desperately wanting something you will probably never have. *The worst pain is not even having anything to want.*

She closed her eyes, felt the whoosh of cool damp air rushing past her face as she fell down, down a tunnel that stretched straight toward infinity.

Bzzzzzz.

It took Lucy's brain a moment even to process what the

buzzing was, that it was not the inside parts of her brain but her phone on her nightstand. Tristan's name was flashing on the screen. *Tristan.*

Her hand reached for the phone before her brain had a chance to stop it, desperately grasped it like it was a rope dangling down the tunnel she was whooshing through.

She lifted the phone to her ear. "Hello."

"Can you come outside?" Tristan said, so quickly it was as though she had caught him in the middle of a sentence; he would have said it whether she'd picked up the phone or not.

Lucy felt herself nodding. And although no words escaped her lips, she somehow knew that Tristan could hear her. "I'll be here," he said. And then he hung up.

Lucy stood up, walked out of her room into the dark hallway. She tiptoed out the front door. The gravel driveway crunched under her feet.

She looked up at the moon, and thought about how far away it was, how much empty blackness was between her and it, how much lonely empty space there was in the universe.

The music came then—a single, sweet mournful note stretching out into the night and curling back, like a long finger, beckoning. She followed it, down the driveway, down the street toward Tristan in his truck.

"Listen," he said, "there's something I need to show you."

Thirty-
Three

They were going fast—Lucy had no idea where, but it didn't matter. "I'm surprised you even want to see me," she said to Tristan. "I'm so . . ." She wanted to apologize, to explain. But there was no explanation she could give.

He shook his head. He wasn't smiling. "Don't," he said.

So she didn't. And they just drove.

She looked out the window. They were in the industrial part of town where the big, flat buildings were pushed back far from the road. Tristan pulled down a wide driveway into a huge parking lot filled with row after row of school buses.

Tristan parked and got out. He snaked between the buses

and stopped in front of one. He curled his fingers in the crack between the bus door and the edge of the bus and pried it open. Without saying anything, he disappeared inside, and Lucy followed.

Tristan walked to the back of the bus, sat in the last seat on the right, slid over to make room for Lucy. She sat. He took out his phone and used it to light up the seat.

There in black Sharpie on the green vinyl was written: *THE HAPPY SEAT.* "Remember this?" he said.

Lucy raised her hand to her lips. Of course she did.

In the middle of fourth grade, Lucy's parents had told her they were getting divorced. It was the first time they'd said that, so she'd thought their proclamations meant something and had stayed awake most of the night crying. The next morning she'd boarded the bus with red puffy eyes, wanting to hide from everyone. And this kid Tristan was there, eating two lollipops. She did not know him then, just knew that he was the kid whose mom had died a few years before. That he always seemed to be joking and trying to make people laugh. "It's your lucky day, you know," he'd said. "No matter what you're sad about, it's no match for the happy-ing power of the happy seat." And she'd asked him what the happy seat was. And he'd just smiled. "You're sitting in it!" He'd taken a marker out of his bag then and started graffiti-ing on the seat to prove it. Lucy had been scared he was going to get caught but he didn't seem to care.

They'd been best friends ever since.

Lucy turned toward Tristan, stared at him in the moonlight that was shining in through the dust-caked windows. She reached out and touched the sticky vinyl. "How did you find this?" she whispered.

"Fate, I guess," Tristan said. And he sort of smiled since they both knew he didn't believe in that kind of stuff. "Or maybe magic. I was driving around the other night and I saw this place and I just drove in. . . . I know you're upset about . . . what happened and everything, but I thought if I brought you here . . . I don't know." He paused. "Here," he said. He handed her his harmonica. "I don't suppose there's a cure for a broken heart, but I hear playing the blues helps sometimes."

Lucy took it, so grateful for him, for his friendship. She pressed the harmonica to her mouth and blew it. A sad whine escaped. It didn't sound sweet and haunting and mournful the way it did when Tristan played.

Lucy took the harmonica away from her lips. "I think it's bro—" she started to say. But then something happened— her lips began to tingle. They started to warm and then just kept getting hotter.

Lucy raised her hand to her lips.

"What's wrong?" he said.

She tasted cinnamon.

"No," she whispered. She put her hand over her eyes. *No.*

Tristan started to reach for her. "You okay?"

Lucy nodded.

"Lucy," Tristan said. "I didn't bring you here to show you the seat. I mean, that was part of it but . . ." And he sighed then, that heavy sigh that often comes right before someone says something they know they probably shouldn't, as though their own lungs are trying to force them to wait one more minute, before ruining everything. "I have to tell you something."

Lucy closed her eyes. She begged the world, Mother Nature, the universe herself to please, please, please not let him do it. Not let him tell her what she had just realized he was about to.

But anyone who has lived even one day knows that they seldom intervene in situations such as this.

Tristan was looking at her, looking at her so intensely. He reached for her hand.

"I've . . ." He looked down. "I . . . um," he laughed suddenly. "There's something I've needed to tell you for a long time. . . ."

Lucy started shaking her head and pulled her hand away.

Tristan was still staring. "Lucy?"

Her entire body was pulsing along with her heart.

"Wait!" Lucy called out. "Wait!"

Later Lucy would wonder if she had been wrong to stop him. Sometimes things need to be knocked down so they can be built back better. Sometimes fire needs to wipe out everything so new life can bloom. Sometimes people just need to say what they need to say even if what they need to say is "I love you" to their best friend who does not love them back.

But she was not thinking of that then. All she was thinking was that if he told her, things would change, their friendship would be ruined. And in that moment, it was truly all she had.

Lucy looked at his profile. At the curve of his always-smiley mouth, at the reddish stubble growing out of his chin, at his brown hair flopping into his eyes. He was so sweet, and kind and funny. He had always, always been there for her. If only she could love him the way he wanted her to.

What would it be like if his face made her heart squeeze the way Alex's did? What if it was his voice that made her stomach tighten with love?

Everything would be fixed.

The problem is, we can't choose not to love someone just because they hurt us. And we can't choose to love someone either, no matter how perfect they might be.

"Tristan," Lucy started off. "You are my very best friend. . . ." And then she went from there, just opened her mouth and let the words fly out.

She thanked him for being such a good friend and apologized for being such a bad one lately. She told him how much she cared about him, how lucky she was to have him in her life. She took a breath and turned her head and stared out the dusty window at the moon. She wanted to get off that bus, to run out into the moonlight. To feel her legs pumping faster and faster until her body lifted up and she floated away.

But she had to finish this.

So she went on. She told him: So many things in life were messy and complicated, but what was between them was perfect and simple. A pure friendship, deep and true with nothing mucking it up. She told him gently, and with love, that what she was most grateful for, maybe in this entire world, was that in finding him on this bus all those years ago, she had not just found a best friend, but a brother.

She hoped that would never ever change.

She was finished then, emptied out. He was quiet and she sighed with relief. She had stopped him from saying something they would both regret. She had saved them both.

But she turned toward him and was suddenly struck with the horrible understanding of something. Her words had not been simply words to him, but shards of lead, sharp and heavy, shot like bullets from her mouth. They sliced through his skin, through every part of him, and clattered together, filling up his insides. She felt his body sagging against her shoulder, as though all of those shards of lead had given his body a sick and terrible weight.

He nodded numbly and turned toward the window. "But

I love you," Tristan choked. There was such longing in those words. Lucy gasped, she thought her heart was too broken to break again. But it did, right then it broke for him too. "I mean . . ." He paused. "You know, as a buddy, buddy. So, that's what I wanted to say too so that you would never forget it. That I love you."

They sat there together, the two of them. And they felt, for maybe the first and only time, precisely, exactly the same. That there was no hope, that it was all over.

By the glow of the moon Lucy could see Tristan wipe his eyes. And then, he reached out and just for a moment grasped her hand. She felt something on her finger, something wet.

He let go of her then. She raised her hand; a tiny droplet was on the tip of her finger. A single curved droplet shimmering in the light.

Thirty-Four

We learn about ourselves from the tough choices. We might think we know who we are because of what we think is right, but we don't really know if we'll give the wallet back until we find one, if we'll help that slow old lady until the building's actually on fire.

Lucy had always believed, always wanted to believe, that when faced with a friend in pain she'd be able to put herself entirely aside for a while and do whatever she could to help.

But that night, sitting in that bus staring at that tear when she wished she would have been thinking of her friend and how best to help him, she was only thinking this: it was 11:51

and there were still nine minutes left until midnight.

Tick.

She pressed her lips together. And felt the rough and ragged hole in her heart. Later she would be tortured by her choice, what it meant that she'd made it. But she was not thinking of that yet.

"Tristan," Lucy said. She watched herself and she learned just what she'd do. . . .

Thirty-Five

hey were back in the truck driving fast, the wind whipping in through the open windows. Lucy held on to the vial on the chain around her neck.

Tristan was staring straight ahead, jaw clenched, gripping the steering wheel tight. She was racing toward something. He was only racing away.

11:53.

11:54.

Lucy could feel the seconds ticking in her stomach, her chest, her head, her heart. A bomb was set to go off inside her. And any second it would.

It was 11:58 when they pulled up to Olivia's house.

"Thank you, Tristy," Lucy whispered. And she reached out to hug him. But when her hand touched his arm, he pulled back. "Thank you, Tristy," she said again.

He tried to force a smile. "No problem, buddy." His voice was all wrong.

"Don't wait for me," she said.

She got out of the car and shut the door behind her. By the time she got to the gate, he was already gone.

Thirty-Six

Through the gate, up the driveway. Clouds had rolled in and the air was thick with a storm on its way. Velvet black sky and not even a moon to guide her. The pumping in her chest led the way. She ran.

TICK TICK TICKTICK

At the front door she flung her body at the thick old wood. The sound of her thunking against it echoed in the cavern inside.

She waited, breathless, for the door to creak open. It didn't.

It was dark. The sky was dark. Her phone was sitting in her room at home. Tristan was gone.

She knocked again. Nothing. And there was no bell. She

tried to turn the doorknob. Locked.

"Olivia!" she shouted. But there was no answer. "Gil!" she shouted.

She felt the ticking inside her still, harder, louder, faster. How much time was left?

TICKTICKTICKTICKTICK

It was happening now, to every cell within her.

Body pumping blood, face pumping sweat.

This was it. Something was moving through her muscles and her blood. Up through her skin. Working its way out.

For a moment she was aware of only pain, searing through her. How strange it was to feel this pain, how strange it was to have so many nerves right inside you capable of such things, but to never have them fire. *And then fire all at once.*

She felt her body crumpling in slow motion then.

Gravity tugged her down and she did not resist.

On the ground, in a heap, too late, Lucy wondered, *What have they done to me? What have I let them do?*

It was her last thought before the ticking finally stopped and everything went dark.

Thirty-Seven

Seconds before midnight, there was Lucy on the ground in front of Olivia's house. She could not move. She could not speak. But could feel everything. She was nothing but nerves now.

There was: the pinch of fingers under her arms as someone lifted her up, the feeling of her heels dragging lightly against the slate as she was pulled up the stairs, the feeling of her toes being bent back as the heel of her flip-flop caught against the step and was yanked off. She wanted to look up, to see who was pulling her, but the muscles in her neck did not listen when she told them to move. Her head bobbed heavy like an overripe fruit.

What had she done? What the hell had she done?

Panic seized her, but her heart didn't speed up. It just pounded slowly, a drum for a death march. No sound left her lips, not even a ragged gasping. Air flowed smoothly in and out.

She heard voices, but her ears weren't working right because all she could make out were foreign sounds blended together. Her brain would not turn these sounds to words.

The moon came out from behind the clouds. She could see her own body below her now, lit by that silver light. She felt grass under her feet, soft and cool. Then felt herself laid down flat on her back on something hard. They were inside the gazebo and now Lucy could see Olivia's face leaning over her, surrounded by a halo of candlelight.

"Well, it's about time," Olivia said. "We'd almost given up on you." Lucy tried to say something. But her tongue lay limp inside her open mouth.

Olivia lifted Lucy's hand, which was still clutching the vial.

Lucy felt her fingers being uncurled and the vial taken away. Off to the side she heard the clink of glass against metal.

"Hurry," someone said.

Liza was there then, smiling widely, holding a terrifying contraption made of copper and brass. It looked like a gun with a long needle protruding from the barrel. Olivia unscrewed the base of the vial, and passed it to Liza. Liza pushed it onto the end of the machine. Then flipped a switch on the contraption's side. A sickening buzzing filled the air.

Someone pulled Lucy's shirt down at the neck, exposing the skin over her heart.

Liza leaned over, her long hair tickling Lucy's cheek. She held the machine up over Lucy's chest. *This is it. It's all over now,* Lucy thought. Somehow in that moment she knew that they were going to cut out her heart. That was what they'd wanted all along.

Lucy tried to close her eyes so she would not have to see the blood, the thick redness of her own beating broken heart. But eyelids stayed open.

"Don't move," Liza said sweetly. As though Lucy had a choice.

Olivia laughed. That tinkling, tinkling, terrible laugh. It sounded, Lucy realized then, nothing at all like a door being opened. It was the sound of the end of everything, of a door creaking forever shut.

And then that long needle went in, through her skin, and the muscle below it, popping her breastbone like a punch through leather.

The needle went farther, through all that inside human jelly, and finally, finally the needle pierced the slick, sloppy, flabby, fat, broken, bloody, ragged red meat of her heart.

It stabbed Lucy's heart, again and again, over and over. Thick warm liquid pooled in her chest. Hot pain radiated out.

The buzzing and whirring went on forever, getting louder and louder.

And then finally there was a silence. A silence few people will ever hear—the silence that comes when that quiet but insistent pounding that you've heard every second for your entire life stops.

Lucy's heart was not beating anymore.

But her eyes worked as they always had.

Lucy saw a thin curl of smoke rising up out of her own chest.

Images formed in the smoke.

First, a pair of lovers, in a swirling dance. Apart, together, apart. Their bodies moving in perfect harmony. Fingertip to fingertip and toe to toe, the space between them formed shapes. Apart, together, apart, together. Until they turned their backs on each other and twirled away.

Then there was Alex. The plane of his cheek, the sweep of his hair. His eyes shrunk down to gray dots. His face hung there, cartoonish now. Repulsive even. It collapsed in on itself. The smoke morphed into a translucent tornado swirling faster and faster. As it swirled, something was happening inside Lucy's chest, something new was being built, one cell at a time clicking into place.

The smoke drifted into the shape of a heart—red and proud and stronger than anything. And behind it her own face, calm, powerful, and beautiful.

The smoke cleared then. The candles flickered.

And inside Lucy's chest her new heart began to beat.

Lucy sat up slowly, blinking.

Everything was quiet. Olivia, Liza, and Gil were glowing in the moonlight.

She took a deep breath, breathed out as though exhaling smoke. She raised her hand up to her chest. She pressed where her broken heart had been. Where there had once been so much pain, there wasn't any longer.

Her heart was beating, and that was all.

"How do you feel?" Gil said.

"I don't know," Lucy said. But she reached up and felt her own face and it was smiling.

Gil reached out and squeezed Lucy's hand.

Lucy looked down at the skin over her heart. There was a deep red heart, edged in gold, locked shut, a purple ribbon swirling across it with *SECRET SISTERHOOD OF HEARTBREAKERS* inked on in black. And dripping off the point of the heart was a topaz teardrop jewel.

Lucy touched the tear with her fingertip. She was one of them now.

"The tattoo is directly on your heart," Gil said. "It's invisible to everyone except for other Heartbreakers."

"There are others?"

"Obviously," Liza said. "What did you think? That it was just us?" She rolled her eyes, but her tone was jokey. She was talking to Lucy the way you talk to a friend.

Lucy looked at her and smiled. And she noticed something coming out of the top of Liza's green-and-white-striped dress.

"Your tattoo . . . ," Lucy said. It was identical to her own.

"We all have them," said Gil. She pulled down the front of her T-shirt. Olivia pulled down the front of her dress.

"And now," said Gil, "our family is complete."

"What does that mean?"

"That means there's no room for anyone else. Four seasons, four elements, four sisters." When she said the word *sisters,* she smiled.

"But what happens now?" Lucy asked.

"Well, lots of things," Olivia said. "But there's time to talk about all of that later. Plenty of time now. Tonight go home and rest." And then she smiled. "Tomorrow we celebrate . . ."

Gil reached out and hugged Lucy. "I knew you would do it," she whispered. "We've been waiting so long for you." And she squeezed Lucy again. "We're sisters now," she said.

Lucy smiled as they helped her walk toward the car. "We're sisters," Gil said again. "We're sisters!" She repeated it over and over. And by the time they got there, Lucy believed her.

Thirty-Eight

That night, alone in her room, for the first time since her heart broke, Lucy picked up her guitar. Then she sat on her bed and started to write her second song. It was different than the one she'd written for Alex. It was slower, more complex, with sweet warm notes emerging from the cracked wood and swirling over and under and all around her voice. It would take a while to finish, this song would. But Lucy was in no rush.

When she was tired, she lay in her bed, quiet and still, thoughts gently resting in her head. And a full and whole heart beating soundly in her chest. She felt the softness of the sheets under her skin, the smoothness of her pillowcase against her cheek. She opened the window, and a breeze blew, fluttering the curtains and carrying in the scent of night-blooming flowers that had probably been in her yard all week, but she hadn't been able to smell them until now.

As she breathed in the sweet air, felt the soft sheets, she suddenly felt something that can only be described like this: she felt as though she was falling in love.

Deeply in love, but deeply loved too. Not with or by Alex, or her new sisters, or anyone in particular. No. She was in love with the whole world, the entire universe, every wretched, beautiful, lumpy, slimy, whispering, dark, sick, soft, twinkling, sharp, scented, smooth, rough, magnificent bit of it. Equally, wholly, and completely, every bit as much as she'd ever loved Alex. Maybe even more.

She thought: maybe this feeling was what we were before we were born—not bodies or spirits exactly, but just this feeling, this love.

The rest of what we are is just layers, wrapped around that feeling, layers of who we think we are and what we think we are. But at the core we're all just this. The rest doesn't matter. The rest isn't even real anyway.

With this thought she smiled. And she wondered why she had never realized this before, felt this before, since it had always clearly been this way. Everything she'd ever worried about, or been nervous about or scared about or sad about didn't matter. Not because life is meaningless, but because it's too big and too wonderful and too precious to spend it like that.

Suddenly the feelings she'd once had for Alex—that out-of-control top of a roller coaster sick and crazy feeling seemed silly, juvenile. It wasn't that she hadn't really loved him because oh, she had, she had. She'd loved him the best she could then, but she'd loved him the way a baby loves, full of longing and need. It was a love that made the lack of him feel like death.

But she could not love that way anymore. She knew that then. And she was glad for it.

She thought of all the people out there in the night, their broken hearts beating as they lay in their beds, on their floors, curled in sleepless balls of ache. She felt so touched by all of this, so sad for all of them, that she wanted to cry in that moment, but laugh somehow too. She wanted to hug them all and hold them all gently and then let them go.

As she drifted off to sleep, she wondered if this was now the permanent state of things for her. If *this* is what being a Heartbreaker meant? And if so, how would she go around in the world with a heart so full, with a heart just barely this side of bursting?

Thirty-Nine

*I*n the beginning, there was Lucy Wrenn, walking into school on the eighth day of her sophomore year, with a tattoo on her heart, which no one could see. And a smile on her face that everyone could.

The world felt brand-new. She was brand-new in it.

The feeling from the night before had gone, but she had the warm memory of it. And that was enough.

Without her own pain, her own need, her own anything acting as a veil between her and the world, everything seemed different. There was Jessica Wooster, a girl from her homeroom. Lucy used to feel so sorry for her, for her frizzy hair, her short neck, her too-round face, her propensity for doing everything subtly wrong. But somehow that day Lucy didn't feel that stab of pity anymore. She felt instead a kinship, the kinship that comes from realizing that that sack of cells walking around over there is a human. *And I am a human too.*

When their eyes met Lucy smiled. And Jessica looked shocked for a moment, confused by this smile. But there was such warmth in the gesture, such genuine feeling that a moment later Jessica smiled back.

Behind Jessica were a couple of freshmen. The boy was trying so hard to impress the girl with some story. Lucy stared at them. She thought, *Well, isn't that sweet.* But it was as though she was watching a video of something that happened a very long time ago. Something that no longer applied to her life at all and never could again. And that both delighted and scared her.

Lucy found Alex at lunch. He was right where she thought he'd be, at the edge of the junior section, sitting against the wall eating a sandwich.

He had a glob of mustard in the corner of his mouth, a bright yellow spot which would have once sent her into a frenzy of loving him back when everything did. She felt nothing at all.

It was as though he suddenly just ceased to matter.

"Hey, Alex," she said. He looked up, a little wary, then sorry.

"Lucy," he said. "About yesterday . . ."

"Old news," she said. Lucy shook her head and waved her hand. "I have something of yours." She reached into her bag and took out his photograph of the girl in bed. She put it on the table in front of him. He stared at it and Lucy saw a deep red blush creeping up his neck, right to the tips of his little baby ears.

"It really is a nice picture," she said. "The best one you've taken by far." And Lucy looked down at it, at the girl's delicate shoulder, the top of her breast. There was something there. A mark on that smooth skin that Lucy hadn't noticed before, that she hadn't seen because she *couldn't see it before.* A heart, locked shut, teardrop dripping below, and a banner across it on which was written SECRET SISTERHOOD OF HEARTBREAKERS.

How funny, she thought. How funny that someday soon Alex's heart would be broken too. And what a strange, *strange* coincidence. She hoped it wouldn't hurt him. Well, not *too* badly . . .

She looked back up at Alex, who was staring at her, this guilty look on his face, like he was wondering exactly what she knew. But she just smiled.

"Good luck," Lucy said.

Alex tipped his head to the side, trying to figure out what she was wishing him luck for. Lucy turned to go. She raised her hand up to her chest as she walked away from him. She pressed her new heart, and it pressed back against her hand. It was only hers now.

Forty

ut what was healed in Lucy had broken in some- one else.

Tristan. After school that day, there he was, walking so slowly like he was waiting for her but not waiting for her too.

She caught his eye. He tried to smile in that easy way he always did. But something was not the same. When you know someone well enough, when you've stared at their face long enough, that creates a familiarity that is its own kind of magic. He was different.

And it was all her fault.

No, she hadn't broken his heart on purpose and taking that tear hadn't hurt him any more than he already was. But the simple truth was this: she was free because he wasn't.

Now that she knew what he was feeling, had been feeling for so long, was it fair to ignore it? Was it fair to still be friends with him? Tristan was his own person, Lucy knew. Capable of making his own decisions of course. But isn't being in love an altered state? Like being drunk or sick or high or crazy? And shouldn't one protect one's friends from bad choices they might make? But what if the bad choice your friend is making, what if what is hurting them, is simply being friends with you?

There were too many questions, and Lucy didn't have answers for any of them. Not then at least.

Tristan was standing right in front of her, twirling a lollipop stick in the corner of his mouth.

"You know what," Lucy said. "I think we need to find you a girlfriend." She tried to sound cheery when she said it, as though this was a fun idea she'd just had.

Tristan squinted like he couldn't quite see her. "Lucy, what are you even talking about?" he said. His voice was flat, bitter.

Lucy shrugged. "I don't know," she said. "It just popped into my head, I guess."

"Well, whatever," he said. "Let it go."

"Sure," she said. But she knew she wouldn't. She made a silent promise to him then, to fix this, to fix everything. It was a promise she knew she would not soon forget.

Forty-
One

When Lucy came home after school, her parents were cuddled up on the couch. She stopped in the doorway and looked at the two of them, her mom's feet resting in her dad's lap. They were holding up sections of the newspaper, reading out loud in hushed voices, laughing quietly.

Nine days ago, watching this scene would have filled Lucy's heart with such a mix of emotions: a pang of hope that things would just stay this way, a stab of sadness because she knew they wouldn't, anger that they couldn't and loneliness that of the three of them she was the only one who seemed to know this. It had always felt like a burden, that knowledge, too heavy to carry alone.

And three days ago when they'd first returned from their trip, she'd been too wrapped up in her heartbreak to really even see them.

But at that moment, standing there watching them, all she felt was a calm sense of perfect understanding: they were not stupid, they were not careless, they were not ignorant, they were just afraid.

That's what kept them in this cycle going around and around—it was the fear of the crushing pain of a broken heart, fear that if they entered into that abyss they would never make it to the other side. That's what kept them locked in their rubber-band dance. Looking at them, now knowing this, she felt nothing but a great warmth toward them and a deep sense of compassion for the two sad people in this situation, which she now felt so far removed from. They didn't know any better. They were doing the very best they could. But they were fragile, breakable, after all, only human.

"Lucy!" her mom said. "You're home! We took the day off just for fun!"

"That's nice." Lucy paused, smiled at the two of them. "I really love you guys."

Her mom smiled like she was surprised to hear Lucy say it. "We love you too, honey."

"Seems like you're feeling better, huh?" her dad said. "Your mom was worried about your stomach." He turned toward her mom. "See? I told you it was just a bug."

"You were right, Dad." Lucy nodded. "I'm only here to drop my stuff off and then I was thinking of staying over at my friend Gil's house. We have a project to do if that's okay."

"Have fuuuuuuun," they sing-songed in unison. And they looked at each other and broke into giggles.

Forty-
Two

*S*itting in the back garden of some faraway restaurant, under a string of colorful silk flags, next to a white stone fountain filled with flickering floating candles and bobbing purple flowers, drinking from the jug of red wine that Liza snuck in in her giant purse and glugged into their crystal water glasses, Lucy was struck with the sudden realization that that night, the four of them, Olivia, Liza, Gil, and Lucy, really did feel like a family.

Liza raised her cup. "To sweet little Lucy, who is maybe not quite so little and sweet anymore."

"To Lucy," said Olivia.

Gil grinned. "To Lucy, our brand-new sister."

They brought their glasses together and then Lucy drank deeply. A hot server was standing there watching them—early twenties, swimmer's body, close-cropped hair. He looked at their glasses and raised an eyebrow at Lucy. Her stomach tightened. But then she remembered who they were: the Secret Sisterhood of Heartbreakers. All jangling bracelets and sweet-smelling hair and glowing skin and ruby lips. The regular rules, well, they didn't apply anymore. She cocked an eyebrow and raised her glass in his direction.

When he did finally approach it wasn't to tell them to stop sneaking wine, but to offer to take a photo of the four of them after he'd seen Lucy snap a picture of the other three. "You're way too pretty to be left out of the shot," he said. Lucy didn't even blush, just sat back down and blew a kiss at the camera when the flash went off.

"Looks like you're celebrating something," he said. "What's the occasion?"

"It's Lucy's birthday," Olivia said. She pointed at Lucy, her silver rings glinting in the candlelight.

"Well, happy birthday, Lucy," he said. "How old are you?"

"I was born today," Lucy said. "Just after midnight."

He looked at Lucy and tipped his head to the side. "You are very tall for a baby," he said.

"Yeah," Lucy said. "Must be something in the water." She tapped her glass of wine. He looked down at it, then back up at her. When their eyes met, she winked.

He grinned. "Well, then I hope you're having a happy birthday, baby."

"Oh believe me," Lucy said, "I am."

"Toast our sister?" Gil pointed to an empty glass and then down at the wine jug.

"I shouldn't." He looked behind him. "My manager is around here somewhere."

"He won't come out here," Gil said. "I promise."

He looked around again, bit his lip.

Gil lowered a glass into her lap, filled it from the jug, and then took out an emerald dropper and squeezed a drop of something into his wine, where it let off the tiniest curl of silver smoke. Then she refilled Lucy's glass and put a drip from the dropper into it too.

"To you, birthday girl," he said. He raised his glass and clinked with hers. He never broke eye contact as he took his sip. A little bead of purple clung to the corner of his mouth. He licked it off and then his mouth spread into a slow smile.

She took her own sip, her lips tingling.

He's pretty damn sexy, Lucy thought.

"He's pretty damn sexy," the server said. And then he looked around, suddenly embarrassed.

"Yup," said Gil.

Lucy raised her eyebrows.

Gil grinned and nodded.

You are all very beautiful, except for you, Liza, who looks a bit like a frog, Lucy thought.

"You are all very beautiful, except for you, Liza, who looks a bit like a frog," he said. His eyes opened wide as he heard himself. He brought his hand up to his lips. "I'm so sorry. I have absolutely no idea why I just said that." He looked around in every direction. "I think I should get back to work now." He walked away, blinking and shaking his head.

Liza shot Lucy a look. "You!" she said. She pressed her lips together and pointed. "You're going to be trouble, aren't you?"

"Guess you'll just have to wait and see," said Lucy.

The four of them burst out laughing. It sounded like the jingle of bells when a door is being opened. A few minutes later their food came—giant copper dishes full of fragrant stew, saffron rice, and other things Lucy did not know the names of. Olivia, Liza, and Gil seemed different than she'd ever seen them before, smiling and laughing and joking just like regular girls, well, almost. It was, Lucy realized then, not just a relief and a joy for Lucy to be one of them, it was a relief and a joy for them to have her, too.

Lucy leaned back against her seat and looked at her new sisters, at the tattoo emerging from Olivia's gunmetal-gray silk dress, from Liza's black halter, from Gil's green tank. That locked heart, the ribbon, the jewel tear. Identical to her own.

She was filled with a million questions.

But that night, for the first time maybe ever, she was content to have her questions and just let them be. To let the vast and mysterious future simply stretch out ahead of her. To let it unfold when it unfolded.

When they were done eating and their plates cleared away, the cute server came back with three others, each carrying pieces of some fancy-looking cake, with a long, skinny candle burning in the middle of the slice. They all sang happy birthday to Lucy, their voices melding together. And she wasn't embarrassed when every single person in the garden turned to stare at her and some joined in. She got up and sang right along with them, loud in beautiful harmony. And when the song was over, she stood there enjoying the feeling of all eyes on her. She waited an extra second before she blew the candle out.

Acknowledgments

Thank you so much to:

All the fantastic people at HarperCollins, including Elise Howard, Catherine Wallace, Erin Fitzsimmons, Marisa Russell, and Sarah Landis. Extra special thanks to Farrin Jacobs and Zareen Jaffery for being wonderful editors.

(Cousin) Aimee Friedman for all the help when this idea was just beginning. Alyssa Reuben and Lydia Wills for the great agenting.

Micol Ostow and Siobhan Vivian being fabulous writing buddies.

Tigerlili Cavill for, amongst many other things, the gorgeous drawing.

OST Café (and the lovely people therein) for the ultimate coziness.

Cheryl Weingarten and Donald Weingarten for being my mom and my dad!

Elise West (and Muffy) for much assorted delightfulness.

Aaron Lewis for the brainstorming, the author-photo taking, and being all-around awesome.

Christopher Prince-Barry, Mary Crosbie, Melanie Altarescu, and the rest of my very marvelous friends for the snacks, jokes, karaoke, and dance parties.

And Paul Griffin for you know exactly what.

♡

JOIN
THE COMMUNITY AT

Epic Reads
Your World. Your Books.

FIND
the latest
books

DISCUSS
what's on
your reading
wish list

CREATE
your own book
news and
activities to share
with friends

ACCESS
exclusive
contests and
videos

**Don't miss out on any upcoming
EPIC READS!**

**Visit the site and browse the
categories to find out more.**

www.epicreads.com